The Tuzla Run

The Tuzla Run

By Robert Davidson

The Tuzla Run

Printed by CreateSpace

ISBN: 1456513699
ISBN-13: 9781456513696

For Wendy,
whose belief and support made it possible

PROLOGUE

"In every transaction there must be trust. Naturally, you are aggrieved because it is you who must do all the trusting. However, consider. You cannot officially obtain customs documentation, bills of lading and transportation for the consignment. An end-user certificate would be impossible in light of the embargo against your country. You have no chance. I would suggest to you that I am your only opportunity for the specific weapons you so earnestly desire."

The diffused light from the desk lamp gave the sallow features an ethereal glow. A misshapen lower lip curled in the semblance of a smile as Stösser leaned forward.

"But, since we are having this conversation, you know all this. Why else would you be here? Do not overlook the fact that, should we agree to conclude this transaction, I can arrange that the consignment will be delivered to Tuzla."

The man sitting opposite took a deep drag on his cigarette and narrowed his eyes in question.

"You can provide exactly what I have asked for?"

"The Stingers with projectiles, the M136 AT-4s also with projectiles, AK-47s with ammunition, grenades and all in precisely the numbers requested? Yes, most definitely. Some of the weapons may not be new but knowing that they have been used before must provide some reassurance as to their reliability?" He smiled again. This was definitely his market, a seller's market, and he had no doubt whatsoever that this deal would go through.

"Transportation?"

"The consignment will pass through Croatia—"

"The whole point of my coming to you is that we can no longer afford to allow the Croatians to make off with twenty-five per cent or more of our supplies."

"—and will not, I assure you, be subject to examination by the Croatian authorities," the dealer continued, ignoring the interruption. He paused. "I can commit to 'best effort'."

"Best effort?"

"There are no guarantees in this business. I can promise that every reasonable effort will be made to accomplish delivery but sometimes a *force majeure,* unexpected events or bad luck all conspire to render our intentions futile." Again, there was a confident pause.

"We do business?"

There was no immediate response. However, this deal was not going to go away. He waited.

"Agreed."

ONE

Doctor Denis Macaulay, a senior lecturer in Political Science at Queen's University, had likened Belfast to Beirut in his lectures and writings. The presence of danger, often intensified by the acrid smell of burning rubber and petrol, together with the pervading sense of fear, conjured up the Lebanese cauldron. The bombed shop-fronts and burnt-out buildings, the tense unforgiving air of permanent conflict, heightened the similarity. Macaulay was a streetwise academic who had taught at Beirut's American College. He had, however, read the handwriting on the wall and left before the spate of kidnappings caught the world's attention.

That morning he awoke in a foul mood to find his Red Setter lying across his ankles. Pushed off the bed, she grunted in complaint but waited on the landing to accompany him downstairs. In the spacious kitchen, the academic prepared breakfast for them both. Wagging her plump rear quarters, the dog waited, knowing she would eat first. Macaulay put the bowl on the floor and pushed it with his foot to meet her lowered nose.

He went to the hallway to pick up the morning paper.

Back in the kitchen and seated at his breakfast bar, he scanned the front page then leafed through to the book review section. His mood lightened as he read the review that was of most interest to him.

Thirty-five minutes later, he opened his garage door, slid behind the wheel of the BMW and drove off towards the University. Unnoticed, a Ford Escort followed as he filtered into the stream of traffic on the Malone Road.

As a lecturer in Political Science, his life was neither demanding nor overly exciting. He had published once again and, as a result, had made an appearance on television to promote his most radical book to date, To Cure the Ills. The theory espoused was extreme. It had caught the attention of the more right-wing members of Ulster's elected representatives at Westminster. He was cognisant of, and unashamedly pleased by, the rumour that the Unionist political machine in the province had pencilled him in as a prospective parliamentary candidate.

However, he was unaware that others in Ulster had also taken note.

One element of Northern Ireland's many divides found his premises and solutions particularly unacceptable. True, the postulations expounded were no more rigorous or harsh than those they had tried to enforce in the many years after Partition. They, too, did not consider tolerance to be a virtue. They abhorred non-partisanship, detested compromise, and wasted little time on political solutions. Macaulay was therefore an annoyance that could well represent a threat in the future.

Accordingly, they had scheduled an appointment for the doctor with the "Removal Man."

"I wonder who he is?" Marie McCracken asked, indicating the room above, with a jerk of her head towards the smoke-darkened ceiling. Despite the apparent naiveté of the question, she was aware that the types of lodger they accommodated always had a connection with the Provos. The nature of this one's stay appeared no different from that of previous 'guests'.

"Shut it, woman," growled her husband through a mouthful of food. "Just shut it. It's no business of yours. You should know better than to get nosy over this kind of thing." He scowled and shovelled another forkful of beans into his mouth.

"Aye, but—"

"No bloody buts. Just shut it." He had half risen, brandishing the fork.

She sighed, spread another slice of bread with margarine and passed it to him.

The weak light partitioned the McCracken's dingy upstairs spare room with blocks of broken shadow. Mingled, in the light's feeble strands, indistinctive back-street sounds drifted upwards and into the gloom. Declan Rath sat motionless on the edge of the bed staring at the head-and-shoulders photograph of a middle-aged man smiling assuredly from the dust jacket of a book. He put the book aside.

As always, he would prepare thoroughly. Methodical, painstaking preparation eliminated error. Standing before the flyspecked mirror of the wardrobe, he checked his appearance. The sleeves of the woollen shirt reached the backs of his hands and the dark green corduroy trouser-cuffs hung adequately over his scuffed suede boots. A circular movement of his muscular neck confirmed that the tie was not restrictive. Blending with the milieu would be paramount in the approach phase. The reflection revealed the epitome of a mature student.

From a side pocket of the long sports holdall beside him, he removed a small bottle of olive oil. Pouring a small amount into his cupped palm, he rubbed both hands together. After massaging his face and ears, applying the lubrication evenly, he rubbed his closely cropped hair vigorously until the excess was gone.

As soon as possible after the hit, he would shower to remove all traces of cordite, and the oil would make the job easier. He would burn the clothes.

After closing the bottle, he returned it to the pocket of the bag and removed a pair of surgical gloves, dulled with talcum powder, from the same compartment. Pulling them on, he then made sure his wrists were covered and, threading his fingers together, eased the rubber into place.

He reached into the body of the carryall to grasp the Ithaca Model 37 pump-action shotgun by its pistol grip. Positioning the weapon vertically, butt end on the floor, and gripping it with his knees, he unscrewed the top of the tubular magazine. He took a handful of cartridges from the holdall and spilled them onto the bed beside his right thigh.

The size 4 cartridges contained a heavier shot than those used for game. He wiped each cartridge with a small cloth before feeding it into the magazine. When the tube was full, he inserted the threaded end of the cap and screwed it closed.

Rising effortlessly, he then pulled the canvas sling over his right shoulder and released his hold, allowing the weapon to hang barrel downwards close to his body. He reached inside the wardrobe for the dark duffel coat and adjusted the fit over his shoulders. With it unbuttoned, his reflection returned his critical stare, looking for tell-tale signs of the gun. Satisfied, he placed his feet apart, flexed his calf muscles and slightly bent his knees. A short, sharp backward movement of his hand flared the coat open and the same hand unerringly located the pistol grip to swing the shotgun forwards and upwards. His waiting left hand confidently grasped the slide action to cock it with a pumping action as the muzzle swept up into the firing plane. The barrel was now pointing at the torso of his reflected image. After a prolonged pause, he applied the safety catch and dropped the weapon to its previous downward position. A cursory flick of the coat swiftly masked the gun. He removed the coat and laid it on the bed, placing the shotgun next to it.

It was unusual for a specialist to keep his own weapons due to the danger of detection, but he enjoyed the added risk. Reaching down, he removed a toilet bag from the holdall and took out a Smith and Wesson. He slid the released magazine from the butt, then, using the ball of his thumb, flicked the 9mm rounds onto the cloth spread across his thighs. Painstakingly, he wiped each brass shell with the cloth. He reloaded the mag, designed to hold twelve rounds, with just eleven, to lessen the possibility of jamming. He confirmed the resilience of the spring by pressing down on the uppermost bullet with his thumb.

Replacing the magazine, he chambered a round, applied the safety catch and placed the automatic in the right-hand patch pocket of the duffel coat. The lining was heavy, durable plastic. The fingers of an open hand would go unfailingly to the grip, the thumb to the safety catch and the gun would clear the pocket effortlessly. The plastic lining ensured a snag-free release.

Unlike those who preferred revolvers, he believed the advantage of the additional rounds far outweighed the possible disadvantage of a stoppage. High quality ammunition, maintenance and frequent practice reduced the risk of such failures.

The radio clock on the bedside cabinet showed half past seven in the morning. Twelve more minutes and it would be time to leave. He made a final check of the textbooks, ring binder and Queen's scarf in the shallow wicker-shopping basket beside the bed.

"All set, Doctor. Ready when you are," he murmured.

Stretching out on the bed beside the coat and shotgun, he put his gloved hands behind his head and stared at the ceiling. He smiled and shook his head when he heard the raised voices and sounds of a scuffle downstairs that culminated in the thud of a body against furniture.

Her man had already left for 'work' and she was alone.

Thank God!

She heard the creak of footsteps on the stairs, then the sound of the front door closing. She crossed to the front window in time to see the duffel-coated figure of their lodger.

Wearing one of those college scarves. Fancy!

As she watched, her thoughts eddied to her own problems. She touched her nose gingerly and saw the blood on her fingers before she wiped them briskly on her apron.

Money, always money. Or drink. A woman was entitled to ask for her housekeeping without fear of a beating.

"For the last time…" she swore to herself, but recognized immediately that it was hopeless.

Jesus, though, they were paying him for putting up the hard men and she had to do the cooking and cleaning!

It was not as though he had no money for *his* drink… but hardly ever enough for food and rent.

Oh no, that came a poor second. No money for that. Well, it is going to stop.

She nodded emphatically as though she had spoken aloud.

But how?

She had hated McCracken for years but how could she change things?

Considered himself to be a big, big man, he did, because they trusted him to—

The answer struck her forcefully, like a bolt. She remained motionless, her face flushing. The idea grew. She felt giddy with the enormity of it flood her consciousness.

Would she dare?

Just you wait and see, Billy McCracken.

She scuttled over to the dresser and rummaged through the drawer for the seldom-used writing pad and envelopes. With a stub of pencil, she started to write.

Parked several yards from the newsagents at the end of the road was a dark blue Cortina. Stealing a Cortina was child's play, and for that reason, they were a great favourite with the young joyriders of the city. The vehicle was nondescript enough for its intended purpose—a simple delivery. It would not draw undue attention.

Scrutinizing the man who was nonchalantly eating crisps and leaning against the left side of the bonnet, the Removal Man noted that the air of disinterest shown was overdone. It faded as he drew nearer.

The fellow moved from the car, crumpled the crisp packet in both hands and dropped it. Both hands remained in full view and his posture stiffened. The gunman glanced at the other side of the street and saw the watcher, located twenty yards diagonally opposite, ostensibly reading a newspaper. His job would be to report that the car and occupants had left for the assignment. The driver nodded, and opened the rear door of the car. Ignoring him, the big man climbed into the front passenger seat.

With a glance at the other side of the street, the driver shrugged and walked round to the driver's door. The Removal Man casually noted the ripped housing round the steering wheel and watched the driver start the engine by joining the loose wires.

In less than a minute, they were on Newtownards Road and heading south on Short Strand towards the Ormeau Bridge. The car negotiated the right turn onto the bridge and headed to University Street where it pulled into the kerb. As the passenger got out of the car, the driver said,

"Our day will come."

The Removal Man turned, stooped to look back into the car and stared stonily at the other man, then smiled in return, an unexpectedly boyish grin.

"*Tiochfaidh ár lá.*"

He straightened, draped the scarf around his neck and scanned the surrounding area for uniformed police or Army patrols. With none in sight, he started to walk towards the Queen's Film Theatre.

Macaulay paid scant attention to the other vehicles in the traffic streaming towards the city centre. His thoughts were on the reception his latest effort was having on the reading public. The doctor, in no way commercially naive, accepted that furore created, or at least improved, marketability. He had dutifully followed his agent's advice and increased the rhetoric to the point of rabidity.

While he did not desperately need the money, it was nonetheless welcome. Exceptional sales confirmed his professional competency to those he wished to impress and unveiled his hitherto low-key reputation to the masses.

In political circles and academia, there was not so much admiration as respect, albeit tinged with envy. In debate, he had a sharp acerbic wit, which, together with his undoubted intellect, he used to deadly effect.

As an analyst of policies and their probable effect in both general and specific terms, he was infallible, or so his supporters claimed. Even his detractors said he had the ability to see behind political smokescreens and identify the secret agendas. He himself would say that he was aware and unashamed of his visionary prowess.

However, he failed to register the Ford that overtook him and led the way to the University car park.

Earlier that morning, in Palace Barracks, Holywood, on the outskirts of eastern Belfast, the sergeant major of the Special Air Service contingent had strode down the hallway of the unit's accommodation and opened the door to room six.

As he reached for the light switch he sensed, rather than saw, the movement in the darkness; they were already awake and watching him. As the dim light came on, legs swung to the floor.

"The Queen's job is on. There's an 'O' group with the Boss in twenty. Christ, can't you people leave a window open?"

Expecting no reply, or a ribald put-down, he left the door open and strode along the corridor to the main door. The four occupants gathered up towels and soap and made their way to the shower cubicles at the end of the hallway. While in the showers no one spoke. Back in the room the tallest of the four lit a cigarette and said,

"Made up your mind about extending, Spider?"

The individual addressed was slightly above medium height with the lithe muscularity of a competitive swimmer. He shrugged and threw his towel onto his bed. Rolling an elastic band round his fingers, he pulled his long fair hair into a bunch at the nape of his neck and fixed it in place.

"Miss me, will you, Lofty?" He grinned at his questioner.

"Piss off! But you do need to think about it, mate, seriously. You want your head looking at. You'll be lost without the Regiment."

Spider smiled but did not answer. He finished dressing, and then joined the others as they removed weapons, together with spare magazines, from the steel lockers and laid them on the trestle table. Spider stripped his Browning 9mm pistol and examined the components. The weapon was quickly reassembled, then holstered.

"Time for Oscar Charlie," said the red-haired member of the group.

He stood aside as the others came out of the room; then he locked the door. They crossed the tarmac road to the prefabricated briefing room. Inside they gathered round the urn. After each collected a mug of tea, they took their places at the table.

Within a few minutes, the Officer Commanding entered the room.

"Morning gentlemen," he said as he laid his map case at the head of the table. "Get me a spot of tea, Piebald, will you."

The fourth member of the group, slim and mousy-haired stood, filled a mug and silently placed it in front of the officer.

"Right. Further to last night's briefing... First, the summary sheet. Info is still rather skimpy I'm afraid. We know that Macaulay, a lecturer in Political Science at the University, is the object of their attention.

The hit will take place at the University—we don't know precisely where in the grounds or in which building. A couple of hours ago an RUC informant confirmed that they have brought in the Removal Man. He's been here in Belfast for," he paused as he squinted at his watch, "almost nine hours now. The description available remains sketchy. We do know that he is big, and well-built.

Intelligence believes that he is one Declan Rath, a former denizen of Londonderry.

"We've been more than lucky on this one because coincidence has played a part. For some time now, Echo 4 Bravo has been placing tracking devices in the cars of selected IRA sympathizers on the off chance that the cars might be 'borrowed' for jobs then belatedly reported stolen.

Late last night, a local businessman's Rover saloon car parked up for the night in Whiterock, but the owner, one James McKinley, lives in the Ardoyne and is there at this moment. What we don't know is when Rath will arrive or if he will have back-up.

"During the operation, use standard radio procedures. Roddy Ewan's section will be providing follow-up support, if needed. They'll be in the blue Volkswagen van. Sometime after eight o'clock this morning, we'll ensure that the area is free of our uniformed colleagues. After completion, Roddy will handle the evacuation. Any questions?"

"Whereabouts in the University will the doctor be, most of the day?" asked Lofty.

"In the main block, where he teaches. We've had it and the approaches under observation. As far as we know, no one is pre-positioned from their side and we've made sure there's been no entry during the night."

"Weapons?"

"The choice is yours," replied the OC. "But let me emphasize that Macaulay's safety is paramount. No unnecessary risks with his well-being."

The group at the table smiled at each other with humorous resignation.

"Not knowing for sure if Paddy will have back-up, it's imperative that you be on the lookout for outside inter-ference. I do not have to remind you that the Provos are well-versed in sting operations. The possibility does exist that this could be a set-up. Body armour is your own call.

"Well, that's it. Roddy's crew has been briefed. I rec-ommend that you get together with him now." With a curt nod to the group, he added, "I'll be back in an hour to hear your plan, Stewart. Thank you."

Despite the large map of Belfast and its environs on the wall, Lofty went to a table in the corner of the room, leafed through a pile of Ordnance sheet maps, and pulled one free.

"Sticking with the doctor without being spotted is going to be difficult. On the other hand, if we try to do it from too great a distance, we could be circling around when the action takes off."

Spider pulled the fact sheet towards him and scanned it.

"He lives in the Malone residential area."

The others identified the street on the map.

"He comes to town on the Malone Road. What time is he due at the University?" he wondered aloud.

"You've got the fact sheet, Bonehead," said Piebald.

"Bollocks," retorted Spider, without feeling, as he referred to the sheet again. "Normally, he's scheduled for lectures at nine in the morning. Leaves home at about a quarter to nine."

"What's he drive?" asked Lofty.

Spider searched the sheet as the others gave the map their attention.

"BMW. Maroon." He thought for a moment then suggested, "It might be better if Lofty and I were already at the University car park. As one of the staff, he'll have reserved parking, and we can check out the immediate area."

"Makes sense," said a grinning Stewart, "but you'd better make sure you look like students 'cos you're both too thick to pass for teachers!"

They discussed their plan for a further fifteen minutes, finally agreeing on the two vehicles they would use, one for Piebald and Stewart as Macaulay's escort and the other for Spider and Lofty, who would wait for the arrival of the lecturer at the University.

They would all wear Kevlar body armour. Three of them would carry MP5Ks, the shortened version of the Heckler and Koch sub-machine gun, with thirty-round magazines. Spider would take a Remington shotgun.

Shortly afterwards, Roddy Ewan's back-up section joined them. Following a review of the main points of the plan, the discussion centred on radio procedures, the use of call signs, and emergency codes.

When the briefing ended, they remained in the room until the Officer Commanding returned. He sat at the head of the table then, with a curt nod, signalled to Sergeant Stewart to begin the presentation.

Rath walked towards the opening in the low wall that bordered the wide lawn fronting the main building. Macaulay's reserved parking space was close to a narrow pathway between the lawn and the imposing edifice of the North's premier seat of learning. He would arrive in the next few minutes to walk this path from his car.

Rath took in the cluster of students gathered at the entrance, as on most days, to smoke or discuss lecture notes or last night's television.

A battered Ford drove past, then turned into the car park. Its occupants were engrossed in a spirited conversation but the rapid raucous clatter of a Scout helicopter drew all his attention. His scalp prickled, galvanizing a rash of goose pimples on his neck.

Why the chopper? Did they know? Think, he told himself calmly.

Worst case scenario, it could be scouring the immediate area as a final check for uniformed forces. The security people frequently did this when a covert security action was imminent. They would not want to be involved in a gunfight with their uniformed colleagues.

However, it could also be on its way to or from some other tasking somewhere else in the city. He weighed the probability of their knowing of the job and decided the chance was minimal. His people had only decided the timing of this operation late the day before yesterday. The Brigade Intelligence Officer had assured him that only he and one other, the driver of the getaway vehicle, knew precisely where it would take place. He scanned the area again but detected no trace of a security presence. If the helicopter made another sweep—

The arrival of another car pulling into the car park interrupted his train of thought. The occupants of the previous vehicle had climbed out, and the taller of the duo waited while the other locked the Ford. They continued to argue.

Turning his attention to the last arrival, who had left his vehicle carrying a holdall, he watched him make his way to the entrance. Rath watched intently, the bag arousing his suspicions. The obvious acceptance, displayed by smiles of greeting and mild horseplay from the cluster of students at the bottom of the steps, convinced him that the man presented no danger.

A burst of adrenalin boosted his anticipation as he saw Macaulay's BMW pull into its allotted space. Rath walked without haste towards the main building as the doctor left his car and strode briskly along the path. The pair of students with their thermos flask and books had reached the group at the entrance, some forty yards ahead of Macaulay. They continued their animated conversation.

Two other late arrivals trailed Macaulay separately, at a distance of thirty and fifty yards respectively. The gunman noticed that the leading student had a textbook open and was mouthing the words as he walked along. Probably following the words with his finger too, he thought with a wry grin.

The group at the bottom of the steps started to break up and, in huddles of twos and threes, began to wander into the building.

"Did anyone see who left this?" the inspector asked.

The desk sergeant raised his head from the register and looked at the letter.

"Afraid not, sir. It was lying on the desk when I came on duty. I brought it in to you unopened and—"

"Yes, okay." The inspector turned from the desk, then paused for a moment. "Get me the I.O. at Army H.Q. Lisburn. Put it through to my office."

In the Ops Centre in Palace Barracks, the O.C. faced the I.O

"How reliable is this description?"

"I would say no worse than any other info we get from informers. The people in Montpelier Police Station think it is genuine. And anyway, it only confirms what you already know."

"Yes, but confirmation is a commodity we so rarely have." The O.C. thought for a few moments, then wrote briefly on a yellow memo pad. Tearing off the sheet, he crossed the room to the sergeant operating the radio.

"Get this out to the detail at Queen's. Now!"

Macaulay bustled to the entrance and elbowed his way through the slower moving students. Behind him, the big

man dropped his basket, threw open the duffel coat and, as he was bringing the gun to bear, called in a clear voice.

"Doctor Macaulay, a moment please!"

Macaulay turned to face him. His eyes widened and apprehension swirled into raw shock when he saw the shotgun. He dropped his briefcase. Arms windmilling, he backed away and turned simultaneously. Mouth distorted, he tried to shout, but no sound came. A riser caught his heel, and he crashed backwards onto the stone stairs. In terror, he rolled and scrambled on his hands and knees up the cold granite steps.

The Removal Man strode forward but the pit of his stomach vaulted upwards as he saw the two erstwhile students, one on each side of the fallen doctor, throw aside their books and rip open their anoraks.

The taller of the couple threw the thermos to one side, placed his foot in the small of the fallen man's back and pushed him down. Both men screamed, "Down! Down!" Those students still outside milled and pushed in confusion.

On the entrance landing, a panicked student blocked the gunman's view of his target but also obstructed a clear line of fire for both escorts. A second before Rath saw the weapons, he caught sight of the bulky body armour, as the anoraks were torn open.

He knew with sickening surety—they were SAS.

He fired at the chin of the one on the right, pumped the slide action and swung the Ithaca towards the other trooper. He snapped off a shot and saw the man buffeted into the sidewall. As he pumped a third cartridge into the breech, animalistic self-preservation screeched its awareness of danger from the two who had been following the lecturer.

The sledgehammer impact of the 9mm bullets slamming into his left thigh spun him around and drenched that side of his body with a freezing numbness. He fired at the man in front but missed. The second man, however, closely following the first but to his right, dropped down heavily onto one knee.

The wounded gunman lurched towards the entrance, seeking the protection of the hallway, but dropped onto the steps. He rolled awkwardly to the nearside wall into a firing posture. The remaining trooper jumped into a wide-legged stance several feet away from the bottom step and sought his target.

The second taken by the SAS man to scan the figures above him cost him dearly as Rath's fourth shot tore into the flesh of his lower face. The fallen assailant reached above his head, caught the metal handrail and pulled himself upright. He dragged the scarf from his neck and knotted it around his thigh high against his crotch. As he pulled it tight, bile surged up through his mouth and nasal cavities.

He gripped the handrail to fight off the faintness that threatened to engulf him. Thankfully, he knew that his femur had somehow not been shattered. As he struggled against the nausea, he saw the wiring and microphone on the chest of one of the downed SAS troopers.

He spat and then, gritting his teeth, forced his head to clear. The argument and the mouthed words had been mere pantomime, to mask their radio communication. Turning, he looked down at Macaulay who crouched against the opposite wall. The frightened target put his arm across his face and cowered even more closely to the grey granite as the shotgun swung in his direction.

The fifth and final shot ripped into his huddled figure.

Pulling himself to the top of the steps, Rath pushed through the swing doors, and crabbed his way down the corridor. Thankfully, none of the students had attempted to stand or tried to stop him. As the doors swung closed behind him, he heard the screech of brakes, and knew, with chilling certainty, that more security forces had arrived.

After driving through several streets in the immediate area to locate the Rover saloon car, the Volkswagen van containing Ewan's backup section turned into Upper Crescent.

With confirmation earlier that morning that McKinley's car was on the move, it had not been difficult to monitor its progress. The van stopped alongside the saloon car. Three of the section jumped out and walked to the front of the vehicle to detain the driver and immobilize it.

The sudden sound of gunfire crackled from the direction of the University. In the van, Ewan shouted at his driver.

"Go, go, go!"

The troopers barely had time to leap back into the vehicle. It lurched away with a scream of rubber and rear doors still swinging, along Upper Crescent and onto University Road.

Calum, the getaway driver, stared mesmerized at the departing vehicle. The shaking in his legs would not subside. Arriving with several minutes to spare before the attack was to take place, he took a casual glance in the side mirror. Shock blanched his face, and riveted his body at the sight of the trio of masked figures heading towards the car with their weapons at the ready. Unexpected warmth washed over his crotch and thighs.

Looking down at his lap, blood flooded through his neck and face as he saw that he had wet himself. A trembling hand went to the ignition and started the engine.

The primary urge was to get to safety as quickly as possible, but he could not control the shaking.

The ignominy of fleeing, with urine-sodden trousers, unable to give a concise report, caused his youthful face to flame even more. He struggled to master the panic, to stifle the desire to escape.

His terror faded slowly as he sucked air through his open mouth, and the trembling ebbed. Calmly, or at least slowly, he would take the Rover saloon car once round the block to find out what had happened to the Removal Man. If he could not do the job and evacuate his man, he could at least try to gather some worthwhile intelligence.

Yes, that is what the hard men would do. That is what Liam would want. The great and almighty Liam would expect no less from him. Licking a bead of sweat from the soft down of his upper lip, he knew there was no choice. Calum McDermot put the car into gear, released the handbrake and made a wide U-turn.

Rath lunged along the corridor, brandishing the empty shotgun and roaring like a wounded animal to intimidate the watching students. He threw the gun to one side. Pulling out the pistol, he caught the blur of pale, terrified faces peering from lecture room doorways.

He barged through another swing door.

"No heroes please," he prayed.

The pounding of rubber-soled boots along the hall behind him spurred him on. There were no hallways or passages joining this one. A large sash window set in the wall at the end of the corridor loomed ahead. Panting and groaning, he pulled the gun up in a two-handed grip and fired repeatedly at the casement panes. The glass spewed outwards and, with an extraordinary effort, he heaved himself onto the sill and toppled out, oblivious to the remaining shards.

The heavy fall onto the pavement caused him to scream noiselessly. The force of the fall robbed his tortured lungs of air. Groggily, and using the wall for support, he clawed upright. With glazing eyes, he tried to run. Through the enveloping fog of dizziness and nausea, he heard, as from a distance, a voice shouting.

"Big man! Big man! Over here, for God's sake, over here!"

Someone grabbed his arm and pulled him towards a black car. He stifled the reflex urge to struggle. He keeled over, then felt his legs pushed up into a foetal position. Somewhere in the numbing, enveloping mist, he heard a car door slam.

TWO

The wooded crest of the hill looked out over a panorama of uneven roofs in the middle distance and the undulating patchwork of fields beyond it. Far to the right, the circular fourteenth century keep of Clough Oughter spiked the mist that partially clouded the small island on the Lough.

Rath had made good time today on his daily walk and was satisfied that his rate of recovery from exertion had improved. Lowering himself stiffly onto the mossy slope, he gazed across the moist green and blue hues to Cavan.

His customary cynicism, which coloured most of his thoughts, was dormant. In boyhood, scenes like this had encapsulated an Ireland worth dying for; however, the reality of callous violence and precipitate death, which now saturated life, tainted any such reveries.

His wound, no longer painful, had left no lasting damage, aside from the initial stiffness each morning. He grinned wryly. He should be proud to bear the stigmata of a soldier, a battle scar, as proof of his contribution in the struggle against the tyrants. At least, that is how Father O'Brien back in Derry would see it.

He remembered very little of his escape from Belfast. The flight was a jumble of disjointed actions, shrouded in haze, glimpsed as a drugged observer rather than an active participant. Clouded images intermittently floated past a black wall of comatose consciousness. He recalled toppling over into the car, then nothing until he had felt the tourniquet tighten on his leg.

At some indeterminate time, strong hands lifted him despite his large frame, onto the wooden cargo bed of a truck. He felt the prick of the needle, and he plummeted into an abyss of oblivion. An aeon passed before a frayed rope of tattered awareness dragged him slowly, to the surface of consciousness.

He was aware of a harsh, grating sound filling the cavernous darkness about him. They were piling bricks over and around him. Panic flared briefly but subsided when the concomitant surge of adrenalin merged with the anesthetic. It swept him from his precarious raft of consciousness back into the void.

Much later, the smell of horse manure featured prominently in his recollection. He had been delirious when they had led the horses from the horsebox, uncovered him and lifted him out of the manger.

The ensuing days of treatment and convalescence had provided hours of solitude—time to think, review and re-evaluate his life. Boyish, idealistic illusions, fostered by his father's tales of the Famine, the Easter Rising, and the War for Independence, had gone the way of the adolescent passions roused by stories of his grandfather's role in the struggle against the English.

The establishment of the English-controlled Six Counties had betrayed his grandfather, as it did many Irishmen. His father had felt the same sense of betrayal years later on his return to the North from England's war after debilitating years as a prisoner of the Japanese in Burma. Nothing had changed. The reality of an Eire whole and free in constitution, spirit and politics faded— but never the hope for it.

As a youth, his reading had been single-minded and voracious. Everything he read had been about Ireland, her people and their struggles. At the age of fifteen, he had moved with his parents, his brother and younger sister, to Derry. Something then occurred which eroded his idealism, turning it into an implacable pragmatism, fuelled by a fervent hatred of the system. Recollection of the eviction caused an unholy anger to rage within him.

His unemployed father had had great difficulty in putting food on the table for the family. The rent for Number 13 Kinnard Park was often in arrears. Nevertheless, they always managed to pay, though not without a sense of shame since the money was more often than not from social services.

Reallocation of the house to an unmarried Protestant woman working on the Council changed his shame to hatred. Relatives took in the boys. They sent his sister, who went without protest, almost willingly, to convent school.

Within days of going to live with his grandmother, the RUC had badly beaten his father during a demonstration. Three weeks later, he died from complications related to his injuries. Four months after the death of his father, the Army shot his oldest brother Sean. The so-called tribunal, one solitary English judge, determined that his killing had been lawful.

With the help of an aunt who worked in the Job Centre, he attended an interview and gained a position as a copyboy on the *Irish Times*. He started night school, where he met others who shared a desire for a unified Ireland. Many were convinced that a political solution was not possible.

One evening a recruiter for the IRA approached him. The youth had confirmed that he was ready to help rid the island of the British. The proposition, shortly afterwards, that he should join the British Army—and the Parachute Regiment at that—surprised him. However, finally convinced that there was no better training opportunity, he travelled to England to enlist.

His dedication and will to learn, together with his dispassionate competence, impressed his instructors. Several months later, basic and airborne training behind him, his battalion was warned for duty in Armagh. He knew that soon he would be required to use his newly acquired skills against his compatriots.

He deserted.

Back in Ireland, he was soon operational. At first, his task was to watch and record the daily movement of troops and local Royal Ulster Constabulary members, but he soon took part in the elimination of Ulster Defence Regiment volunteers. He had killed his first soldier when they had ambushed a detachment on its way from Belfast docks to Long Kesh.

More active service followed, and the command structure soon recognized his ability. Within months, he had graduated to assassinations, often as member of a team but more frequently as an independent operative.

Due to his success, the seeds of dissatisfaction were slow to wax into disillusionment, but grow they did. He still believed in the Cause, but any regard he had for the men directing the liberation efforts had dissipated. Doubts germinated relentlessly. He believed the policies were ineffectual and thought they had no real hope of success. They achieved too little at too high a price. The leaders also compromised with time. There was a *mañana* complex.

Nevertheless, he was convinced that the Provisional IRA provided the only hope for a unified Ireland. The numerous setbacks suffered by the Officials and then the Provos over the years did not diminish his enthusiasm nor cause him to question his beliefs. The number of deaths, casualties and captures among his fellow combatants did not compel him to challenge the validity of the means used to free Ireland.

He continued as a team member and, on many occasions, as the sole activist in executions and assassinations. He was proud of the part he had played in such actions, since he saw them as distinct targeting of the enemy. The shootings, properly planned, were direct actions in which the risk for uninvolved innocents was minimal.

More and more, he had even begun to enjoy them. Due to the adrenalin flow beforehand, the feeling of power, and the sense of accomplishment, that followed a successful mission, was satisfying.

The first seeds of doubt, fertilized by a lack of faith in the command structure, gradually grew stronger. The validity of armed struggle and violence was not in question, but the methods chosen to pursue it, such as the specious and indiscriminate use of the bomb as a weapon against soft targets, became abhorrent.

He had listened, at first with patience, to the justifications made for the attacks—how fear and mindless terror would convince the public that the current authorities could not preserve their safety.

However, more and more, the disinterested, almost callous, newspaper reporting of the bombings, couched in terms of bored impartiality, angered him.

"A bomb exploded in a restaurant in Belfast today. One person was killed and eight injured."

The horrific finality of the dreadful wounds hidden behind that bland summary of "eight injured" nauseated him. There began to rise in him a conflict of passion and guilt. The increasing number of disabled, deformed victims among their own Irish people weakened his resolve: there were amputees, wheelchair-bound cripples, and many others maimed and disabled by the haphazard use of the bomb.

He began to challenge the use of bombs to free Ireland. In the name of Independence, the guileless became sacrifices for no reason beyond expediency. The dead and injured over the years counted as irretrievable collateral damage that was unfortunate but necessary. He started to think that the price for recognition of Sinn Fein and its acceptability in the political life of Ireland had been far too high.

It was soon to become a belief.

The rain streamed down the outside of the bus's window and, forming a double layer with the cold condensation clinging to the inside surfaces, reduced visibility. There was nothing picturesque to see outside; terraced houses and ragged gardens that fronted them, littered gutters and overfilled bins. This area was not scenic Belfast. The interior of the bus smelt like drying dog as the warmth caused the passengers' wet clothing to steam.

Not that this bothered young Mrs. Devlin this Saturday morning; she had lived too long in this part of the North for the weather to influence her mood or disposition. Besides, she was on her way to the city centre shops.

She loved shopping, and not only "buying" shopping but "just looking" shopping as well. She knew she had good dress sense and enjoyed seeing the latest trends.

This was the first time she had come downtown alone since her wedding six weeks ago. Up until now, they had come to the shops together every Saturday, but today Dr Devlin was the on-duty GP in the practice he shared with two other aspiring young medics. She did not really mind because, much as she loved Gary Devlin, he did tend to get under her feet, and he certainly had no patience for her way of shopping. He did not seem to know that looking a lot, without necessarily buying, was an integral part of the enjoyment.

Saturday in town was agreeable, though today it might be even more pleasurable, she thought, as she stepped down from the bus. The rain seemed to have deterred some shoppers. The shops and streets would not be so crowded.

She made her way quickly from the bus stop to the entrance of the nearby department store, to shelter while opening her umbrella.

She had her back to the shop when the bomb exploded. Shoes, pullovers, ornamental window dressings and plastic limbs of the dissected tailor's dummies hurtled into the street in a cruel immediate parody of the butchered human bodies inside the store.

Mrs. Helen Devlin, née Rath, felt the blow in the small of her back before she blacked out.

Death came from a huge shard of granite masonry that severed her spinal cord.

The news stunned him. His jaw hung open, and he stared unseeingly at the wall of the darkened room. The letter fell to the floor between his legs. How long had he been there? He had no idea. Images flashed across his consciousness but kept him from thinking the unthinkable.

He saw her as a little girl, clutching her battered suitcase and wearing a dark blue raincoat, waiting at the end of the road where the bus had dropped her home on holiday from the convent. He saw her on the homemade swing at their Gran's, one hand holding the rope support, the other a thick slice of bread, her chin and cheeks covered in plum jam.

Another picture jostled for place and she was giggling with her friend Mary, both dressed as bridesmaids, as they walked up the path to the church for their aunt's wedding.

In myriad flashback clips, he saw her laughing, crying, giggling, pouting, and sulking. Running, skipping, jumping, dancing, singing...then .her image as a beautiful, radiant young bride filled his head.

Now, she was dead. Those fucking mad-dog, indiscriminate swines of bombers had killed her.

He knew that he could not stay in Ireland. The carnage he had caused on the University steps was reason enough for the authorities in the North to leave no stone unturned to find him. Their efforts had not slackened.

Informers had always been prevalent, and it was not beyond the bounds of possibility that one would provide the information that could allow a paramilitary or SAS group to come south and kill him. His leaders could barely hide the frustration and annoyance they experienced because the Security Forces had remained at high-level readiness.

The IRA postponed or curtailed many planned actions. It was not comfortable knowing that he was categorized by some on his own side as a hindrance.

Discussions on his future had taken place, but not without acrimony. His value to the cause had vastly depreciated.

The few belongings he had accrued in the last few weeks were already packed. However, where could he go? Should he wait for the organization to move him? According to the scant information he had, his handlers had made arrangements, but these were in abeyance pending final clearance from the Council. Going wherever they had in mind might not be acceptable if, in the interest of expediency, his departure should be permanent and cost no more than a .45 bullet.

He rose stiffly, then started to walk back to the cottage, his mind occupied with thoughts of how he could leave safely.

The sound of the car stopping outside caused him to rise from the chair and cross to the mirror. The angle captured the path and the gate outside the house, and the reflection showed Doctor Gillis, in the company of another man, opening the gate. He recognized the other man—Belfast had decided.

He opened the door to the men and stood aside as they entered. The second man stayed in the kitchen as the doctor examined him, somewhat perfunctorily, but not without care.

"Everything has healed up nicely. Good clean scar tissue. No problem when you walk?" asked the doctor as he stood up and returned to his bag on the kitchen table.

"None,"

Apart from the initial greeting, the visitor from Belfast had said no more but had watched the examination closely.

"Good. Excellent. Then there'll be no more reason for me to see you." He smiled and closed his bag. "He's fit," he said to the visitor. "You'll be able to make your own way back? Good, then I'll show myself out."

The front door closed. The sound of the car starting and pulling away faded.

The late afternoon sun slid behind the hills and the kitchen darkened. Both men remained seated; then the visitor stood and filled the kettle at the sink.

"Where do you keep the tea? No, don't get up, I'll make it." He opened the cupboard and stretched up for the tea caddy, apparently unaware that Rath's eyes ran over his torso searching for the bulge of a weapon. "We're delighted with the progress you are making. And despite any misgivings you might have, the Army Council's highly pleased with your success to date."

He set out the mugs and resumed his seat. For a few moments, only the sound of the gas mingling with the slow burble of water as it started to boil disturbed the silence.

"Have you wondered yet how and why they were waiting for you?" He clasped his hands on the table and leant forward.

"I never gave it a thought," the big man lied. "But I knew that the rat catchers would be looking. When you got here I thought maybe you were one from Security."

"And now?"

"Well, you could still be, but as I've got to be the last person under suspicion, since the job was completed, it means you still don't know who did inform."

The pale-grey, Belfast eyes blinked once behind rimless lenses.

"But we think we do. Oh yes, we think we do. That's why I'm here." He got up, took the kettle off the stove, poured the steaming water into the teapot, and returned to the table. "We've another job for you," he. 'If you are up for it..."

"I'm listening."

"Well, it looked straightforward at first; the number of people who knew was limited. Fortunately, we were able to sequester all those involved as soon as possible after the action—"

"Sequester?"

"Isolate for questioning. It's the official terminology now."

He smiled sheepishly then shrugged.

"Be that as it may, we interrogated everyone connected with the mission and all the others that might have suspected. We thought we had a result when we found out that the RUC knew where you stayed overnight. We followed that up and settled with the family you stayed with, the McCrackens. The woman admitted informing. However, when the findings were reviewed it became obvious that her info would've been too late for them to set up that ambush.

"We started the investigation again, but somebody we wanted to talk with had already left Belfast. We tracked him to Airdrie, in Scotland, and then we lost him. We want him back to finalise the matter."

"So where do you start looking?"

"Well, that's where you come in. We believe he is now in Frankfurt. Germany."

Rath said nothing.

"There was a feeling that he could still be in Scotland, but we put out a general alert and the word filtered back from Germany that there had been a sighting over there. Our people in Frankfurt are looking for him."

"If they find him then surely they can interrogate him?"

"It's not that convenient. Our people there are pretty low profile, and we have nobody in place with the necessary interrogative skills. You see, McDermot is only under suspicion—for the moment. We would like him back here for questioning under the proper conditions. We need to; in fact, we have to be really sure about him."

Again, Rath made no comment but looked at the other man, who he thought seemed uncomfortable, with a trace of sheepishness in his demeanour.

"He's the younger brother of Liam McDermot."

Rath could not smother the smile that spread across his face as the realization dawned on him. The grey eyes flickered and the man from Belfast made a wry face.

"So that's why he's getting the soft treatment! Shaft him, without being, sure and you'd have one very pissed-off Armagh Brigade Commander." He grinned at the investigator then, with difficulty, subdued the smile.

"And I should bring him back?"

"Well, yes and no. We want you to go to Frankfurt. Speak to our people over there, get whatever you can, see if he has moved on or not. Contact him, talk to him—overcome his reluctance, if you will. If you need help, our people there have been told to be ready."

"Where do you think he's likely to be?"

"All the indications are still Frankfurt. He has probably taken work. With the number of Irish over there, it should not be too hard to get a line on him. He believes he is in the clear so it should not be too difficult.

However, be that as it will, we want you to find him, wherever he is. While you are not fit for a full-scale operation, you could handle this. You will be out of the area and it will give you a low profile. So, find McDermot, and make sure he packs his wee suitcase and comes home."

The thought that he could also be more secure abroad and out of the direct reach of his own organization was not lost on Rath.

"And if he doesn't want to be persuaded?"

"It's important to us, for the sake of discipline that he does. There is time enough, so no need to rush things, but we cannot ever condone flouting General Order 5 part 5. We punish treachery, with no ifs or buts. If he is innocent, he has nothing to fear and should come back willingly, undergo investigation and be a free man.

On the other hand, if he persists and wants to stay there, you should make contact here and get fresh instructions. Things might change in the command structure, in which case we can cut the pussyfooting around, and you will have the go-ahead to make his stay permanent. That would be with the full backing of the Chief of Staff.

"So, are you ready to get back into action?"

He stared unblinkingly at Rath.

Rath tried, most of the time very successfully, not to allow personal feelings to affect his professional judgment or, more importantly, his ability to carry out his assignments. He believed he was devoid of feeling and had no emotional hang-ups, conscience or remorse over his actions for the Cause. His sister's death, however, was the catalyst that changed everything and, together with his suspicions of those whose orders he carried out, had created a seismic re-evaluation of his beliefs. This assignment could very well facilitate his own personal 'road to Damascus' transformation and give him the opportunity for a new start.

"Make the arrangements and give me the details, I'll be ready."

THREE

Cheatham looked across the room, out into the descending gloom. Dark clouds of an impending storm gathered, blackening the sky and smothering the last rays of early evening sun. A rising easterly wind whipped spirals of sand across the deserted yards and chivvied them towards the cluster of vehicles gathered round the headquarters building of the United Nations High Commission for Refugees (UNHCR) depot in Metkovic.

Determined not to reveal his excitement, the convoy manager struggled to control his heavy features. However, he could not chase the thought of the money from his mind. This convoy would make him rich. The chance of a lifetime!

Just say it is going, just give us the word.

His tongue flicked over his fleshy upper lip as he glanced, with feigned disinterest, at the others and was reassured that none appeared too eager.

A wide oval of shadow surrounded the mahogany table centred in the conference room where seven other dark figures sat in overcast silence. The dim light from the wall lamps reflected both light and shadow from the dark pool of its surface, transforming strained faces into gargoyle masks.

Tension was palpable, accentuated by the occasional fidgeting of one or more of the seated figures. The grey-haired woman at the head of the table, slowly tapping a pencil on the pad in front of her, looked at each of the seated figures in turn. With one exception, they refused to meet her gaze. She cleared her throat and flicked the pencil onto the table.

"Gentlemen, the purpose of this meeting is to decide on the composition of a convoy to deliver food and medical supplies to Tuzla." She paused, noting that the table-top retained the unfocussed interest of several pairs of eyes, while one or two could not resist glances at the faces of their colleagues, opposite.

"The situation up there has worsened considerably. The population has swollen to 250,000, and that does not include the recent influx of displaced persons from the east, mostly women, children and the elderly.

"There are 6,000 in makeshift shelters at the air-field alone. The Non-Governmental Organizations are barely able to cope," the Head of Office continued in a monotone.

"An air-bridge has been established with helicopters ferrying relief supplies from Split, but it's spasmodic and the capacity is limited. Zenica is also in a bad way although the numbers there are lower. As of today's date, the airlift into Sarajevo has been out for three months. Surface convoys are reduced to a trickle, and the Serbs are adamant in their refusal to allow safe access."

The majority of heads at the table were bowed; the rest attempted to meet her eyes but looked away sheepishly when they failed to answer the question mirrored there. Nearly every convoy manager wondered what justification he could put forward to avoid the commitment.

Only one waited with a sense of anticipation and eagerness that he struggled to subdue.

"This crisis is not characterized by a lack of food but by a denial of access. We have several thousand tons of food and medical supplies in the warehouses here, but each convoy is subject to attack. Delivery targets of 16,000 metric tons of food and at least 178 metric tons of non-food is just unachievable in the current situation.

Despite assurances of safe passage, the Norwegian and Danish convoys of three days ago were shelled and turned back."

"We had an UN military escort," interjected the Danish convoy manager, "that drew fire it didn't return."

Heads around the table lifted to look at him, but the faces remained expressionless. The HoS raised an index finger to discourage further comment.

Cheatham shifted impatiently and waited with inward eagerness for her next words while trying to maintain a non-committal outward show of qualified interest.

"This morning I received a cable from Geneva. Everyone there is fully aware of the sterling efforts you have made to date and the importance of the contribution made by your convoys, despite our lack of success in recent weeks. We have asked much of your drivers up to now, and they have responded admirably. UNHCR is grateful."

She shuffled a pile of papers in front of her, then, as she carefully chose her next words, returned them to the manila envelope.

"But it's not enough, not nearly enough," she continued quietly. "We've got to make a breakthrough. The world is watching our effort and, more importantly, the survival of thousands of Bosnians demands it. They are waiting for us.

The pause caused the others in the room to glance in question at each other. Would it be a direct tasking or would she ask for a volunteer convoy?"

Get to it, thought Cheatham, *get to it! Just give us permission to go.*

"Our convoys here have the best chance of reaching Tuzla and, despite the perceptible dangers that exist, I intend to get one through. Therefore, an initial convoy of twenty vehicles will be loaded on Wednesday, to remain on standby to pull out with a maximum of three hours' notice.

"We will take two actions to reduce the risk to the safety of that convoy. Firstly, stemming from the recent experience of the Scandinavians, there will be no UNPROFOR escort. Secondly, we have offered several large convoys of food and material out of Belgrade, to Pale, transported by the Russians, as an inducement for safe passage. There has been no definitive response from the Serbs, but we are confident that our overture will be successful. Based on that optimistic, but realistic premise, we have decided not to wait for their response. I will authorize a move at the first optimum moment."

An immediate buzz of agitation was stifled at once with an admonitory forefinger from the Head of Station.

"Do I have any volunteers?"

She probably expected the ensuing silence to be long and drawn out; since they would not volunteer men and vehicles lightly. However, the pause was brief. Cheatham stood without hesitation, and in a firm voice accepted the assignment.

He was sure the HoS could not contain her surprise at the swiftness of his response, but she showed no emotion.

"Thank you, gentleman."

The managers got to their feet and started to file out of the room.

"Roy," the director said, with a smile, using Cheatham's given name for the first time, despite ten months of previous association, "stay behind. I've some more details for you."

Cheatham was jubilant as he swung the jeep around the sharp curves of the coastal road northwards to Gradec on his way to back to Zagreb. A heavy hood of low cloud shortened the vehicle's main beam, already diffused by the sheeting rain. He had a drive of several hours ahead of him, but nothing could deflate the sense of exhilaration he felt.

The glass of whisky shared with a delighted Head of Station had left a warm and pleasant glow, despite the smallness of the measure. He could not believe his good fortune. How could it all have fallen into his hands like this? The tentative arrangement made by Ovasco and his

German contact, Stösser, worth thousands to himself and the Croat, had been brought to the verge of fruition by his efforts in Metkovic at that all-important briefing.

"You're rich," he told himself, "you're rich!"

That morning, several weeks earlier, things had not looked so bright.

He had woken to stare blearily at the ceiling, his mouth and throat parched from the nicotine and alcohol of the previous night. What had started as a periodic review of the company's invoices, with a courtesy cold beer, had developed into a hard drinking session lasting until well into the early hours of a vile wet morning. Nothing that stormy, wet and bleak bore any relation to the start of a day. How he had driven back through those walls of sleet he would never know. A bed for the night would have been preferred, but despite all the outward bonhomie, the backslapping and laughter, Ovasco, his Croatian host, had not invited him to stay.

"Probably just as well," he thought as he stretched. Throwing the duvet to one side, he sat up and swung his legs over the side of the bed. He scratched his stomach as his feet searched for the trainers that doubled as slippers.

He quickly pulled them back onto the bed, his face forming a grimace, as his bare soles met with the cold vomit congealed on the bedside rug. With distaste, he remembered that he had woken from a stupor during the night but could not get out of bed before the gush of evacuating beer and steak tartare drenched the floor.

The abrupt movement caused a well of dizziness to fill his skull, and waves of nausea ebbed and flowed in his empty stomach. Taking a deep breath, he stood unsteadily to go into the bathroom.

He stepped into the shower cubicle hoping that hot water would dispel the fuzziness in his head. Turning on the tap, he peered at the showerhead, waiting with scant patience for the water. When the water did not materialize, he twisted the tap viciously, first in one and then in the other direction.

Damn and blast! This was not the first time the system had failed, but the property owner had said that he had checked it and repaired the defects. Proved how deceptive the locals could be!

Bloody Croats!

"Careful, Cheatham!" he warned himself. "Don't ever say that out loud." A few drinks too many, like last night, and that could slip out. That would never do. If they did not all speak English, they certainly understood enough.

They were a volatile, unforgiving bunch and thought nothing of using knives to settle a debate. Moreover, Ovasco was probably the most implacable of them all.

Back in England, he would never associate with anyone as dangerous as the hard drinking Croat. Here, however, a very productive relationship made them the most unlikely of bedfellows.

For a convoy manager, with the quantity of trucks that he controlled, he had the opportunity to make money, lots of money. However, to make that amount of cash, he had to make sacrifices. If it were not for the stakes, he certainly would not keep company with the service station owner. Still, there would be time enough to be selective in his choice of friends when he returned to England.

The firm, having entered a cost reimbursement contract with UNHCR, left him pretty much to his own devices. On the ground, *he* determined who got the business for repairs and maintenance, and, because of the illicit returns offered by Ovasco, they were now partners. It meant profit for both of them and, because of that, Cheatham could tolerate less than ideal personalities.

As he stepped out of the shower cubicle, he stubbed his toe against the galvanized bucket that held the cleaner's rags and brushes. Slamming the opaque plastic door shut, he snatched up his watch from the windowsill. Blood rushed to his face and pounded in his head. The movement brought on another giddy spell. He grasped the sink to steady himself. Inhaling deeply he turned, reached for the toilet lid, slapped it down and sat on it to put his trainers on.

No water! Bloody inconvenience of it all. Godforsaken armpit of Europe.

Still, he reminded himself, it was worth it for the money. He started to feel better.

Yes, the money! And with more to come... He was glad now that he had had the balls for Ovasco's proposition.

But then, what balls are needed.

A problem did exist, however. Hardly any convoys had been able to complete their assignments and get through the Serbian blockade. True, they had made successful runs into Bihac, Cazin and other destinations relatively near to Zagreb in the North, but Sarajevo, Zenica and Tuzla were a different kettle of fish due to distance and the proximity of the Serbs. These were the main urban centres of Bosnia Herzegovina, and the Serbian military, commanded by General Mladic, had a stranglehold on the arteries into them.

The Serbian focus seemed to be on Sarajevo because of its cultural and political importance. This only lessened, but in no way eliminated, the risks or dangers involved in trying to break through to Tuzla or Zenica. Too many times in the past, convoys had set out only to return fully loaded at the first sign of hindrance or obstruction. This action met with the full approval of UNHCR, who dreaded casualties.

However, Cheatham was aware that UNHCR could not sit on its hands for much longer. Geneva was not happy with the apparent impasse. The bigwigs there were applying pressure to the local management of the aid organization.

There would be a change of direction and the norm of caution would be abandoned. Of this Cheatham was certain. He just had to be ready when it happened.

He would need someone to lead the convoy, an individual prepared to press on; a leader who had the guts, the will to succeed, and who would not balk at the first hurdle. He remained confident that he would find someone.

More important, at this point, was that UNHCR should start the convoys again.

In the kitchen, he grabbed the unplugged kettle and stuck it under the tap before he remembered that the water was off. With a curse, he dropped the kettle in the sink and turned to the fridge.

There had to be risks involved but he could not think of any.

So why the unease?

Leaning forward, he gripped the neck of a plastic Coca Cola bottle and, leaving the door open to enjoy the coolness on his lower body, he unscrewed the top, adjusting his one-handed grip on the bottle to compensate for the change in its shape as the pressure equalized. After a long, greedy swallow, he burped noisily. The effect of the alcohol he had consumed the night before, especially the shots of *travarica*, the local "poteen," had taken its toll. He was drinking too much and promised himself, yet again, that he would stop, or at least cut down.

The telephone rang, breaking into his reverie.

Picking it up on its third ring, he said politely, "Good Morning, this is the Aid Convoy. How can I help you?" One never knew when it might be the head office.

"Roy, Dayan. *Kako ste?*"

Cheatham deflated to curtness, now that this was not an important call but merely one of his employees at the site office. Despite the boy's physical attractions, he had no intention of relaxing the manner in which he treated employees; at least not during working hours.

"Never mind how I am. What's up, Dayan"

"There are some people here asking about the drivers' vacancies. They saw the advertisement in a German paper and travelled down from Frankfurt. Hold on."

Cheatham heard Dayan ask someone in the background what type of licence he held.

"Yes, they say they've both worked with heavy vehicles. When do you want to see them?"

Cheatham expelled his breath with impatience.

"Later, not now. About ten. Do they have paperwork? References? Previous employment? No, do not ask them now if you don't know. Check 'em out, and I will get together with you before I see them. Send them over to the drivers' restroom until I get there. Okay?"

Cheatham replaced the phone and stood for a moment looking out of the window that faced onto the main road. Despite his curtness on the phone, he was glad that these applicants had turned up in person.

He had deliberately not included the telephone number in the advertisement, so choice was limited. It said come in person or write, and the drivers he knew would not rely on a letter to get them a job. This way it saved a lot of time and inconvenience. There was rarely the need for letters responding to an initial inquiry. There were no appointments to arrange.

If they were not suitable, there was no need to refund return travel costs since no offer or agreement to do so existed. The advertisement had not invited personal visits.

He dragged a chair away from the table, and sat down. He did not feel like work yet.

He reflected on the invoices examined the previous night. As agreed, Ovasco was billing for maximum labour hours for every job completed. Unused repair parts and replacements that had not actually taken place all helped to inflate the cost of the work. Vehicles went to the service station with their main tanks, and reserve tanks, filled with diesel, and with oil levels topped off.

When they came back, each truck had no fuel and no oil. The return on the fuel and oil, on the black market, due to national shortages and high prices, was substantial.

Every little bit helps.

The drivers of the vehicles obviously noticed the deficiencies, but due to the uncertain tenure of their employment, which Cheatham kept to the forefront of everyone's mind, they did not make a big issue of the discrepancies.

Yes , a nice little scam."

He finished the cola. He would have murdered for a coffee but felt immensely better. He could now face the day.

"Funny what wonders a few thou in the bank can do," he mused aloud as he stood up and walked upstairs to get dressed for work, "and a lot more to come with this new deal."

The rain had lessened, and the beam picked out the series of pontoons forming the bridge at Zadar. Ninety minutes later, he negotiated the road climbing through the trees up to the mountain pass.

With Senj far below and behind him, before he knew it, engrossed with his mental spending spree, he joined the ring road that encircled Karlovac. After a minimal delay at the tollbooth—with his UNHCR identity card, he was exempt from paying the road toll—he passed onto the main highway to Zagreb.

He had made excellent time and, although it was late, he would call Ovasco to confirm that the "cargo" would be going.

FOUR

The kiosk attendant deposited the bottle on the counter and reached for one of the Marlboro plastic carrier bags.

"Is that everything?"

The traveller nodded curtly and pulled his wallet out.

"How would you like to pay?"

"*Deutschmark, bitte. Sie nehmen Kreditkarten?*"

"*Aber natürlich.*" She smiled and accepted the proffered card.

Zagreb airport was not busy today—at least her tobacco counter was not. A glance at the Arrivals Area directly opposite had confirmed that the approaching customer was one of the disembarking passengers from the morning flight from Frankfurt. She swiped the card and waited for the receipt to emerge.

"*Schreiben Sie bitte hierunter.*"

She pushed the receipt across the counter and handed the ballpoint to the man who, after signing, took the copy and picked up the bag.

As he left, her smile faded. She quickly examined the credit slip once more, and then followed him with her eyes. Thin, gaunt and with a pronounced stoop, he entered the main concourse and looked around as though expecting to see someone.

She caught the movement as he straightened and lifted his arm. Following his gaze, she saw a short, stocky man hurrying toward him. *Ovasco!* They shook hands, and then hurried towards the exit to the car park.

She picked up the telephone and dialled.

"Colonel Paroski, Marika here, Stösser's arrived."

Stösser leaned back against the leather upholstery.

"How was the flight?" asked Ovasco in German. as he rolled down the window of the Volkswagen to pay the parking fee.

"You have flown before?" asked Stösser in the same language without turning his head.

"Yes, many times," responded the Croat, somewhat puzzled.

"Well, it was like that."

They were soon on the main road to Zagreb.

"Where are we going first?" Stösser asked, as the car caught the traffic lights at green and climbed the incline of the slip road to the Autoput.

"I thought we would lunch at the Gracanka. Cheatham will be there. Afterwards I can take you to your hotel."

"The hotel won't be necessary. I am due back in Köln this evening. Have you fully discussed the transaction with this Cheatham?"

"Yes. His vehicles will go to Tuzla any day now—definitely before the week is out."

"He's aware that this is to be a long-term arrangement."

"He's delighted."

They remained silent as the car travelled through the modern suburbs of Zagreb with its glass-fronted office blocks and utilitarian apartment high-rises. They followed the wide avenue shared by the city tramways until they saw the twin spires of St Stephen's on the hill in the centre of the city.

"You too have a church with two steeples in Cologne, no?" asked Ovasco to break the unnerving stillness.

"Are we nearly there yet?" countered the German ignoring the question.

The Croat shrugged as he took the road below the cathedral leading to the wooded slopes that bordered the city on its northern side.

Ovasco swung on to the gravelled car park and pulled on the brake. Both men climbed out of the car, circumvented the hedge, and climbed the steps of the main entrance. The restaurant, set back amongst the trees, was a low single storey building. As they entered, the *maître d'hôtel* hurried over to greet Ovasco.

He beckoned the men to follow and led them through the main dining area. Ovasco, conferring with the restaurateur in Croatian, broke off to turn to Stösser, whose sharp ears had caught the name Cheatham.

"He's already here," he said.

The small group passed the open screening and moved on to the mezzanine floor to a table that had been reserved for them. As they approached, a short, plump man with bushy eyebrows stood up.

Ovasco greeted Cheatham and made the introductions. Stösser extended a limp hand then sat down.

They ordered drinks and, after some desultory small talk, examined the menus that the *maître d'* had left. They said little as they ate the *hors d'oeuvres* and had begun the main course when Stösser interrupted the silence.

"You are acceptable to the proposition? German marks?"

Cheatham made a quick mental calculation and tried to envisage the amount of money Ovasco had mentioned. He stopped, smiling self-consciously, as he saw the Croat grinning knowingly at him.

"So you have agreed to pay what we asked for the move?" he asked.

"You are certain that your vehicles will depart within the next few days?" Stösser countered without taking his eyes off Cheatham.

The convoy manager nodded.

Stösser closed his mouth around a forkful of grilled pork, then pointed the prongs towards Cheatham.

"Of course, for the total payment there would eventually have to be several shipments. But I'm willing, as a measure of good faith, to make a substantial first payment with nothing more than your friend's recommendation." He indicated Ovasco with a nod of his head.

"And for this I simply transport your items amongst the loads we take north?"

"Exactly. The cargo is already packed, in palletized UN boxes and cartons, and guaranteed indistinguishable from the real thing." Cheatham shot a quick look at Ovasco, who continued to grin. "How will you make payment?"

"I already have made the first payment." Stösser again indicated Ovasco with a brief nod.

Cheatham tried to control his features but was unable to hide the frown. He stared myopically at Ovasco, who just smirked. He leaned forward and gripped Cheatham's wrist with a powerful hand,

"Be happy, my friend, we both share equal risk." He squeezed, and then roared with laughter. "None at all!"

Cheatham did not join in but continued to watch Stösser. There was truth in what Ovasco said. He would not be on the convoy. Even if the arms were discovered, no one could prove his involvement.

"Where is the cargo now?"

"I take it then that you agree?" asked Stösser.

Cheatham nodded and reached across the white linen to shake Stösser's hand. Stösser waved him away with an empty fork.

"I will tell Ovasco later today, as soon as I confirm the details with my people at my storage point. I will phone with those details before five. However, understand, and understand clearly, delivery must be in Bosnia. Tuzla. Unequivocally."

Cheatham remained silent for several minutes, busy with his thoughts.

The darkened warehouses were spacious and wide with long rows of loaded pallets stacked to the roofs with

diverse supplies. There were bulging jute sacks emblazoned with the bald eagle logo and filled with flour from the prairies of America's mid-west, medical accessories from Stuttgart and Munich, down-filled sleeping bags and camp beds from Norway, and boots and shoes from Italy and the Czech Republic.

Spider watched as the pallets of flour, lowered onto the cargo bed of his truck, completed his load. Waving to the driver of the forklift, he swung lithely up onto the truck. The forklift crossed to the side of the warehouse and slid its prongs under the stack of heavy metal truck sides, lifting them high in the air while on the move back to Spider's vehicle.

Several minutes later, they were back in place with the tarpaulin roped over them. He removed his work gloves and wiped a heavy sweat from his face and forehead. Although direct sunlight was only visible at the shed's doors, the dry heat inside was oppressive. It seemed as though he waited for hours to get to the point of loading in these depots, but once the process started, ten or twenty tons of stores were loaded in fewer minutes.

The powerful engine growled into life, and the loaded truck rolled slowly but easily into the white heat of the yard. Maintaining a walking pace so as not to create clouds of dust for the waiting drivers, he drove towards the gate and then onto the road back to Metkovic.

In less than fifteen minutes, he would be back at the site and could have a meal before going for a swim. A sense of well-being that had until recently been absent rested easily on him and there now seemed to be a purpose to life. Feeling satisfied, he drove over the bridge spanning the Neretva in the centre of town and turned towards the firm's site in Opusan.

Despite his customary cynicism, the job of convoy leader had been fulfilling from day one. Prepared for a certain amount of disillusionment, he had been surprised when his doubts had not materialized. The variety in the work and the miscellany of tasks pushed the trauma of Belfast, and the period of mind-bending limbo that followed, to the back of his consciousness.

Who would have thought that he would consider himself fortunate to have met up with Cheatham again? Yes, as the truck swung past the open vegetable market and accelerated into the long stretch towards the site in Opusan, it had certainly been worthwhile keeping the appointment in *The Three Bells*.

He stood at the bar in the lounge. Ingrained habit made him survey the other occupants of the room. The voice of the barmaid broke through his thoughts.

"And you would like?"

"Bitter. A pint, please."

The scar drew the woman's eyes, and she started on seeing it for the first time. The barmaid did not, could not, look away and flushed to the roots of her tinted hair. She forced her attention to the taps. Placing the brimming glass in front of him, she took the proffered money to the till. Refusing to meet his eyes, she concentrated on his hands as she passed him the change.

"Thanks," he said curtly, and turned towards an empty table near the door.

The scarred tissue on his lower face and neck, his own Phantom-of-the-Opera deformity, had this effect on strangers. Their aversion, mingled with pity, angered him.

The wound had caused him physical pain for some time after the shooting and he wondered, especially when depressed, if it would have been better to wear the Kevlar body armour that morning.

The protective padding had shielded his torso but the discharge from the shotgun had shredded flesh and ligaments in his neck. It had shattered part of his jaw and torn up the lower side of his face, which had healed to a white toadstool, puckering the cheek below his left eye.

The extensive treatment afterwards meant he had endured many painful hours. The ligaments were functional again and most of his face patched up, but the refusal to undergo further surgery, which would have brought some semblance of normality back to his features, did not stem from any dread of pain or misguided pride in his wounds.

His unwillingness defied definition. He had tried to analyze, rationalize, his reluctance, but that only resulted in the vague feeling that somehow it was the price of survival.

Expressed verbally, the rationale would be suspect, but he could not shake the notion that the burden of the scar in some minor way ameliorated the lost lives of the others.

The Regiment played down deaths and serious injuries of a frequency not known to the public or the rest of the Army. Dark humour and caustic cynicism were masks used to disguise the faces of emotion and grief. They rarely displayed raw anguish, sorrow or distress. A professional force dealing with death and destruction on a daily basis could not afford the debilitating and eroding effect of overt grief. The morale of those remaining would not, could not, survive it.

Nevertheless, the sense of loss, when told that two of his closest friends were dead, was total and immutable. Try as he might, he was not able to build a protective facade. Morbid mental replays of the action disturbed nights of long—interminable—hours. *What if... if only I had... what if...* played in constant loops in his thoughts. Then, on visiting his sergeant in hospital for the first time, several weeks after the action, he broke. The NCO's total paralysis from the neck down, with a zero recovery prognosis for this family man with the sweetest kids he knew, caused a wave of extreme nausea that engulfed him. Tears blinded him. Spider believed that disfigurement was not equal to the price the others had paid, but it was his contribution.

Wounded twice before, he had healed, but this time it had destroyed something irretrievable; shredded fibres left his psyche unsupported. It engendered a vulnerability, not linked to physical fear, but one that shrank from the challenges of fate. He could not go on with a motivation no better than that of a mercenary. He needed more, a belief, a greater moral purpose; but none existed in an abstract political concept. There was no shame, and he had felt none, in being a warrior, but now he needed a belief to sustain him; a personal justification for pride other than being a professional, trained to kill, for pay and pension. His attention came back to the beer. It should now be warm enough to drink. The scything pain usually prodded into action by cold liquids was absent. After a tentative sip, he took a longer swallow.

After hospital, the return to Hereford made him aware all too soon that the sense of belonging, previously felt as an active member of the elite special force, had gone. Nevertheless, he had felt hurt when his

Commanding Officer told him that psychiatric examination had determined him to be unsuitable for continuing active service.

Refusing the offer of a position on the instructing staff, he had opted instead for a clean break. He had not exercised his option to extend, and left the Army.

Although he had been back in Basildon for three weeks, he had not tried to get work. Despite contacts with old friends and acquaintances, some of whom had offered him jobs, there was no desire to start something new. His financial situation would not allow him to remain unemployed forever, but tomorrow, or the next day, would be soon enough.

Each day had passed in a slow drift of lethargy. Although he rose early, by force of habit, sound sleep had been rare. An initial cup of coffee, the newspaper, and more coffee until midday had become routine. Then, providing the weather was dry, he would leave the flat and wander through the town, invariably ending up in one or other of the local pubs.

Today would be slightly different.

A couple of days earlier a friend from his pre-Army time had mentioned that Roy "Cheat" Cheatham had expressed an interest in looking him up and gave Spider a contact number for the man. With only mild curiosity, he had rung Cheatham and they had agreed to meet in *The Three Bells*.

"Spider? Spider Webb?" The voice broke into his reverie. He looked up to see a vaguely familiar face, and took the proffered hand as full recognition flooded to the fore.

"Cheat," he said half-standing, "how's it going?"

"Can't complain." The newcomer took a seat opposite Spider. "So what's been happening? Working yet?"

Spider shook his head as he raised his glass and looked at Cheatham over the rim.

They had been members of the same childhood gang as boys, worked in the same garage on leaving school, but the relationship had waned during their mid-teens. A security check at the garage, initiated because of extensive losses, had uncovered theft but no culprit.

Nevertheless, both had to leave. Cheatham had gone to work at the Ford factory in Dagenham. Spider had seen less and less of him, and they had finally gone their different ways, losing touch just before his enlistment.

"So what are you doing now?" asked Spider.

"I'm on a break from Zagreb for a few days. We're running relief convoys down there. I go back on Thursday."

"Big change from Rennie's Garage, then?"

Cheatham coloured and looked at Spider to see any intended malice. Satisfied there was none, he grinned, almost shyly.

"Yeah, you could say that. I'm the main man now with twenty ten-ton trucks and twenty-five people working for me. Keeps me busy, but it's got its compensations."

"Where'd you run the convoys to?"

"All over. It's mostly in the north of the old Yugoslavia. We've done some runs to other parts of Bosnia, but not so much. Mind you, I'm rarely on the road with them. There's enough to do organizing things and that," said Cheatham.

"That's a fair old gash you've got there, Spider; looks painful."

"It has its moments."

"Are you going to leave it as it is?"

"I'd rather not talk about it."

"Understood. No sweat."

There was a break in the conversation as both men turned their attention to their beer.

"So, any plans for the future?" Cheatham asked in a conciliatory manner.

"Not really."

"Married?"

"No. And you?"

"No. Never really fancied it." Cheatham appeared ill at ease with the question and looked around the bar as though to deflect further questions. The noise level had increased as the lounge started to fill.

Cheatham leant forward.

With luck, my convoy leader problem is about to be solved, but softly, Cheat, softly.

"Have you thought about working overseas?"

"Can't say I've given much thought to working at all. Wouldn't have a hang-up about working outside the UK though," shrugged Spider. "Are you offering me a job?"

Cheatham did not return his smile but nodded.

"Besides the leave, one of the reasons I'm back here is to find a convoy leader, a sort of working manager on the road, so to speak, down there. How would you feel about that?"

Spider looked speculatively at Cheatham. On the point of saying that he did not really want a job at this stage, he changed his mind.

"Why not?"

He nodded.

Cheatham leaned back, somehow more confident.

"Y'know, I like coming back. In fact, I look forward to it for weeks but no sooner am I here than I want to be out of the country again. Weird, ain't it?"

"It's natural enough, affects a lot of people that way."

Cheatham took a sip of his drink.

"I work for a firm that has a contract with the UN to provide transport for relief supplies and fuel to different parts of northern Croatia and Bosnia. Banja Luka, Cazin, Bihac, with a mixed bunch of drivers. All nationalities."

"No locals driving?"

"Can't use 'em, 'cept as interpreters."

Cheatham rested his arms on the table.

"Local drivers can't be employed because we cross into different war zones on a daily basis. Serbs will not accept Croats, in their areas and vice versa. The driving isn't straightforward because of the different factors that affect it, like bad road conditions, drunken idiots with weapons, flare-ups between the different sides and other 'embuggerances'."

Cheatham sat back, his empty glass spinning idly between his fingers. Spider smiled, reached across to remove it, and then picked up his own, before walking to the bar for another round.

Left to his own thoughts, Cheatham felt a surge of optimism. He had no doubt that Webb was capable. If everything continued to go the way it seemed to be heading, then he had his man to oversee the convoys. Moreover, for nothing. There was no reason to cut Webb in. He did not have to know what he was escorting.

Spider returned to place both glasses on the table as Cheatham closely watched a youth in skin-tight jeans playing solo pool.

"You were saying, Cheat."

Cheatham wet his lips, then brought his eyes back to Spider.

"About six weeks ago, the firm got a supplementary contract to make runs into Tuzla, Sarajevo, Zenica and a few other places down the other end of the country. We have been running out of Zagreb, but it could prove to be uneconomical in terms of time, money and fuel.

"So, I've opened up another base down near Metkovic, on the border with Bosnia, that'll cut the time of each convoy by at least four days. Problem is, I need someone down there that I can rely on.

"He must be capable and able to organize the office so that it will run for the few days that he is out on convoy, keep track of the major taskings, all that sort of thing. I need someone who can think on his feet. Someone who appreciates that in this business, you have to take the rough with the smooth."

Despite a spark of interest, Spider did not respond immediately. There was no doubt that he had the abilities Cheatham had mentioned. With no ties in the UK, maybe it was time to get involved in something worthwhile.

"How long would it be likely to last?"

"Well, like anything of this nature, permanency is not part of it. We only get a six-month contract from the UN but, if you were interested, I could give you the same, regardless of when the situation bottoms out. Any extensions would be dependent on the firm getting further contracts. Interested?"

"It sounds as though it could be something. When would you want me to start?"

"Providing we could agree on terms, I'd want you as soon as possible. My scheme would be to have you work alongside me in Zagreb for a couple of days to get the hang of things. Then I'd travel down with you to the other place to get things set up and running."

Spider asked some desultory questions about the other employees, aspects of the work and location of the site, then recognized that he was interested. At an undefined point in the discussion, both men grinned at each other, both knowing that Spider had taken the hook. Impulsively, they reached across the table and shook hands.

"Another one?"

Spider nodded.

"I fly back to Zagreb on Thursday, day after tomorrow, but I can arrange your flight from that end and get you there within a couple of weeks. Suit you?"

"Go for it." Spider, felt a new enthusiasm for life.

Cheatham smiled smugly.

Suits me too, right down to the ground.

The River Main, absorbing the leaden reflection of the sky, its surface peppered by the continuous drizzle, flowed silently past Frankfurt's YMCA. Calum could not shed the sensation of thousands of dull, opaque eyes, set in the stone faces of the city's banks and commercial offices across the width of the river, watching him. Here and there, a point of light would flash on the yards of chrome and glass set in the grey concrete. The tree-lined street below was deserted, and the leaves and branches glistened in the closing dusk.

In Frankfurt, he had found a driving job, making deliveries for a catering contractor who provided canteen services for several factories and office blocks. Finding a place to stay was not so easy. The work was black market, of course, no deductions or social contributions were paid on his behalf, but at least it gave him the where-withal for food and the twelve marks per night for the hostel.

Weekends here in Sachenhausen were wild, and although the Guinness would never be as good as that back home—they did not know how to pull a good one—you could forget the loneliness in the crowds in the pubs. The *craic* with the other expats—an unbelievably big community of his own folk were here—helped minimize the empty feeling of being homesick. Still, nothing could beat the pubs on the Ormeau Road of a Friday night.

"Get bloody real," he snarled at himself. "You're here and in a damn sight better health than you would be at this very minute back there."

Christ, would they be looking for me again?

They had to be; the investigation must have come to a dead end days ago. It would be too much to hope for that they had come up with somebody else, but maybe, just maybe, they had.

However, he could not be sure that they would not be looking for him again. After all, he had been questioned and, surprisingly, had satisfied them; surprisingly, because of his guilt and because he had really believed his time was up. Told to go about his business, he knew deep down that if the investigation did not produce a result, they would come full circle and start again.

He had no plans, no strategy to run or hide, but it made no sense to hang around there waiting for them to pick him up. If they did get him again, it would not be as easy as the first time; that had been a nightmare because of his own fears.

He prayed they would accept a display of naiveté—he had not stayed around, because he wanted to travel. If only he could get away with it! Sometimes when his spirits were high, he really believed he could; other times stark reality stomped on any spark of optimism.

He turned from the window, and crossed the sparsely furnished room, with its bunk beds and very little else. He folded his sheet, which with its returnable ten-mark deposit was currency, and placed it in the small metal locker that he shared with Kurt.

The German would probably be in the TV room.

Wonder if he's going out tonight?

At the very least, it would be a distraction of sorts, being in someone else's company, instead of alone with his own stark thoughts, which only lashings of mind-bending alcohol could numb.

The TV high in the corner of the bar had the sound turned off. Since Calum didn't understand a word, it made no real difference. Watching it as he sipped the Guinness, his interest rose when the screen filled with pictures from the former Yugoslavia, showing a convoy of white UN trucks held up at a barrier.

Uniformed men wearing strange blue camouflage outfits and carrying guns climbed all over each truck. The camera picked up a group of men, at the side of one of the vehicles, and he grasped from their dress and postures that they were the drivers.

They were civilians!

Kurt had been right; soldiers were not the only ones driving down there.

Kurt had worked for some big transport firm just outside Wiesbaden and had travelled all over Europe. He had apparently had a big bust-up with his girlfriend several days ago and was now dossing in the YM. He reckoned that the relief convoys, the official ones, paid the real money and that they were crying out for drivers.

Calum watched the drivers mount their trucks before the news programme moved onto another subject.

Might be the place to be, at least for the immediate future. But, how would I get in touch with the people who do the hiring? Kurt'll know.

Carrying his beer, he pushed through the crowd in the bar and stepped outside to find the German earnestly conversing with a young woman.

FIVE

They walked across the gravel of the yard to the drivers' rest room. Inside, three men, obviously off-duty drivers, were playing darts.

"We've been told to wait here until the boss calls for us," Calum said to no one in particular. All three nodded in acknowledgement.

The newcomers flopped onto the empty bench, leant back against the wall, and watched the play. Calum wondered if long practice at the game led to any constructive advantage in other fields or skills.

"Possibly mental arithmetic," he thought and grinned.

With half an ear, he listened to the conversation. Kurt's interest also appeared to deepen as they gathered that the drivers were discussing the movement of their personal effects to a new site.

"Are you moving then?" Calum asked.

"Metkovic, down by Dubrovnik. Any time now. We already have an operation up and running down there. Been going about a month now."

"How's the driving down there?" asked Kurt.

"Trips are a lot shorter, couple days off at each end."

"Yeah," contributed the tallest of the three, "means we don't have to drive two days down the coast road to get to the start point. The new place is right on the border."

Conversation dried up and the players' interest returned to their game. Calum pulled a tattered magazine across the table towards him and was soon lost in his own thoughts. He felt tired from the long overnight journey from Frankfurt. He had hardly slept during the trip, although they had been fortunate in hitching lifts without too much waiting. His eyes had just closed when the office clerk looked around the door and said that Cheatham wanted to see Kurt.

Calum began to relax, knowing that he had sized Cheatham up. He did not need to think about his answer. The manager would not go to the bother of checking on the driving claims he had made. Why should he, as long as Calum performed adequately for the wage offered?

In the yard, Calum had shown that he could control the lowering of the heavy spare wheel of the ten-ton truck, held in its bracket high behind the cab. With some difficulty, it was true, but he could roll it into position for changing any one of the other fixed wheels. Jacking up the vehicle had been problematic but not impossible and he had surprised himself, with his tenacity.

Driving the thing, with its semi-automatic gearbox and power steering, had been child's play. Luckily, Kurt had told him to let the engine build up the air in the system before doing anything else, and the rest had come naturally.

The question from Cheatham brought Calum back.

"Yes, that's no problem, I'll write home for the references as soon as possible."

"Fine, fine. That's it, then," said Cheatham, who knew that he could not give a damn if he never saw either one's documentation. The new arrivals were going to fit into his plans very nicely.

"I'll introduce you to Crowther. You'll share a room until Friday, and then you'll pick up a load and travel down to Metkovic.

"But first, let's get you with the admin people to fix you up with UNHCR ID cards."

Calum followed Cheatham back to the restroom where they collected Kurt and made their way across the yard to the main office.

The automatic doors swung open at the approach of the luggage trolley and revealed a bank of searching faces. Without difficulty, Rath picked out his contact. He nodded as the girl with auburn hair indicated the area to his left. Her freckled face bobbed and weaved its way through the press of bodies that thinned, as the distance from the barrier increased.

"Welcome to Frankfurt."

"Thanks." It sounded more abrupt than he had intended. "You've got a car?" H smiled in an effort to appear friendlier.

"Follow me," she said over her shoulder as she led the way on the down escalator. He took in the well-shaped calves and the firm curves of her stonewashed jeans before glancing around to identify possible watchers. They reached the lower level, where the crowd thickened once again in front of a McDonald's, but her pace did not slacken as she continued to walk toward the pay kiosks in the tunnel.

He followed with an easy stride.

She led the way and returned her purse to her bag, keeping the parking ticket in her hand. They pushed through the swing doors then waited with four other couples for the lift.

When the doors opened, they entered the elevator with the others. The woman pressed up against him as the doors closed. He felt an involuntary stirring, but she remained apparently oblivious. Moments later the lift reached the third floor and the others pushed forward to leave. She shook her head, indicating that they had more floors to travel.

The parking hall was empty but for four cars. She walked towards the nearest one, a black Mercedes, and held the boot open. Throwing in his holdall, he waited at the passenger door.

"It's open," she said across the roof of the vehicle before climbing in behind the wheel.

They left the airport environs and within minutes were filtering into the traffic towards Frankfurt city when she spoke again.

"It looks as though McDermot has moved on," she said. Her attention focused on the overtaking cars as she pulled the car over into the fast lane and gunned the engine.

"Tell me I didn't hear right.

"We'd traced him to the YM down by the river about a week ago and found out that he had found a job. Knowing where he lived and where he worked, we didn't think it necessary to keep him under constant observation. The orders from Belfast were just to locate and confirm his whereabouts.

"Most nights he was out drinking with a German friend of his, at pubs in Sachenhausen. Then we were shorthanded...". She sensed him stiffen with impatience or annoyance.

She added in a rush, "Jimmy, one of the watchers, went down with flu.

"A couple of nights ago McDermot did not show at his usual hangout. We were not too concerned. He had been drinking most of the time we were watching. We thought he might be having an early night. When he did not show again last night, we checked. He hasn't been to work for three days now."

"Have you checked out the YM?"

"We're going there now. I've got to pick up Jimmy first."

He expelled his breath forcibly. She looked away as she saw his frown.

The west end suburbs appeared, dominated by the elongated stem of the concrete mushroom of the Main Tower that punctured the skyline. Minutes later, the car passed the nondescript, rectangular grey pile of the German National Bank. Speeding under the trees that lined Miguel, then Nibelungen Allee, she swung the car left at the lights.

"It's just up here."

She turned the car into the flow of traffic on the other side of the dual carriageway. The car slowed and crawled past the line of parked cars, stopping as a man slid through a gap and stepped into the street.

"Jimmy Rafferty," she said, by way of introduction, as the newcomer opened the car door and climbed into the back.

She pulled away.

"Better make for Weissenstein, Siobhan," said Rafferty leaning forward. "It looks as though his friend, Kurt Bierbaum, had a regular watering hole—the *Zur Post* near the U-Bahn stop.

"He's ducked out from the YM; I phoned, but no one at reception there seems to know where or when. If they don't know at the pub then..." He shrugged.

He turned to introduce himself to the big man in the passenger's seat, but the air of frostiness in the car caused him to change his mind, and he sat back.

"So how's things," Rafferty asked, as the barman pulled the first of the three Kilkenny beers that he had ordered. The barman looked up and across to the others at the table beside the window, taking in the presence of the big man, and nodding to Siobhan. Bringing his attention back to his questioner, he gave a non-committal grimace.

"Has Kurt been in lately?"

"He's gone; didn't you know? Him and the young Irish guy." He set the first beer on the bar and started pulling the second. "Pair o'dickheads. Off to Croatia to feed the hungry. Working on those convoys."

"Is that right? When did they go?"

The barman lifted his shoulders, signalling ignorance or disinterest. He set the second tankard on the bar, then relenting, called out to one of the customers seated on a stool at the end of the bar.

"Eh, Marcus. *Wann sind Dicke und Dunne weggefahren?*"

The customer addressed broke off his conversation with his neighbour and lifted his head. He glanced at the barman, looked to see who had raised the question, then, reassured that it was not a police enquiry, answered,

"*Vorgestern, glaube ich.*"

Jimmy and the barman looked at each other as the latter shrugged and said, "Day before yesterday, he supposes."

"Have one for yourself, and Marcus," said Rafferty laying twenty marks on the bar.

He picked up the three glasses in a two-handed grip and took them over to the table. Both Rath and Siobhan had followed the conversation closely.

"I want to know precisely when they left Frankfurt, where they're headed and who they intend working for," said Rath. His companions looked at each other over their glasses but made no response.

After several minutes of silence, Siobhan broke it by asking Rath if he had accommodation.

"No, but I'd appreciate it if something could be arranged."

She searched through her bag and took out a small notebook, which she leafed through then, holding it open, passed to Jimmy.

"Ring the Ramada, Roedelheim. They're big enough to still have rooms available."

Expressionless, Jimmy took the book and went towards the phone.

Every table was occupied. The crowd at the bar stood at least three deep. Smoke, thick and grey from the inevitable cigarettes, hung in slow eddies below the ceiling.. Music from the jukebox, together with the electronic clattering of the pinball machines, vied with loud conversation and the shouted orders for drinks. The two men and the woman in the corner had said little to each other for most of the evening.

Rath looked at his watch and, as he leaned forward to tell the others that he was going to his hotel, a sudden change in Jimmy's posture made him pause.

"The barman's just pointed us out to a fella at the bar." muttered Rafferty from behind his raised glass. Rath glanced at the throng at the bar but was unable to identify the individual. He remained outwardly relaxed but experienced an inner new tension.

"Small guy, open-necked shirt, blue anorak," Jimmy whispered head bowed over the table. Siobhan reached behind her for her shoulder bag and took out her cigarettes leaving the bag unzipped on her lap. The man described looked directly at the group then made his way towards them through the press of people. Stopping a couple of feet away, glass held at waist height, he examined them with a watery but direct stare from pale blue eyes.

"Ye's is lookin' fer McDermot?"

"Ah'm his cousin," responded Siobhan with a brief smile before either of her male companions could answer.

"Is that right now?" sneered the little man, placing his glass down, and pulling the ashtray towards him. Without asking, he stretched a none-too-clean hand to the opened cigarette packet on the table and took one. As he lit it, with her Zippo, he peered at each one of them in turn, one eye squinting under unruly grey eyebrows against the smoke. Siobhan took a cigarette herself then leaned towards him, inviting him to light it. As he did so, fumbling with the cover, she smiled.

"And ye'd be knowing our Calum, would ye?"

"I would," the man responded, not smiling, "and I ast meself how his cousin disn't know where he's at?"

"He wiz supposed te meet us here t'night," Siobhan returned, broadening her vernacular to match his, with a subdued giggle. "Ah'm Siobhan and," indicating Rath, "this is me fella and Jimmy's a pal o' his. So ye're a close pal o' Calum's?"

"How desperate are ye's te know where he's at now?" said the man as he ignored the question and addressed the silent Rath.

Jimmy spoke for the first time. "What's yer point, old man?" he snarled belligerently, locking his eyes on the other's face. Rath remained expressionless as the older man examined his features, disregarding Jimmy, as though he were not there.

"Is it worth anything te ye's?" he persisted.

Rath lifted his glass but said nothing. He nodded to Siobhan who said,

"We're generous by nature. Jimmy, get..." she paused and pointed an opened hand at the older man's chest.

"Niall."

"Get Niall another o' whutever he's drinkin'," she directed, pulling her chair closer to the table.

"So, Niall, what have ye got?"

"I know exactly where they're now," he answered, turning his hand to lie open on the table. Siobhan dropped a hundred-mark note onto the opened palm, enjoying the surprise that flickered across his face. She resisted the temptation to look at Rath but was prepared to bet that he had not seen her get the money out either. Niall put the note into a pocket of his soiled anorak. He pulled out a rolled-up newspaper from another pocket but did not pass it over.

"Him and his pal were selling some things—watches, couple o' rings, chains—to get the scratch together to go to Croatia."

"And did they say where in Croatia?" she asked, her brogue subdued knowing that Rath was hoping for, would indeed want, something more specific.

"No," said Niall, "but I picked this up after they left." He laid the newspaper in front of her.

"And . . ." she prompted, as Rath reached for the copy of the *Frankfurter Zeitung* and spread it open.

"They've circled an ad in the jobs vacant. That's where they would go first."

Rath located the circled entry, then looked reflectively at Niall. After a pause, he nodded his satisfaction to Siobhan.

"So what d'ye want them fer?" Niall asked as he picked up the filled glass Jimmy had brought to the table.

"Just keep your mouth shut about this," Siobhan snapped, all pretence of friendliness gone. "Now fuck off, and remember what I've said." She felt more assured than she had all night, now that they knew where Calum was. The success bolstered her confidence, and she no longer felt like the big man's inferior. She took a long swallow of her drink.

Hell, she was no man's inferior!

Rath opened the hotel room door, then stood aside to let Siobhan pass. His nostrils trapped a pleasant warm waft of alcohol tinged with tobacco and a trace of jasmine. She stood in the doorway surveying the room, her dark hair level with his chest, her scent teasingly fading as she brushed past him. Throwing her handbag onto the bed she widened her eyes at him and gave a long drawn out 'Hmm' of fake delight as she pointed to the mini-bar next to the full-length mirror.

"Drink?" she asked, opening the door and examining the contents of the small refrigerator.

"Cognac, if there is any." She pulled a plastic cup from the tube on the top shelf.

In a glass, if you don't mind."

She threw the unwanted container into a nearby wastepaper basket and walked towards the bathroom, unscrewing the cap of the miniature bottle. He let his holdall fall at the foot of the bed and removed his jacket, which he dropped onto a chair, before stretching his arms in an expansive feeling of well-being. He flopped onto the sofa and removed his shoes, as Siobhan returned with the glasses. Each contained a measure of amber cognac.

"Move up." She lowered herself onto the couch beside him, kicked off her high heels, drew her legs up under her, and passed him his drink.

"*Slainté.*" She sighed contentedly as they touched glasses.

Head tilted back against the sofa, with his long legs stretched out across the rug, he awoke in the darkened room feeling pressure on his upper body. Without changing position, he opened his eyes to squint downwards. Her head rested on his chest, rising and falling with his breathing, her face hidden in the profusion of burnished chestnut curls that billowed across his shirtfront. She must have turned the lights off when he had dropped off, then made herself comfortable. He smiled.

Let her sleep.

He pulled his arm clear and shifted his weight to a more comfortable position. He closed his eyes.

Almost immediately, intense pleasurable warmth swept across his groin. He stiffened, but otherwise did not move as her open palm slid lightly across his lower stomach Her fingers found his zip. As it was opened, it seemed as though an expanding pressure had been vented; released from the restriction of his clothing his now-erect penis was freed by cool, searching fingers and pulled clear.

Her hand was smooth and dry, moving slowly, delightfully slowly, up and down. She shifted her weight, and his involuntary gasp of ecstasy sounded loud as the fingers eased his flesh towards and into the moistness of her waiting mouth.

Unable to control his breathing, he sank his fingers into her thick hair and pulled her, none too gently, up and away, from his groin. He took in her flushed complexion and the excited look in her eyes before crushing her mouth with his.

Seconds later, she pulled away to stand upright before him and, with her eyes locked on his, unzipped her jeans, then kicked them free. Her naked legs, feet apart, joining the firm swell of her lower belly and fulfilling the earlier promise were inches from his face, with the tantalizing scent of her womanhood full and alluring in his nostrils.

Grasping her buttocks, his fingers spread wide across the resilient flesh, he pulled her forward and pressed his face in the cushion of soft, wiry hair. He heard her stifle a moan of unadulterated pleasure before she wrenched his head away.

Grasping both his wrists, she pulled him towards the waiting bed.

Moving slowly, so as not to wake her, he reached across her naked back for the cigarettes and lighter. Lying with one arm behind his head, he watched the smoke spiral upwards, feeling more relaxed than he had felt for months. If things had been different, he would have liked to stay here longer, get to know Siobhan better and, he smiled, get to 'know' her many more times. However, the hunt for Calum was not yet behind him, and in a few hours, he would have to move on.

She stirred and laid a soft forearm across his chest, drawing her body closer to his. Moments later, she made a soft purr of contentment then lifted her head to look at him in the grey morning light.

"Hmm—breakfast," she murmured, taking the cigarette from his hand and taking a shallow drag. "What are you thinking?" She turned to lie on her back.

"About what's got to be done next," he answered, stubbing out the cigarette.

"When it's done, will you be coming back through Frankfurt?" When he did not answer immediately, she sat up to swing her feet to the floor.

"Forget I asked that."

"It's not that I don't want to," he said, stretching out a hand to touch her shoulder, "it's just that—"

"If anyone should understand, it's me, especially in our line of work," Her voice had hardened.

"Just—please," moving his hand from her arm, "no excuses."

He sat up his mind made up.

"Siobhan, for what it is worth, I'll be back. I'd like to see you again."

She looked at him from under her tousled hair and a slow smile lit up her face. It changed into a pout of mock injury, hiding her delighted laughter, when he said, straight-faced,

"And I will respect you in the morning."

She grabbed one of the pillows and began to pound him, in a fit of giggles.

The long train journey from Frankfurt, with a short stop in Munich, across Austria and through Slovenia was uneventful. He had tried to sleep, but with moderate success.

During the long periods of wakefulness, he thought of how he would approach his assignment.

While his doubts certainly did not qualify as a quandary, he was not quite sure how he would accomplish it. He knew he was not going to kill McDermot. Would he, however, coerce the man into returning to Ireland? With force, if necessary?

He knew even that was unlikely, although not doing so would increase the risk to his own well-being. It had occurred to him that he had no great desire to return home. If he did not carry out his assigned task, going home would make it easier for the organization to exact retribution for his dereliction of duty.

His enthusiasm for *The Struggle* had waned. He had belatedly doubted the utility of the bombing campaigns and now he questioned the validity of his own part in The Troubles. What had he or the IRA achieved by the disappearance of those individuals he had eliminated?

He winced as he mentally substituted *murdered* for *eliminated.*

Nevertheless, he had accepted the task and had almost caught up with the errant McDermot. Perhaps, he would be able to clarify his thinking and decide on a course of action when he confronted the man.

Arriving in Zagreb mid-morning on the day following his departure from Germany, he stood outside the railway station and waved to a waiting taxi. He showed the driver the newspaper clipping with the address. The driver threw his bag into the opened boot and within seconds, they had pulled out into the traffic and were heading out on the main road to Varazdin and the base camp of the convoy organization.

He decided that his best option to gain time would be to seek employment with the very outfit that McDermot intended to join. If McDermot had failed to get a job, he would continue to track him, but if McDermot were now working for the aid convoy, then he too would try it. When he found the runaway, he would probably have to implement Plan B, which, at this moment, he had still to devise.

SIX

Colonel Paroski looked at the former Communist behind the desk. His father had served with Radovic long before the general became Head of Intelligence for the Croatian Army. The older officer did not acknowledge his presence, despite the passage of several minutes, but continued to write.

Paroski eyes moved to the framed photograph on the wall behind the man, which showed Radovic with three others in the company of Marshall Tito. Although Paroski and Radovic were both Croats, Radovic had been born in Belgrade, while he came from Mostar, in southern Bosnia. He knew of the soldier from stories his father told and from similar legends perpetuated by other older military men. Radovic was what was referred to, but never derisively, by the younger element in the Army as "one of the old school".

The general, educated in Russia, had served in the Red Army before returning to the Balkans immediately after the Second World War. He became a member of the Central Committee of the Yugoslavian Communist Party and played a major part at the party meeting that passed the sentence of death on the leader of the defeated Chetniks.`

After the collapse of the Axis powers, the Communists had captured Mihailovic in 1946. Radovic showed his ruthlessness with his outspoken and passionate support for the death penalty. The party executive dutifully ratified Tito's demand for the execution of the Chetnik leader.

Radovic's subsequent progress in the Army and the Party was confirmation of Tito's appreciation.

Paroski's father had been an active member of the Partisans but was too junior to have a say in the workings of the Party. He had not been political, or even astute enough, to pretend he was. He remained a tool to implement policies made by others. However, he had caught the attention of Radovic who chose him as the officer in charge of the firing squad responsible for Mihailovic's execution, and secret burial.

Despite the passage of time, and the many changes that post-war Yugoslavia experienced, General Radovic continued to have great influence in the Party. He believed implicitly in the one-nation concept, provided it was under Croatian leadership.

With the present turn of events, his vigour in promoting ethnic cleansing, with particular regard to the calculating terror with which it was enforced, showed that the elapse of time had not diminished his zeal. His place on the decision-making cartel, pursuing the war against the Serbs, ensured that his position of power was stronger than it had ever been.

The colonel had been surprised when he received orders to join Radovic's group in Zagreb. He was even more surprised to learn that Radovic had personally made the request for the transfer.

The general signed the last of the papers in front of him and placed the pen in the skull-shaped holder. Without raising his head, he peered at Paroski from under his bushy grey eyebrows, and then held up his left index finger, indicating a pause for one further action. He reached over to the intercom, pressed a button and said, *"Kava."*

"Well, Colonel," he met Paroski's gaze as he leaned back in his chair, "how is your father?"

The sound of the door opening behind him caused Paroski to withhold his reply. Radovic maintained his level stare as the secretary set the coffee tray on the desk. The general poured two cups from the ornate silver pot and indicated the sugar with a nod and upraised eyebrows. Paroski shook his head. He and reached for the proffered cup.

"He is not well, but at his age that is to be expected."

The general gave no indication that he was aware that Paroski's father was three years younger than he was. He continued to look fixedly at Paroski, without a word, for some time, before he spoke.

"I want you to help resolve concerns we have about a standing arrangement with the Bosnians that allows passage of weapons across Croatian territory into Bosnia. As every schoolchild knows, they have no ports of their own.

"It is also common knowledge that, in order to circumvent the embargo on Bosnia, much of the weaponry and military equipment arrives at our ports of Split, Rijeka and Ploce, to be transported by road into Bosnia through the Neretva valley.

"We authorize passage in return for a percentage of the total. We know that the Bosnians are reneging on the agreement. They still want the weapons but are reluctant to pay the price. Lately, they have also been receiving weapon consignments clandestinely by air. One assumes that this is to avoid parting with any state-of-the-art materiel, such as the Stingers we believe they have, and to prevent the growth of our arsenal.

"We now also know that they have received some covert consignments that do not land at our ports but pass by road through Croatia.

This in particular cannot continue. It must cease.

"Charity transports get the weapons and ammunition into Bosnia. Much of the cargo comes from Germany and Austria. We know who is organizing the shipments in those countries and which aid enterprise is carrying the weapons.

"However, because of the support that we receive from those countries and the perception that we are a reasonable people, President Tudjman does not want any overt action that is anti-Bosnian. Any move made to halt these arms deliveries must not be attributable to Croatia, nor can it take place in Croatia. Nevertheless, we must deny this pipeline to the Muslims in such a way that they comprehend we know of their duplicity and that arms will only reach them under the terms of the previous agreement.

"So, Colonel, how could this be achieved? Your thoughts, please."

Paroski chewed his lower lip for a second, then, setting the cup down on the small table at the side of his chair, he clasped his hands between his knees, and leant towards the general.

"By destroying a convoy on passage through Bosnia on the way to its destination. Do we have any evidence of UN connivance or convoy drivers' complicity?"

Radovic shook his head in answer to both questions. Paroski continued.

"It could not be indiscriminate. Prior to any attempt to destroy them, we would need to know which convoy and which trucks were indeed carrying the contraband. We would also need details of the planned departure and route of the convoy. This in itself should not be difficult."

"Develop it, Paroski."

He reached for his pen, signifying that the meeting was at an end. Paroski stood, inclined his head in salute, and left the room.

He went down the wide stairway from the second floor, left the building and walked across the square. He turned right and entered St Mark's church, where he sat in one of the pews at the rear.

The precise information needed to put an attack into action—times, loads, number of vehicles, updated and current—could only come from within the convoy administration. He would need access to an individual in the organization.

Several days later, good fortune smiled on him beyond his wildest imaginings.

Sweat oozed from Crowther's pores, trickling through the hair on his back to form a rivulet, which flowed into the cleft of his naked buttocks and formed a puddle on the hard wooden chair. Slumped, with head bowed, his glazed eyes tried to focus on his genitals lying limp on the hard-callused palm of the guard. Sparse of hair they looked like a bald, legless squab. He hiccupped as he tried to stifle a hysterical giggle. The thick, teak talons flexed and he screamed, flinching in a futile attempt to escape the impending pain.

Mercifully, the hand did not close fully, and the agony seemed averted. Then, as his terror ebbed, it clamped shut, and the powerful fingers squeezed the flesh, grinding the gristle and his scrotum together. His captors' coarse laughter, at his frightened anticipation, mingled with his screams of pain.

Through a haze of nausea, he sensed the mocking fade. They turned their attention to someone descending the wooden stairs to the cellar. His testicles flopped forlornly onto his wet thighs as the guard and his colleagues stood and braced to attention. Through his tears of shame and fear, he saw the camouflaged uniform of a Croatian Army officer.

The newcomer spoke briefly, and then the voices died as the men ascended the stairs together, leaving him alone to a god-sent respite from the torture.

What had he done to deserve this? He had not wanted to hurt the child. Children loved him, and he loved children. Could they not understand that? It was just that she had been so...well...trusting. Despite his present condition, he felt his penis twitch as the memory of the girl flooded his consciousness.

He had singled her out in the sea of clutching hands and supplicating eyes as the children begged for the candy and biscuits he carried in the plastic bag. Small, endearingly defenceless, she mimicked the actions and calls of the older children to attract his attention.

The suffocating bindweed of longing and desire, which he had restrained for so long and had tried to stifle, burgeoned and strangled his weakening and progressively feebler good intentions.

This had not been the first time the overwhelming urge to caress, cuddle, hug, and squeeze had swamped him. The sound of his grinding teeth broke through his reverie and dragged him back. He sniffed.

Back home, there had been several times when he had taken a little mite away to play with, to love, and had, inevitably, invariably broken.

They were so doll-like, so fragile.

One part, deep inside him, knew it was wrong, and he hated his perversion. However, his swelling lust could swamp decency, overwhelm righteous feelings and drown his conscience. In the company of others, he was able to make all the right sympathetic noises on hearing of the discovery of a tiny, shattered Thumbelina.

He dreaded the thought of capture but could not stop. Rumours that the police were to question all the drivers in the county where he lived caused him to end the lease on his flat and leave the area. Three weeks after his most recent lapse, the sight of an official-looking saloon car in the yard of the new transport firm, and the officious looking men with notebooks questioning the supervisor, spooked him.

Once again, he ran; this time much further afield.

He had come to Zagreb and within days had signed a contract to drive aid convoys in the former Yugoslavia. For several months, he was able to subdue the hunger and seriously began to believe that he had vanquished the desire. He convinced himself that given the chance, or rather deprived of the opportunity, he could conquer his weakness. Somehow, he believed that he would see very few children when working on the convoys, and in this new environment, he would be able to suppress the lust that threatened to destroy him.

He failed. The minute angels were everywhere.

The run to Banja Luka with the diesel tanker that day had been uneventful. He had driven the tanker back in the afternoon's heat, conscious of a stirring of the old desires. Then, just outside Rugavica, he saw the group of children playing at the side of the road and, without conscious control of his faculties, like a robot, he had pulled over.

Eager, sparkling, greedy eyes soon spotted him. They surrounded him. Before long, tiny, grubby hands stretched out, for the candy they knew all foreigners carried.

He had thrown several hard candies amongst them, then, after pulling out two bars of chocolate, had thrown the bag with its contents into the woods at the side of the road. The pack of feverish children, shrilly baying in triumph, with much pushing and shoving, had turned and run after the sweets, leaving the little one, the chosen one, pushed over, at his feet.

Making sympathetic sounds, he stooped over her and held out one of the bars. Her dark-lashed, brown eyes widening as though she could not believe her good fortune, she snatched the chocolate from his hand. Attention fully on the candy, she did not resist as he scooped her up in his arms to carry her to the truck.

The small rounded form under her ragged dress, her only piece of clothing, smelt sweet, clean and milky. He nuzzled his face in the softness of her hair. His body's hunger was so strong he could taste it on his lips. God, how long had it been since he had last fondled...?

Several miles from the village, he pulled the vehicle over into the trees and switched the engine off. As she munched the second bar of chocolate, he furtively unzipped his trousers and then reached stealthily over to tug the frayed hem of her frock above her doll-like waist. He grasped her frail shoulders and pulled her over onto his lap. Her hair hid the soft, doe-like eyes that glanced up at him, then, reassured by his furtive smile, she returned to her prize.

Thick, blunt fingers closed, slowly, gently but as inexorably as a poacher's trout-strangling grasp. He parted her soft, minute, baby-velvet thighs, one in each hand, and then leant back to close his eyes in ecstasy, as the thick, warm redness engulfed him.

Much later that afternoon—he could never be sure how much time had elapsed when the hunger held him—as dusk was gathering, he had tried to hide the small body in a copse. Filled with panic, fear of discovery and the self-disgust that followed, he had not heard the hunters approach.

Their angry eyes had taken in the torn body of the child and read the poster of guilt on his face. They had not believed his protestations that the child had run into the road and that he was unable to avoid her. They went berserk. Battered with the butts of their shotguns he had fallen to his knees.

They had tied his hands behind his back with a belt and beaten him again, relentlessly, before driving him to the police station in the village.

Within minutes, the police had thrown him down the steps into this cellar. They stripped his clothes from his body, even his glasses, without which he was sightless. Their callous, mocking laughter as he had tried to hide his smallness behind cupped hands, echoed in the white-washed cellar.

They had manacled him to this chair and would not release him even to void his bowels. That must have been at least three days ago, he thought, but he could not be sure...

He started at the sound of voices and returning foot-steps on the stairs. Rough hands untied him, dragged him to his feet, spun him round, and pushed him face down onto the rough, unfinished surface of the table.

Horror flooded through him as the largest of the three men grasped one of his wrists in each hand and pulled him forward, pressing his face hard against the table top. Another had secured his wrists and ankles with leather straps to the table legs. Rough hands forced his clenched buttocks apart and another groped beneath him to gather up his genitalia. He heard the snapping sound of elastic and moments later felt the rubber bite into his penis and scrotum. His sphincter shrank as it met a cold, hard round object.

"It is a hose," said the Croatian officer as he pulled a chair to the side of the table, reversed it and leaned forward with his chin on his arms. Expressionless dark eyes inches from his own held him mesmerized like a stricken rabbit.

"Not a very large one." The accent was heavy, but the words were clear.

His head snapped up, and he felt ripped apart as several inches of the hard tube brutally penetrated his rectum.

Through the wall of pain, he saw the officer nod, felt a hand on his left buttock then, immediately, his rear passage bulged and rippled as liquid surged through his colon. His chest constricted as his jaws sprang apart in a silent scream, and his ears caught the sound of tutting.

"Behave. Control yourself. It is only water."

Subdued, gurgling rumbles echoed from his abdomen and his ears popped violently as the water pushed and stretched his bowels. He felt his ballooning stomach harden against the table.

He gagged.

Then a wide strip of adhesive sealed his mouth.

The expansion became unbearable.

He felt his eyes widen, and then bulge.

The shape of the face in front of him lost its definition. It swam before him.

Upward, increasing pressure squashed his lungs.

He sucked and snorted at the air through his nostrils.

Then, blessedly, relief came with the rough extraction of the tube. The speed, due to the abrupt reduction of pressure, at which the well of pain receded, was a reprieve that was short-lived. He struggled to control his bowels.

And failed. The smell assailed his nostrils, and only terror quelled the shame he felt.

He heard several words of Croatian and then felt another insertion before the man asked in a level tone, "Do I have your full attention?"

He stared blankly at the officer.

The shock was horrific.

His body bucked and thrashed so violently that his nose broke when his face hit the surface of the table. Blood filled his mouth. His chest heaved. Lungs sucked, like punctured bellows. He could not breathe.

He felt the dispassionate eyes on him. He nodded. Mingled with the reek of excrement was a strong odour of burnt flesh.

"If others had done what you have done, they would be taken out and shot. But you, fortunately, have an avenue of redemption."

The colonel unbuttoned his shirt pocket to extract a cigarette without bringing out the packet. Placing the cigarette in his lips, his black eyes flicked an order in the direction of the prisoner's feet.

The wall of pain was tremendous. The shock thrashed his body and shook it like a demented rag doll. The violence of the tremors faded but flames of agony scorched his rectum and buttocks. His testicles felt crushed. Through his tears, puzzled, he could see the colonel's questioning look.

Another biting wave surged through his flesh as someone threw the switch yet again.

Awareness flooded through him, before the forest of pain receded. He was supposed to ask *why, how*?

"Tell me, yes, for Christ's sake, tell me," he screamed.

"You are a driver on the convoy that will make the next UNHCR effort to reach Tuzla?"

He didn't know if he would be or not, as he wasn't a good enough cross-country driver to be selected as a natural first team choice, but God, what would happen if he said no? Scarcely daring to breathe in a vain effort to mute the pain, and clenching his teeth to hide the lie, he gave a weak nod.

"*Dobro*. I am prepared to allow you to return to the comparative safety of that organization, providing you are prepared to cooperate. Wholly and without question. You understand?"

The meaning of the words filtered through the wall of agony. *Safety? Oh my God, yes, yes*, his eyes begged as understanding struck home. He blinked rapidly in question.

How? Please, tell me how?

"Good. This evening, before you are released, you will be brought to me and I will instruct you in what I require you to do." The Croat stood and pushed the chair to one side. "Make no mistake. I own you now. To ensure you accept this, you will remain here for," he glanced at his watch, "the next hour while the lesson is reinforced."

The prisoner saw the index finger pointing in the direction of his feet before a breath-blocking, smothering sheet of raging pain enveloped him and his consciousness exploded.

Much later, the buckets of icy cold water revived him but did nothing to disperse the reek of human waste matter. Still face down on the table, he felt the rub of the coarse towelling as they dried his body, manhandling him as easily as an infant. They left him on the table, slumped in a sitting position, with his clothes in a sodden heap under his dangling legs.

He did not remember dressing.

His next recollection was of the session with Paroski, the Croatian colonel. Concentration was difficult; he felt nauseous and his rectum ached, but fear of the man who had the power to hurt him overcame his inattention.

"I am going to retain your passport." The officer, flicked the small red book into the open mouth of an orange-coloured manila folder.

"Together with these."

He winced, but could not avert his eyes as the Croat threw several large black and white prints, onto the desk in front of him, of a small, frail, broken corpse, its lips and cheeks smeared with dark chocolate. He shook his head, when the colonel offered him copies of the confession he did not remember making. The statements joined the passport and photographs.

"The situation is simple, extremely simple. Once clear of this building, should you decide not to cooperate, I will charge you with the child's murder in a Croatian court. You will find the questioning vastly more..." the seated officer searched for the right words, "...more robust than what you have experienced so far. Should you decide to flee Croatia, these documents," he flicked a hand in the direction of the folder, "would be handed over to your country's embassy with the strongest demand for extradition."

Could they extradite him?

He could not afford the passing of those documents to the authorities of his own country. They would be damning, even if the police there did not already want him for questioning.

"Your work for me will be elementary and straight-forward. Put simply, I require you to report periodically the precise location of your convoy on its way north into Bosnia. It is no more complicated than that."

He could not believe his ears; he would soon be free. Overwhelming relief filled him, removing any doubts he might have had about the practical difficulty of reporting the convoy's position. Why they would want to track relief supplies, he did not know, but thank Christ they did. His sense of survival buried any reservations about the logic of the Croatian's reasoning.

"This mobile phone has been pre-programmed." The officer held up a small compact instrument. He pulled out the short aerial and pointed to a button. "One depression and it will ring my number. It has a very wide range. When I call you, it will not ring but vibrate quietly. Carry it with you at all times. Also, here is a map to be used when reporting the convoy's location to me." The Croat sat back, placing both hands wide upon the table. "No questions? Good, you will have no problems. Just do as you have been told."

The interview ended; he had taken the plastic bag containing the map and the mobile phone, and he had been, even by his own standards, sickly subservient.

Please do not call me back, a voice pleaded in his head, as he backed towards the door and freedom. *Please.*

SEVEN

Paroski watched the Serb climbing through the pines towards him. Despite the appearance of being unaccompanied, he knew that the bearded soldier was not alone. Confident that their meeting would be straightforward and problem-free, he nevertheless drew his pistol, thumbed off the safety and concealed the weapon under his hat on the ground beside him.

Even in the days before the war, while both served in the JNA, Kalosowich and he had never been close. They were never friends, just colleagues with respect for the other's strengths and skills. Each believed he knew the weaknesses of his fellow soldier. . Neither had any love for the Bosnians.

Paroski was confident that the Serb would be willing to help. Kalosowich was possessed of the same ruthlessness and cunning as he himself. Despite the Serb being on the other side, he knew he could rely on him to keep his word, provided the return was sufficient. The assistance would be forthcoming.

The colonel ignored the covert hint of movement in the trees behind the approaching figure, who bent forward against the incline. Breathing heavily, the arrival looked up and pantomimed seeing the Croat for the first time. Paroski picked up his cap, with the pistol inside, before standing and moving toward the Serb with an outstretched hand.

"*Dobro jutro*, Kalosowich." He smiled, "*Kako ste?*"

"*Dobro,*" answered the Serb, indicating that he was well. He took off his rucksack and laid it at the foot of a tree, then lowered himself to sit beside it. Taking his cigarettes from a breast pocket, he extracted one and returned the pack to his pocket. He did not offer one to Paroski. Lighting it with a Zippo, he exhaled, and then looked up at the still standing Croatian.

"What do you have for me?"

Paroski bent his knees and sank onto to his haunches beside the Serb. Both men looked into the distance. The Croat took his time in answering.

"To be honest, I need your cooperation to accomplish something that is in our mutual interests."

"I'm always glad to promote my interests, but I assume that you mean national interests?"

Paroski smiled sourly at Kalosowich and his wooden sense of humour.

"But naturally." He paused.

"I have some information that you might want to act upon. In fact, if you didn't, it could be very much to your disadvantage."

"I am listening, Comrade."

"For some time, the Bosnians have been receiving arms shipments in a manner that does not conform to the agreements established at the highest level—"

"And are not sharing with you, as agreed at the same high levels," Kalosowich interjected with a mirthless grin.

"Be that as it may, I am prepared to identify an aid convoy for you that will be carrying weapons for the Bosnians, if you are prepared to agree to destroy the weapons."

"Since you offer me the opportunity to destroy and not confiscate these weapons, I assume that it will not be crossing any territory held by us at this time and that any attack on it will have to be made on Bosnian territory?"

"*Da*. Exactly,"

"And you will give me chapter and verse?"

"Unfortunately, I am not able to say at this stage whether each vehicle has weapons as part of its cargo, but I will pass on this information nearer the time."

"It must be a UN convoy, if you are asking us to destroy it?"

"But of course, Kalosowich. UNHCR."

The Serb was silent. He lit a fresh cigarette from the butt of the first, grinding the stub into the pine needles beside him.

"And U.N. military involvement? This convoy of yours will have no escort?"

"How often do the convoys have military escorts nowadays? Still, if the thought of UN military is—"

"You do not have to try childish goading, Paroski. It's unnecessary. We, the Serbs, will do what the Croats are unable to do. We will catch your pig for you. I need the date, the proposed route and any other relevant information. I will have to clear this with Pale, but I foresee no problems."

Calum baited the hook with the mussel, then swung the weighted end of the line round his head several times, before letting it go. The throw took the lead shot and hook ten or fifteen feet up into the air and thirty yards out into the bay before it started to drop. The plop made by the lure hitting the water sounded loud in the still evening air. Wiping his hands on his jeans, he settled back in the folding chair to wait for the fish to bite.

A slight breeze was building and the surface of the water was ruffling in places, but it was still warm on the end of the jetty. It would not get cold until darkness fell.

"Thanks, Kurt," he said, as he accepted the cigarette from the German who was sitting to his left. Kurt lit both cigarettes before returning to the magazine, a tattered copy of *Der Spiegel* that he had picked up from the barber's shop in Metkovic.

"If it comes off, Kurt, do you think we'll have problems on the run to Tuzla?" Calum, watched the candy-striped float bobbing in the water. Kurt drew on his cigarette then, throwing the magazine to one side, sat forward level with Calum.

"Honestly?"

"Aye, of course, honestly."

"It's going to be very difficult. No convoys got through for three months. We will not know from one minute to the next what is going to happen. To get to Tuzla, we've got to pass through them all."

"All who?"

"Well, who would you like first? There is the Croat Regular Army, then the Croatian National Guard, like reservists but with the same mentality as any other paramilitaries down here. There will be the Bosnian Croat Defence Council—the HVO—and, more of a worry, the HOS with their black uniforms, jump boots and ethnic cleansing. On the other hand, at any time at all, the

Yugoslavian Army, the JNA, who are really the Serbs, could bump us. And, of course, there's the Bosnian Serb Army and their *Chetnik*, the White Eagles, Arkan's *Tigers* or any other bandits who'd cut your throat for your watch. There is a bunch of psychosomatic war victims, disgruntled zealots, sociopathic loners, drunks and intoxicated teens out for cheap thrills just waiting for us to come up country.

"That is saying nothing about the Armija BiH, the Bosniacs, who are the Muslim Bosnians and have the Mujahedeen, Muslim fundamentalists from Iran, Afghanistan and other places. They run in packs. It's even rumoured that there is a one-hundred-strong active unit of the Iranian Revolutionary Guard."

"Like *Ben Hur*. A cast o' thousands."

Kurt grinned mirthlessly.

"The biggest danger is not that they're organized, but the fact that they are not!"

The air became cooler when the sun, almost unnoticed, dropped behind the horizon. The surrounding black mountains edged closer. White horses pranced on the water and threw themselves at the piles supporting the pier.

Calum stood up and started to reel in his line. He had left Ireland to avoid retribution from those who would wreak vengeance on him. Yet here he was, in danger from people who could not care less about him, but who would just as effectively destroy him.

Liam would say he had deserved it. *Aye, the brave Liam; that callous, calculating, cold-hearted bastard. Liam.*

Since he was a toddler in a soaked nappy playing on the warm concrete of their back yard, he had lived in awe of his big brother. As far back as he could remember, they had never been close. At first, it had been a child's fear of ugliness and cruelty; he remembered a grimacing Liam tying him up and setting fire to his socks. His Mam, coming home unexpectedly early from work, had run screaming into the yard, ripped his socks from his feet, and then raised a hand to chastise Liam. His brother had just glowered at her, willing her to drop her hand. His Mam never attempted to rebuke the boy again.

As Calum grew so did his fear of his dour, stocky sibling who never smiled.

Feuds with the neighbours, culminating in the hospitalization of a man whom Liam had beaten unmercifully, brought the hated RUC to the door. When he was away in borstal, Calum and his Mam were never free of the malevolent presence; it hung over their house like a bad smell.

Before long, Liam joined the hard men and became even more menacing. In an effort to conquer his fear of his brother, Calum foolishly tried to emulate him and also joined, but knew, deep down, that none of the others respected him. They used him as a 'gopher,' a message boy, and a watcher of trivialities.

Then one day, because his regular driver was sick, the company commander had asked him if he could drive. He could but was not proficient. Surprisingly, it made no difference. Given the chance to drive, he replaced the other youth.

Later, on his third run, he learnt that the C.O. had a penchant for young flaxen-haired boys. Moreover, to his amazement, despite his initial unease, Calum found that he was not averse to the man's overtures.

They had gone on trips together to the South, where he learnt evasive and proactive driving, while the C.O. had meetings, and he was buggered every night. However, during the course of time, the physical side of the relationship palled.

Several months later, propositioned by a well-spoken, middle-aged man in the bar of the *Europa*, he agreed to sleep with him. The man was the main speaker at a function in the hotel, but he was not a guest there. They went to his home in the Malone, where the more experienced lover had seduced him, gently and almost graciously, in the way that he knew it should be done. The pickup developed into a deepening relationship until Calum fell hopelessly in love.

He had been driving his C.O. and a senior officer to a meeting when he overheard Macaulay's name mentioned as a target. He knew he could not let it happen. Nevertheless, how could he, a lowly foot soldier—not even a soldier, he thought ruefully, just a driver—prevent it?

Simple. He would grass, something that he never believed he would be capable of doing. He had been unprepared for the order tasking him to evacuate the gunman after the job, but it had helped to provide a cover for him.

I wonder if they have any idea where I am now? Turning to speak to Kurt, the black shape of a bulky figure standing behind his friend caused him to gasp and drop the reel, which he caught against his knees in a panicked, two-handed scrabble.

"You've got more to worry about than them, Calum."

He had never heard this voice before and had only seen its owner once, but he recognized the man straightaway.

His stomach somersaulted with dread and he felt winded. His mouth dried up and his legs trembled. Of their own volition, they folded and he dropped heavily into the chair.

"Would you excuse us for a wee while," the newcomer said in a firm tone to Kurt.

"Are you alright?" the German asked standing over the seated Calum.

"Take off, now!" the stranger bit off the words.

Kurt, dubious and uncertain, turned and walked toward the café with frequent backward glances at the men on the jetty.

The big man lowered himself into the seat that the German had vacated. The ensuing silence remained unbroken for several minutes until Calum raised his head and looked at Rath.

"The Removal Man! Oh, Mother of God! How did you find me?"

"Oh, there was no problem there. It was not as though you attempted to hide your tracks. If you did, it was so amateurish it was laughable. Anyway, that is not important. You know why I'm here?"

The youth stared slack-jawed at Rath but gave no indication that he intended to answer.

"Do you know?" the big man repeated.

"You're here to kill me,"

"They want you back."

He could not take his eyes from the big man's face, but shook his head in disbelief.

"There are a lot of questions to be answered. You leaving when you did, and in the way you did, does not look good. You must see that. But if you go back—"

"Why you? Why did they send you?"

"That's neither here nor there—"

"Jesus, are you stupid or what?" Calum shouted, gripping the arms of the folding chair, his knuckles almost luminescent in the growing dusk. "I can't go back. You know it. They know it. That's why you're here, to kill me."

"Grow up. You have no choice. You are going back. Make no mistake. I'm here to see that you do."

Calum's breathing was still ragged, but his determination to control the shaking had a measure of success. He stiffened, pulling his shoulders back and tried to meet the big man's gaze.

"What sort of bastard are you? You owe me. I risked my life to pull you out of Queen's."

Rath stared at the youth, his face blank, then puzzled, before comprehension dawned on him—

Calum had been the driver!

Why had they not told him?

"You mean..." his voice faded as he comprehended the full impact of what the boy had done. "Christ, Calum..."

"You didn't know?"

"No, I didn't know Just let me think for a moment, just let me think."

The big man stared out across the bay his brows darkened in a frown.

The settlement of Nastri curled lazily around the edge of one of hundreds of inlets that serrate the narrow strip of Dalmatian coast of southern Croatia. The ruins of the old village, whose inhabitants were reputed to have blocked the advance of a fifteen-thousand-strong army of Turks in earlier times, nestled in a shallow valley high on the slope of the mountain that dominated the landward side of the hamlet.

Adjacent to the derelict houses the ruined fortress of Smrden Grad stood near a Bogomil cemetery dating back to the fourteenth century.

The road linking Split with Dubrovnik paralleled the coast and bypassing the present day homesteads followed the shoreline towards the nearby Bosnian town of Neum.

From the edge of the road, near the rubble of the restaurant, destroyed by the Croats during an ethnic cleansing operation, the houses spilled in disarray through the greenery of ubiquitous fig trees and indigenous palms.

The red-roofs were intact, showing that, unlike the restaurant, their owners were not Serb. Adjacent to the beach of pale yellow gravel was a holiday camp complete with hotel, restaurant, chalets, and tennis courts. There were few residents and of those, the majority was Croatian police or military. Branched like a sapling from the main road on the south side of Nastri, a steep narrow lane gave access to the beach and the Villa.

The Villa had become the home of the members of the convoy during the hot summer months. Three storeys of a white-stone building, with a spacious patio and a balcony for each of the rooms, faced the road.

The ground floor, divided into two large chambers used as the restaurant and bar area, in more peaceful times, was the convoy's kitchen and dining area. Individual rooms on the first and second floor, complete with shower and toilet, accommodated them. Behind the

Villa was an enclosed area, level with the ceiling of the kitchen, used by the proprietor's wife to dry her tenants' laundry, and where the Convoy Leader parked the Jeep.

The elderly property owner, his wife and grown-up family shared the house next to the Villa. Fronting the house were several fig trees and a small vegetable garden. On the concrete apron that lay immediately in front of their house were several fishing creels, nets, oars and their boat engine, which they removed and brought back in a wheelbarrow, after their early morning and evening fishing trips.

The middle-aged wife always pushed the barrow.

Less than a hundred yards from the house was a small jetty with several tiny slots to accommodate the fishing boats of their neighbours. Bordering the jetty, the local cafe was always busy, many of its clients, including on-duty police, coming in the late evening, from Neum, Opusan, and Metkovic.

During the day and late into the night, the jukebox blared, reminding the residents of Nastri that the café, with its ample stock of beer and slivovitz, was open for business. The bistro looked out across the inlet, which stretched from the open sea to the small ghost town of Neum, with its luxurious but deserted hotel, situated on the curve of the bay. The servers were Muslims, young and darkly pretty, refugees from Sarajevo, separated from their families by the perverse nature of civil war.

There was an envious suspicion among the drivers that both Scouse and Dawke had slept with the younger of the two girls.

The far side of the inlet was contained by the barren hills of a peninsula bisected by the road that continued south across this narrow strip of Bosnia.

Spider spread his towel on the sand, kicked off his sandals and sat down. He opened a book and started to read, but after a couple of minutes, the heat of the sun started to burn his upper body and thighs. Closing the book, he threw it aside and rolled over to reach for the oil.

He gave no indication that he was aware of Rath's presence.

Sprawled in the tilted chair against the café's whitewashed wall, the Irishman's relaxed posture belied the turmoil of his thoughts. The lenses of his Raybans mirrored the Englishman. The watchful eyes saw Webb's lithe silhouette move to the edge of the jetty, remain motionless for a second, and then launch itself into the cobalt-blue water. A long moment later, a head broke the surface and the man swam toward the cluster of rocks in the centre of the inlet.

Rath's misgivings had been strong right from the first time he had set eyes on the working manager.

Later, as there had been nothing palpable on which to base his unease, he was prepared to concede that his Celtic temperament might be lending itself to foreboding. However, his mental agitation reappeared when he heard Cheatham quashing a desultory inquiry from one of the others about the man.

The scarred neck and face intrigued Rath. The disfigurement was obviously the result of a relatively recent wound, at most no more than a year old. He knew enough of such things to eliminate an industrial or traffic accident as the cause; an explosion or blast had caused those raw weals and ridges of scar tissue.

That the scars did not inhibit the man, that they caused him no embarrassment and he displayed no self-deprecation, showed strength of character that Rath respected.

The signs that he was not a trucker, though not blatant, were obvious to Rath. Webb, an experienced and capable driver, devoted extra effort in his own time to improve the comfort of his cab and the standard of maintenance on his vehicle. A muscular body, with an enduring tan, revealed time spent in regions other than the temperate zone of northern Europe. His demeanour and bearing implied reliability.

His quiet yet good-natured willingness to share daily tasks made him popular with the other drivers but it also revealed to Rath self-discipline and maturity not in abundance in ordinary occupations.

The subject of Rath's thoughts was not a stereotypical Londoner. Neither gregarious nor garrulous but also not withdrawn, he took no part in the gratuitous conversations that filled the group's off-duty periods. He listened to the anecdotes, as they all did, but never contributed. Rath felt there were many he could have told.

Only direct questions prompted responses, and even then his answers were lean and devoid of detail. Appearing ever watchful, he was always on guard and alert. Such constant vigilance indicated a conscious awareness of an undefined threat of danger.

The root cause of his concern, Rath realized, was the complete and total absence of interest, feigned or real, that Webb showed in his existence. Since he had joined the convoy, they had not spoken to one another, despite working on the same team unloading supplies into the warehouse. Rath had not initiated any overture of friendship, but Webb had supervised and worked in his presence as if he had not been there. He had not met Webb's eyes and although he had freely studied the man—and he knew Webb had been aware of his examination—he had not detected any reciprocal interest by the newcomer.

Rath picked up the glass and sipped the warm beer. Since the shooting in Belfast, he was unable to suppress the tendrils of apprehension that sprouted when he thought of possible attempts by the British to locate him.

On one side, as a practical man, he felt it unlikely that the British Army would search the world for him. Yet he knew they would view his attack on Macaulay and the resultant carnage as a defeat for the Special Air Service. That, they would not easily forget. He had left Ireland, ostensibly on an operation, but also to minimize the possibility of their finding him.

He was not naive. Neither national borders nor another country's sovereignty would prove a hindrance when they had a score to settle. Their much-vaunted respect for justice was, in reality, negligible; the assassinations in Gibraltar had shown the world that much. Rath thought it incongruous that the British called his people terrorists.

Webb had been a soldier; of that, there was no doubt. Was he still a soldier? Could he—*Jesus Christ!*

He felt as though his skull would rupture.

The thought crashed through into his consciousness as realization exploded.

The chair slammed forward onto all four legs. A shotgun wound!

My shotgun!

The newspaper reports of the action listed two deaths and a serious wounding on the Army side. There was no mention of the fourth member. Rath wiped the bead of sweat from his upper lip.

Damn, there was no excuse for an oversight like this. Concentrating his attention on the matter in hand,

McDermot's treachery, he had overlooked the need to protect his own well-being. Forcing himself to relax, to decelerate, he tried to analyze his feelings. The realization that Webb could present a risk was not fanciful. However, the coincidence did stretch the imagination. He could not be sure that fear was not present.

A strange elation and near savage joy was becoming predominant now that he had a defined challenge to face. Perhaps right from the start, he should have taken the Englishman for what he now suspected him to be; that would have been the safest and least risky option.

Now, he would have to make up for lost time.

Rising to his feet and taking a quick glance in the direction of the bay to confirm that Webb was not yet returning, he set off towards the house.

Spider reached up to the ledge and, without effort, pulled himself out of the water. Seated, he turned in the direction of the beach, leant forward, and vigorously shook his long hair free of water. He leant back against the rock, face his forearms resting on his knees, and watched the distant Rath walk toward the house.

Even now, it was difficult to believe that this man had been the patrol's Nemesis—and even more unlikely that the killer had not yet recognized *him*.

During the previous months, in endless loops of recall, especially at night, he had relived each second of the debacle at that damned University. Breaking out of the cycles of recollection had been impossible. He imagined repeatedly what he would do, given the same opportunity again. What would his action be if he were to come face to face with the gunman now?

Against all probability, with no effort or intent on his part to find him, the man of his nightmares had reappeared. Yet, despite the loss caused by the gunman and the destruction of his own ordered existence, he felt no passion, no hatred for the man; only respect for the single-minded dedication and sense of purpose displayed on the University steps.

The advantage had been theirs, and somehow they had lost it—with disastrous consequences.

Spider had been at the other side of the marshalling yard, partly obscured by his vehicle, as the new driver arrived. He looked up and was unprepared for the tidal wave of surprise that engulfed him on seeing the Irishman. Recognition flooded his consciousness, and a surge of emotions coursed through his being.

To see the man here in Croatia, and in the same company that he had joined, defied belief. The skin on the back of his neck prickled as Spider realized that, as difficult as his primary emotion was to define, it mingled with a sense of trepidation. Not fear or dread, but intense alarmed anticipation. Forcing himself to think, calmly and logically, he had mechanically pulled the rolled tarpaulin to the front of the truck.

He knew that there were other Irishmen employed by Cheatham. Was it inconceivable that the IRA men would use a convoy operation as a bolt hole or sanctuary? It was not beyond the bounds of possibility that they were not resting, but were in fact an operational team on a mission. Weapons, explosives, and ammunition were readily available due to the collapse of law and order in the region.

It would be risky taking action against Rath, without determining whether the others were IRA soldiers or not.

Even if they were not, he reasoned, he would have to be circumspect in any action against the Irishman, since his compatriots' sympathies would most probably be with their fellow citizen. However, what action could he take? Faced with reality, he was not sure that he did want to precipitate or initiate a move against the man.

How long would it be before Declan Rath recognized him? Would there be any overt signs? Not likely. What action would the gunman take? Spider stared at the Villa just visible in the trees.

The obvious thing to do would be to confront the Irishman.

The din from the jukebox in the dim, red-lit café filled the night air. The place was already filling up. The drivers occupied adjoining tables in a corner. The Irish contingent, as he had come to recognize them, was absent, with the exception of Michael at the bar.

After collecting a beer, Spider made his way across to the group. Several of the occupants of the table looked up and made some form of greeting. He raised his glass in a general response and pulled across an empty chair from the next table.

Crowther, a small weasel of a man, who had obviously had more than his measure for that evening, was holding forth.

"Everybody likes German cars—Mercedes, Porsche, and Audi. Their cameras and electronic gear are great. Look at yer Leicas, Carl Zeiss lenses and Braun shavers, and all that stuff." He took a hefty pull at his glass, wiped his mouth with the back of his hand.

"Their beer ain't too bad, either," he paused, "as piss goes." He guffawed and shoved the drinker sitting next to him to emphasize the witticism. "As piss goes."

"The D-mark's strong, more acceptable down here than sterling, so the question is, why don't anybody like the Krauts? D'ye know? Eh, d'ye know?"

Spider thought that even Dennis Crowther hated Dennis Crowther. Kurt had expressed an opinion earlier that the problem was Crowther's bad teeth and the poison their decayed roots generated.

In appearance, Crowther invited comparison with a malevolent gnome. His wrinkled face with its hanging jowls and watery eyes, embedded in inflated pouches, destroyed any pretence of the intellectuality hinted at by his high-domed balding head. His wide mouth, permanently turned down at the corners, when not active, belonged to a sad circus clown. This state, however, occurred only rarely because Crowther was vociferous with an unforgiving and venomous garrulity.

He detested the Balkans, his accommodation, his job, UNHCR and his fellow drivers, regardless of nationality, who were the subject of many of his diatribes. His co-workers made an effort to believe that it was unintended, and that it was Crowther's attempt, albeit heavy-handed, at wit.

The three Germans listened politely, not quite coping with the speed and awkward rhythm of Crowther's speech, smiling hesitantly and waiting for the typical, and often tiresome British put-down, with its hidden, caustic comedy.

"Nah? All right, I'll tell yer." He paused to take several gulps of beer, then peered at his listeners through his wire-rimmed spectacles. "They're a lying shower o' two-faced bastards that we'll have to slap down again in the bloody near future! Yer just 'ave to listen ter 'em going on 'bout not being responsible for the start o' the war, the wreckin' of Europe and trying to convince anyone who'll listen that all the others in the war did the same things. Berks! How the hell can they possibly think they're not tarred with the same bleeding brushes as their fathers?"

The Germans stiffened and exchanged glances, uncertain that they had heard correctly. The other nationalities at the table looked down fixedly at their beers.

"Christ, their fathers probably claimed they'd nothing to do with the atrocities that *their* fathers committed in Belgium during the First World War."

"Hold on, Crowther," said Spider quietly, "even for you that's a bit strong."

"Take any one of them wot's here with us," said Crowther, throwing a drunken look at Spider, then ignoring him. "How many Krauts are there driving? And, where do they drive to? The Serbs hate 'em with a passion and threaten to top 'em if any of their trucks show up trying to cross their territory."

Casting his arm wide to take in the bemused Germans, he continued, "Did you see how they reacted to the chance that a run might be on again? They're crapping themselves! Well, *tuvski shitska,* I say."

"That's unfair, Dennis—" began Kurt.

"I think the educated ones are worse, especially in this outfit. Bleeding Cheatham, why the hell does he need any Huns on the team at all?"

"That's it, Crowther. Wrap it up." Spider stood up. "You've had enough. Apologize to the lads here. Then leave."

With the slow deliberation and the exaggerated movements of a drunk, Crowther swallowed the last of his beer, set the glass firmly on the table, and then got to his feet unsteadily.

Leaning forward he placed both hands on the table, knocking over his now empty glass, and grinned vacantly at the group.

"If I've offended anyone here, I 'pologize." He turned and pushed his chair away with the side of his leg. "But I meant ever' word." With that, he faced the door and, with determined pseudo-steadiness, strode out of the café.

The group visibly relaxed. Those sitting next to the German drivers began to make excuses for the outburst. Spider remained standing, and then reached for his untouched beer before making his way outside. He took a seat at an empty table on the veranda with his back to the café wall.

It was hard at times to offset Crowther's vitriolic outbursts against the need for drivers. Although he was not as proficient as many of the others, his availability made him as indispensable as the rest.

Nevertheless, one of these days, thought Spider, *one of these days.*

Rath walked toward the café. He saw the solitary figure at the table outside and made an instant decision. The big man stopped, and swung a chair across the path, placing it at the empty side of the table. He sat down.

Spider looked at him but made no comment. He lifted his glass to his lips and drank without taking his eyes off Rath. The Irishman returned the other's stony look.

Without preamble, he asked, "Are you still with the Army?"

"I am not," said Spider. "I'm here as a civilian to get a job done, and that job only concerns convoys. But that doesn't mean that I won't settle with you at the first opportunity after we've stood down."

"That's a bit brash, being so open about your intentions. I thought your lot were supposed to be professional?" Rath held Spider's gaze.

"Don't worry about my professionalism. You'll have evidence of that soon enough, but first and foremost there's a job to do."

The Irishman was silent then looked away across the darkened inlet.

"For what it's worth, that's all it was to me."

"What do you mean?"

"Back home, when I came up against you and the others at Queen's."

Spider said nothing. Rath continued.

"You Brits have never accepted that some of us believed in what we were doing, that we considered ourselves to be more dedicated and committed, if not as professional, as you saw yourselves to be. Most of the men did what they did for a cause that they believed in—and still do." He ignored Spider's gesture of disbelief.

"Not for money or prestige; not as mercenaries, but as volunteers. We are fighting for an ideal that in any other circumstances you would applaud and support, if it were not for the fact that we are fighting against you. We're as much soldiers as you are." The big man leaned back in the chair and shook his head sadly. "You've a terrible habit of seeing your opponents as lesser beings."

He had spoken quietly but with a deadly passion. Spider shifted in his chair and made no comment while the Irishman stopped to light a cigarette.

"You and yours have been standing on Irish necks for generations now. Well, it is ending. Your decrepit colonial system, a system that is openly biased, nasty and corrupt, is going to be pushed off the island."

He fell quiet. The silence became heavy and uncomfortable as it hung over the table. Both men's eyes remained locked together. Spider broke the stillness, by setting his unfinished beer on the table and standing to lean over towards Rath.

"You butchered three of my friends on those steps and blasted an unarmed academic to kingdom come. If the shoe were on the other foot and I were to say to you it was only a job, done with competence, that there were no hard feelings, no hatred—that you should take your loss philosophically—your unforgiving, sectarian, perverse megalomania would scream 'No surrender'."

"That's not one of our slogans," Rath interjected, smiling slightly.

Spider ignored the interruption.

"Despite what you've said—and maybe you do believe it yourself—for me that business was personal, very personal. As I said, I am here to do a job, and my professionalism overrides my own feelings.

"But," he said as he leaned even further over the table, "make no mistake, once it's over there'll be a reckoning. Bank on it."

Spider turned and strode towards the Villa Nastri. Rath, expressionless, remained seated for several minutes then went to join Michael at the bar.

EIGHT

Due to the intransigence of the Serbs, and often of the Croats, changes to procedures and projects prevented regular scheduled transports, on many occasions. Each relief run was determined on its own merits; and the self-interests and not-so-secret agendas of the controlling bodies of the areas through which the convoys had to pass.

As a result, the supplies from the donating countries were restricted to an ever-narrowing conduit. Huge amounts of essential food and medical relief poured into warehouses—and stayed there.

Crowther looked down at the mountains of pallets filled with supplies in the central receiving area of the darkened warehouse and wondered how on earth he would be able to pick out those Colonel Paroski wanted him to find.

He switched on his torch, keeping the beam of light directed at the floor. It was doubtful, he thought, that the old man at the main gate, deep in a slumber induced by long daylight hours of labour in his fields, would awaken and notice anything. Most of the convoy personnel, including Spider, were in the cafe.

Stopping at the foot of the wooden stairs, he was undecided as to where to start.

He looked along the rows of racking. Professionals had assembled most of the pallet loads; neat compact cubes of strong carton containers, enveloped in thick polythene wrapping and bound in place by substantial steel or plastic banding. However, keen but unskilled amateurs had assembled the others. Many of those boxes were torn, squashed and battered. Quite a few had burst and their contents protruded like the intestines of an alien. These would require repacking by the warehouse people before they could go anywhere.

Wouldn't like any of my stuff to be in those.

Of course! He knew immediately where to look! No one shipping clandestine cargo could afford the risk of exposure by rough handling; therefore, it had to be in the well-packed containers. He scanned the rows. Pulling his knife from his pocket, he snapped it open and climbed up the outside of the racking of the nearest batch.

Soon after he started, Crowther realized that he would find what he was looking for by feel and common sense. He need not open any boxes that looked too small or felt too light. Having climbed down and collected the material he would need to close the boxes, he soon developed a method of checking. He was pleased with his progress. However, it was only after three hours of searching, cutting each box open, removing the contents, examining and repacking, and finally resealing with heavy-duty adhesive tape, that he found the first items.

Pulling aside the huge flaps of one pack, which the stencils stated contained processed peas, he removed the top layer of cartons and was about to remove the second when the weight indicated something far more substantial than peas. He undid one of the individual boxes and was nonplussed to see that it did indeed contain tins, each with a colourful illustration of peas.

However, as he lifted the tins out, he noticed that the individual cans were too heavy.

He glanced at his watch. Damn! It would soon be dawn. Fumbling in his haste, he clawed the tin opener blade free and gouged one of the tins open. Crowther almost whooped with glee but stifled it.

Success!

A dense cluster of 7.62mm bullets filled the tin. Spurred on by his find, he redoubled his efforts to find the rest of the contraband. By four o'clock in the morning, he had located the anti-tank launchers, the truncated folded skeletal frames of the Kalashnikovs and more 'vegetables', which he knew by the weight were small-arms ammunition.

A new thought struck him, and he felt like kicking himself at how obvious it was! Those expecting the shipment must have some way of identifying the consignment. Going back to the last pallet in which he had discovered weapons, he examined it, comparing it closely with a nearby box that had proved free of arms.

Then he found it; the spelling of one of the words on the logo on the outer packing was different from the others. He decided to confirm his findings by looking for the same word on another of his previous finds.

Match! After about an hour, he had identified the entire shipment.

Spider woke, wide awake and alert; head still on the pillow, his eyes quickly focused in the darkened room. He listened for a few seconds, then sat up to look around. *Nothing shifted, added, disturbed or removed.* Relaxing, he swung his legs over the side of the bed.

The confrontation with Declan Rath the previous evening, and his immature admission that he already knew who the Irishman was, now appeared foolhardy. The cliché *forewarned is forearmed* had particular relevance in this case. Despite his claim to being professional, he had shown a total lack of control by warning Rath of his future intent to settle the score. He would now have to be more vigilant to avoid the terrorist preempting him.

Spider was aware that what he was looking for when he checked his surroundings was unlikely, especially here in the base area, but it was a force of habit developed in the Regiment. After leaving the Special Air Service, he had been unable to sleep through the hours of darkness without an alarm being set in his system. It caused him to wake, without effort, at the slightest change in his surroundings. It was as if he had a sensory surveillance system installed in his body.

He could not remember when he had last slept through eight hours of darkness. Even when he was dreaming, no matter whether the dream was pleasant or not, the alarm system would override the dream, causing him to awake and check his immediate surroundings.

Still in a sitting position, he raised his arms and stretched, turning his flexed neck first to one side and then to the other. He yawned, flinching as the spasm rippled from his jaw into his shoulder. Disregarding the pain he stood, and with his feet apart, began twisting his torso from side to side.

After several minutes, he started forward trunk bending. Eventually, he brought his feet together, and then fell forward with his arms extended and hands spread into the prone position for press-ups. With his breathing under control, he completed one hundred press-ups then, rolling over, he performed his daily one hundred sit-ups. Without effort, he rose to his feet.

His lower body was a catalogue of the places he had been and the actions he had seen. Scars on his legs were the result of bullet and shrapnel wounds.

Picking up his running shoes from beside the door, he walked over to the chair where he had laid his shorts and athletic supporter the night before. He dressed quickly and left the room, after locking the door. He slipped the key into his supporter. He trotted down the concrete stairs to the road, turned right and ran up the hill.

As he ran, Spider thought of the preparations they had made for the tasking. They had spent less than an hour in the United Nations High Commission for Refugees depot, loading the eight-wheeled trucks. The loading crew was proficient and worked as a team to load the supplies without wasted effort or time. The drivers spent a further hour tying down the tarps and completing the various checks on the vehicles back at base. They parked the trucks close together in a line side to side, so that just the outside doors of the end vehicles were accessible. Only by moving the end vehicle was it possible to gain entry to the cab of the next vehicle.

When they had stayed overnight in Velika Kladusa on a previous run, they discovered their tool kits had been stolen and the diesel in the main tanks siphoned off. A large part of the consignment was no longer there. The Convoy Management had reported the loss to the local UNHCR officials, minimized to prevent the report reaching a higher level.

However, despite the loss, no one bothered to devise a viable way of protecting the cargo for future taskings. He shook his head at the naiveté.

Spider believed that Convoy security was paramount. What could they accomplish in Serb territory with no fuel and no tools? Breakdowns had increasingly become the norm, rather than the exception, in the last few months. He made a mental note to tell Kurt, the reserve Convoy Leader, about the first aid box and the additional items the British Liaison Officer at UNHCR Metkovic had given them.

Turning at the top of the hill to run along its crest towards Osmo, he reviewed the list of equipment still needed. It caused irritation when one thought of the gear, considered everyday necessities in a wartime environment, that other sponsored convoys possessed and they did not. He knew that the main problems with their convoy were twofold: the rank amateurism of its management and some of its drivers, together with their motive for being there, namely, profit. No one had altruistic motives.

He accepted that profit was not always a bad thing. However, it had soon become obvious that bribes and kickbacks were an integral part of its acquisition. These paved the way to disregard shoddy or non-existent workmanship; they were the incentive to delay purchase of essential items and spare parts, and were the inducement to buy shoddy and inferior materiel. There was no area in their operations that did not result in some personal monetary benefit. Services were billed that were either not performed or were inadequate. Huge sums were available for the payment of inflated invoices.

At the same time, legitimate needs, such as first aid items, sufficient body armour, flak jackets, functional winches and chains together with other recovery equipment, continued to be ignored. Promises for the purchase of new equipment on extension of the contract never reached fulfillment.

As he loped past the ruined restaurant, Spider increased his pace and felt the pump action of his heart increase. Today was the big one. Today was T-1. Today they would make the run into Tuzla.

Everyone was apprehensive, but none more so than the Germans in the team. The Serbs who operated the many of the roadblocks upcountry did not welcome them. These militiamen were often drunken old misfits and hopped-up teenagers.

He remembered how fearful Kurt had been at the barricade on the way to Banja Luka. A grizzled ancient, festooned with bandoleers of ammunition, an antiquated rifle in his left hand and a well-depleted bottle of *slivovic* in his right, had sprayed his bitter hatred into the driver's face. The man threatened to kill any German who ventured into the new Republica Srpska. Kurt was no coward and not easily intimidated. However, when the geriatric gunman fired a shot, shattering the windscreen and showering him with shards of glass, he burnt rubber and U-turned the Toyota, almost in its own length, to get away.

Spider blew the sweat off his upper lip and increased his speed as he headed into the home stretch towards Nastri. He hoped the trip would be uneventful and that awareness, together with good convoy discipline, would be sufficient to outweigh or at least minimize the possible dangers.

He would soon know whether this was likely or not. There were thirty minutes before he was due at the seven o'clock security briefing.

At nine o'clock, after roll call, Spider reminded Crowther that it was his turn to go to the post office in Opusan to collect the mail. The man took the jeep and soon reached the arched sandstone bridge leading to the village square.

He decided he would have a coffee later, but now was an ideal time, free from discovery by anyone in the convoy, to call Paroski. Without leaving his vehicle, he made the connection.

"Yes?"

As usual, the colonel did not identify himself, but there was no mistaking the gruff tones.

"The trucks are loaded for Tuzla."

"*Dobro*. Are you sure you located everything?" There was no change in Paroski's voice. Crowther detected no surprise, no elation, and no thanks.

"I believe I found it all."

"Do you know at this stage when they plan to move out?"

"Later this morning. They've emptied the warehouse. It's possible that it might not—"

"Once loaded," Paroski interrupted, "if the convoy doesn't go, would they unload?"

"Unlikely, but the—"

"Let me know if anything changes." The connection was broken.

Crowther shrugged, then collapsed the aerial. What the colonel intended to do with the information he did not know, but he had closed his mind to the question. Leaving his vehicle parked next to the church, he walked over to the café.

As Crowther deposited the official and personal mail in the main office, he overheard Spider on the phone confirming that the convoy was ready to pull out. The call gave the all clear from UNHCR. Spider immediately gave instructions for the drivers to assemble.

Crowther left the office and entered one of the toilet cubicles, locked the door and dialled the mobile for Paroski.

"It's definitely go,"

Expecting the usual, abrupt termination of the call, he was unprepared for the other's next remark.

"You have the numbers of the trucks on which the items have been loaded?"

His own silence seemed to last forever.

"Did you hear me? Which trucks?"

"I don't know! You never said you wanted... I couldn't be there when... Just confirmation about the stuff..." he finished lamely and dreaded Paroski's response.

"Are records kept in the office of the individual truck loads?"

"Yes, but only of general categories, not individual consignments—medical, food, hygiene supplies. Often, they carry mixed loads..." Crowther's voice died.

"Think carefully, very carefully. You are sure there is no way to show which trucks are carrying the goods and which order they will be in convoy?"

"Only if the trucks were searched again," his voice rising as the panic increased, "and they leave at any time now."

"I don't care how you arrange it, but I need to know which vehicles are loaded with the weapons."

"There is no way I can. I don't know the order of travel, which is leaving first, which truck is next... It's just not... The stuff could be spread over all the trucks!"

"Make sure you are on that convoy. Call me again when you are underway."

The line went dead.

Dejected, Crowther stared at the mobile.

In the HQ operations room in Pale, Kalosowich stepped back from the wall map and, in response to its persistent beep, picked up the mobile phone lying next to his pistol belt on the desk.

"Kalosowich."

"Paroski."

The Serb pulled his chair round and sat down.

"Unfortunately, I have not been able to get the information I promised you. It looks as though you will have to eat all the apples."

"Comrade Paroski," Kalosowich bared his yellowed teeth in a grin, "I always intended to."

Following the right-hand fork out of the centre of town, the road reached the border crossing into Bosnia Herzegovina after only a few minutes of travel. The aid convoys, however, together with the commercial trucks heading north, could not use this crossing. The noise of heavy vehicles and density of traffic inconvenienced the local residents.

An alternative border crossing for the aid convoys was established at Mali Prolog, a group of buildings too few to be termed a hamlet, on a hillside twenty miles from Metkovic. During ceasefires and moments of calm and inactivity, a column of waiting vehicles would stretch, for several miles, from the valley floor up to the crossing. The majority of drivers had long accepted that a 'gift' of cigarettes, whisky or money no longer expedited a crossing, but failure to do so could ensure days of waiting.

Normally the official relief convoys, those sponsored by the United Nations and other recognized charitable groups, were not delayed or subjected to excessive inspection, since they had already agreed to pay 'tribute' of a percentage of cargo to the regional government. This levy was not from each truck, but periodically the entity in question had to make a complete convoy available to the Croats or the Serbs.

The UNHCR convoys did not blatantly display their preferential treatment in crossing priority. When they arrived at Mali Prolog, their vehicles, with the exception of the lead jeep, would tag on to the end of the line of parked trucks, sometimes as much as three miles long, to wait their turn. The Convoy Leader would go forward to the head of the line, process the necessary paperwork and then, using the radio, call the convoy forward.

During the waiting period, which could be as long as three hours, the drivers would brew tea or coffee and reminisce about other missions and other crossings.

Today was different. After just twenty-five minutes, Spider radioed that they had clearance for crossing. The convoy pulled out in sequential order and rolled in low gear down to the barrier, then onward down the steep slope into Bosnia Herzegovina.

Safely through the first of many checks, the convoy picked up speed and was soon heading southeast to Capalijna where, dependent on Spider's instructions, it would join the main road north to Mostar or head northwest to Ljubusk.

Crowther checked the mobile phone in the glove compartment for the umpteenth time. They had travelled thirteen miles, but he still had not given a location fix to Paroski. Then almost as if on cue, the radio crackled and Spider said curtly, "Convoy Leader to all Vehicles. Mostar. I repeat Mostar. Out."

Secure in the isolation of the cab, Crowther took a deep breath and, with the mobile lying on his thigh, hit the prescribed number to contact Paroski and pass on the information.

On the southern slope of the seventeen thousand metre-high Mount Orfinka, a gun team of the Bosnian Serb Army was finalizing the changes to the howitzers' sightings. The commander pencilled in the new angles on the map, adjusting his previous calculations and marginally altering trajectory and direction. The gun crew moved the bombs closer to the gun to reduce the load interval, and a radio check with the observer verified that the radio was operational.

Preparations completed, the men waited for the whistle that would signal stand-to.

The first villages encountered by the convoy after the crossing showed no sign of the wanton destruction that disfigured the rest of Bosnia. However, after Capalijna and less than seven miles south of Mostar, the signs of war became evident. The countryside had the same appearance as those areas of the Krajina where the more numerous Serbs had evicted the less fortunate Croats and destroyed their homes.

However, in this region the Serbs were not to blame for the bulk of the damage to the dwellings. The devastation here was the result of the conflict between ethnic Croats and Bosnian Muslims. The wrecked homes, systematically looted then destroyed by the detonation of explosive charges, more often than not landmines, were blight on the landscape.

At varying intervals, groups of people, standing with bowed heads at the sides of the road, would raise their faces to glare up at the relief trucks to reveal their deep loathing; they detested the well-fed drivers and hated the unknown recipients of the aid, with the bilious antipathy that only natives of the Balkans can display.

At last, the convoy reached the outskirts of Mostar. The column of relief trucks snarled its way up the steep gradient of the route north, passing the remains of the monastery, which overlooked the river and the city. The extent of the destruction and desolation of the shattered buildings bore stark testament to the ferocity and brutality of the conflict between Muslim and Croat.

Each truck in the convoy had been equipped with a YAESU vehicle-mounted radio with a power output of 50 watts that was sufficient to allow communication between each of the vehicles in the convoy. In addition to its YAESU, the convoy leader's jeep had a CODAN HF radio for long-range communications with its own base station and UNHCR or UNPROFOR bases throughout the country.

Spider used the YAESU to alert the drivers.

"Convoy Leader to all vehicles. That is Mostar down there on the left. We will be at the checkpoint shortly. This part of the route to Jablonica is dicey; it is open and exposed and well within range of the Serb guns. We will all, I repeat, all, put on helmets and flak jackets at the checkpoint. Keep the gear on until I give you the word to remove it. Out."

The UN eastern boundary checkpoint was at the southern edge of a cluster of wrecked houses, blackened and stained like decayed stumps in the infected gums of the landscape. The villagers had been prey to the Black Swans, an element of HOS, a Croatian paramilitary unit whose members legitimately boasted that no living thing existed in their wake.

As the barrier came in sight, the trucks slowed, then stopped as each driver achieved the requisite fifty yards between vehicles.

The late morning sun had reached its zenith. An oppressive heat haze swathed the unkempt abandoned fields and the ruptured walls of the ruined dwellings, and the encircling ramparts of the mountains seemed to increase its intensity.

A couple of Spanish troopers indulged in lazy, half-hearted horseplay to the feigned amusement of three girls who had come to the checkpoint to cadge cigarettes. The remaining soldiers, some openly and some surreptitiously, ogled the females from the meagre shade provided by the ruins.

A stationary Spanish BMR-600, or *Blindado Medio de Ruedas 600* Infantry Fighting Vehicle, was several yards to the right of the barrier pole of the checkpoint. Due to the heat and the presence of the teenage girls, the carrier, which could carry eleven fully equipped infantrymen, was empty. The cupolas and rear doors were open; the externally mounted 12.7mm machine gun was unmanned. In motion, the three-axle BMR-600 powered by a Pegaso 9156/8 diesel could achieve a road speed of 110 km/h. Its British all-welded aluminium spaced armour would give adequate protection to the occupants from 7.62mm ball and armour-piercing rounds.

The Convoy lead vehicle, as directed by the short swarthy guard, who appeared wider than he was tall because of the bulk of his flak jacket and helmet, had halted close to the barrier for the standard check. Spider left the Toyota and, after conferring with the corporal of the guard, briefed the waiting drivers on the latest known conditions for that day's route.

The sun directly overhead maximized the heat and eliminated all shade.

The drivers, some grumbling because of the helmets and body armour, were all wishing they were underway again. The movement of the trucks would create a reasonable breeze. They paid scant attention to Spider as they watched the Lotharios at the barrier.

"Have we got time for a brew?" Scouse asked with his ubiquitous portable gas cooker and kettle already in place. Spider pretended not to hear as he turned toward his vehicle.

Abruptly and shocking in its immediacy, a violent, invisible pressure buffeted vehicles and drivers, pulling and stretching exposed skin downwards and bludgeoning eardrums in turbulent frenzy.

As swiftly as it was compressed, the ambient atmosphere then expanded.

It was sucked into the white Infantry Fighting Vehicle, which pulsed, reverberated, and then with vicious force, regurgitated the air, now converted to thick black smoke, through the hatches and cupolas.

Dark fumes rose in a column streaked with items of military equipment and chunks of the vehicle's interior.

The belated thud of the explosion gusted through the airwaves as the drivers dived for cover.

Calum and Spider collided as they lunged towards the edge of the road and the bordering ditch. They lay there face to face. Calum stared, glassily, as Spider yelled, "Stay down! Down! Everyone! Keep your heads down, but check your neighbour. Look around you. Anyone hurt?" The words sounded muffled and dull against the numbness that wadded his eardrums.

"I'm going to shout names. Answer up if you can." He called the names of each driver, repeating those to which there was no immediate response. Michael had not answered.

"Michael, c'mon! Let's hear it!" bellowed Spider.

Kurt screamed, "He's down! Oh Christ, he is down! They've killed him. The bastards have killed him; he's down."

The scream died down into a warbling moaning.

"Kurt. Kurt, steady! Don't lose it! Get it under control. Can you see Michael? Kurt, gimme an answer!"

The sound of sobbing reached Spider. He noticed that the glazed look had left Calum's eyes but tears were streaming down his face.

"Kurt, I'm coming over to check Michael out. Get down and stay down!"

Spider tensed his arms, braced his legs, raised his body clear of the bottom of the ditch and then, taking a deep breath, hurtled up from the cover and threw himself across the road.

At that moment, the second shell crashed into the third convoy vehicle. The cab disintegrated.

A huge, unseen hand swatted Spider and volleyed him into the ditch as metal, cartons and wheels streamed from the sky to litter the area around him.

He tried to breathe but, although severely winded, he was not bleeding. With extraordinary effort, he gathered his strength and, knowing that it would be at least a few more seconds before they fired again, he threw himself once more across the road.

He reached the shelter of the opposite bank.

Nine of the drivers were within feet of each other.

"Okay, Spider?" Dawke asked.

Spider could not hear him but understood the mouthed question. He nodded, then, realizing that Kurt was not one of the group, looked along the bank towards the end of the convoy. The man was sitting on the bank, some twenty yards away, with his head in his hands and his body wracked by deep shuddering sobs. Spider crawled through the group and rolled along the bank until he reached the German. He pulled the distraught driver down to the bottom of the bank, grasped the other's face in both hands and turned it towards him.

Kurt did not resist but gulped air through his opened lips. He pointed in silence at the road. Spider followed his finger and made out the crumpled figure of Michael lying near the front of his truck. He patted Kurt on the shoulder, and then climbed over him to leopard-crawl further along the ditch until he was opposite Michael's inert form.

The man lay on his back with his arms spread wide and his feet pointing away from Spider. His head tilted at an impossible angle and a sharp, well-defined crease ran across the crown of his Kevlar helmet. From where he lay, Spider could see an ever-widening pool of blood.

"Michael?" he called without expectation of an answer. As he braced himself to run out and pull Michael to the side of the road, the third shell crashed down.

The strike was within feet of the Irishman's vehicle. The blast buffeted the truck and yanked it clear of the ground before slamming it back to earth, where it bounced and shuddered. Spider felt the reverberation through the bank, then looked back to Michael.

The body had vanished.

Leaping to his feet Spider ran towards the cluster of drivers.

"Get in the trucks! Move out! We're sitting ducks. Move it! Into your trucks. Go! Go!" He crashed into a couple of bemused men who remained sitting in the ditch.

"Get in the trucks! Drive! Drive!" he roared, tugging at the shoulders of the two men with each hand and pushing them back up into the road.

As he reached the front of the convoy, the agitated buzz of Spanish voices reached him through the thick, soupy silence. The drivers had climbed back into their vehicles when four of the soldiers, with much excited arm waving and rifle brandishing, indicated that the convoy should leave, and quickly.

Spider scrambled into the Toyota and snatched up the radio mike.

"Start your vehicles. Move it! Let's get the hell out of here! Radios remain open for communication!"

The barrier swung into the air. The white Toyota started up and pulled rapidly away, closely followed by the line of accelerating ten-tonners.

The observer for the Serb gunners counted the speeding vehicles, noting that the direction of departure indicated Jablonica, and radioed that information together with the number of strikes to his headquarters.

Minutes later, Kalosowich was reviewing the resources available to him. The situation report he had received earlier showed that one Chetnik paramilitary element, the White Eagles, was operating several miles to the west of the Jablonica. This detachment was engaged in what the world press euphemistically called ethnic cleansing; they were killing and maiming in Grabovica, a predominantly Croatian village, which lay astride the convoy's projected route.

Kalosowich drafted a brief message and passed it to his radio operator.

On receipt of the message, the leader of the Eagles in Grabovica handed command over to his deputy, climbed into a van with four of his men, and took the road to Mostar to intercept the convoy.

The valley narrowed.

Spider decided to use the overhang of rock as protection for the convoy while he checked the crew and decided on a plan of action. The vehicles closed up and pulled over into the concave shadow offered by the mountain.

Crowther's thoughts ran amok.

His hands and knees shook; he broke a cigarette and dropped one more before he could successfully light it. Like the others, he believed that he had just escaped death back at the barrier. His nerves jangled at the memory of the hole in the road that had been Michael. Now, like crazed lunatics, they were driving further into Bosnia—towards more danger. He dragged on the cigarette and struggled to quell the nausea of panic.

The Serbs often fired small arms at the aid convoys. After the initial attacks on convoys, with no one killed or wounded, it soon became clear that the firing was pure harassment. Their small-arms fire remained clinically accurate. It was the same when they shelled the convoys; near misses, close on occasions, but consistent misses.

Today had been different. One shell could be in error, but more? It was almost as if they had known about the contraband.

The temperature in the cab seemed to plunge, and the perspiration on his skin turned to ice.

Of course, they knew!

He shuddered. They did not intend to let the convoy through! But, how could they know? Was it possible, that like Paroski, *their* intelligence sources had uncovered the arms conduit? Or had Paroski informed them?

He felt an unreasonable sense of betrayal. Paroski had drawn the Serbs' attention to the weapons, but had also ordered him to go with the convoy. It was obvious that Paroski knew they were all in danger—and just did not give a damn.

But then, why should he? To the Croat, he was dross and therefore expendable. He slammed his hands against his steering wheel in frustration. The colonel still had his passport and the evidence. What could he do?

Crowther started when the radio crackled, reminding him that Paroski had told him to disable the long-range radio, but he still had not done so. He would have to cripple the CODAN soon.

Sod the man!

"Convoy Leader to all vehicles. Update. I've been in touch with Base and given them the situation. They said an UNPROFOR helicopter ambulance team is on its way to Mostar. Our only course is to continue through as best we can. If we try to turn back, those gunners will be waiting on the same stretch of road. There's every chance that it was a one-off and that the way ahead is clear," Spider lied to bolster his own courage as well as that of the other drivers. There were two legs, fortunately short ones, of the remaining journey, that were within clear view of the Serbs.

The convoy routes ran on a parallel course between the Bosnian front line and another more fluid demarcation known as the Approximate Line of Confrontation. The main supply route had several sections where alternative roads and tracks led to the same destination. It was considered that the Serbs could not cover all of them.

The geography of the area was also in the convoy's favour. There were stretches on the way where narrow, winding, steep-sided gorges on both sides prevented a clear view of the road. Spider knew that most of the approach was over high ground through dense pine forests on woodcutters' tracks. There would, there should, he corrected himself, be no clear field of fire for gunners.

He felt confident that they could negotiate them without danger.

"Any questions? Then everything's clear. Out."

As he closed down, Spider saw the next checkpoint coming up. The news of the earlier attack had reached the soldiers, members of the Malayan contingent, and the barrier was up. The trucks swept through and swung left onto the track that would lead them towards the suburbs of Jablonica.

Once into the cover of the thick woods, Spider accelerated, widening the gap between his vehicle and the convoy. The distance would increase the warning time for the convoy should any surprises crop up.

The heavy convoy's momentum did not slacken. Rath's truck led the way, bouncing and swinging on the deep ruts of the track, and the others followed eagerly. As the ground rose and they climbed more steeply, the track narrowed, following the contour of the mountain. The drop on the outside edge of the track increased in depth, falling away sharply. Several hundred feet below, a swift-flowing stream rushed over crags and protruding rocks.

Rath, a competent driver, refused to allow the terrain to intimidate him. Despite the high speed at which he travelled, he drove defensively and kept his eyes on the track ahead as the steering wheel bucked and spun in his capable hands.

He enjoyed the thrill and adrenalin swirl of fast convoying. The challenge of the task vitalized his whole being, mounted on this high-strung stallion of a ten-ton cross-country truck, which had a spirit and character of its own. It was a jarring battle of sinew and nerve, physique and instinct. Snaking double-S bends, narrow tracks and the rapidity of the change of gradient, rising, falling away, rising, all added to the sense of a roller-coaster ride.

The shelling had honed his already keen awareness to a degree even he did not think possible.

As the truck bounded across the slope, swinging around a ninety-degree, left-hand bend, to bounce onto a saddle joining the next mountain, he snatched a glance at the side mirror. The rest of the convoy was still with him. The first four continued in line, and as he spun the wheel to negotiate a right-hand turn that appeared almost immediately, he saw the remainder of the column clawing itself upward in his wake.

Another brief look revealed that the tail vehicle was lagging. Without decreasing speed, he manoeuvred his truck over to the left until the lower branches of the pines were brushing and scratching the side of the vehicle.

The image in the mirror confirmed that the last truck was fading—probably a clogged diesel filter. However, its particular driver would push it until it died. The Irishman knew that several hundred yards ahead, just before the crest, the track would widen to allow timber trucks, in better times, to pass in opposite directions.

This broadened track continued for one or two hundred yards. Spider would be waiting there for the convoy to catch up. Rath decided to pull over at the start of that stretch and wait for the lame duck without impeding the progress of the others.

He pulled the radio's microphone down.

"Rath to Convoy Leader. Message. Over."

"Convoy Leader to Rath. Send. Over."

"Dawke looks like he's got a fuel filter problem. I'll wait to check it out. Suggest you go on through with the others. We'll catch up. Over."

"Convoy Leader. Understood, but fix it quickly or let's know ASAP if you can't. You don't want to be stranded here. Out."

The remainder of the convoy roared past as Rath pulled over. Dawke's truck, belching thick black smoke, hiccupped and shuddered its way up the slope, and dragged itself into the side behind the waiting truck. Jumping down, Rath made his way to the faulty vehicle, shaking his head in disgust as he saw the driver's rueful expression.

"Use your goddamned radio when you've got problems—that's what it's for. I won't even ask if you checked the damned filters before we left."

He swung up on the truck and wedged himself between the cab and cargo bed. After unscrewing the reservoir cap on the fuel tank, he removed the sleeve-like inline fuel filter. It was heavy and thickly coated with dark sludge. Rath threw the filter to Dawke.

"Get your bucket and give me a length of hose." He stretched down for the plastic bucket the driver had removed from the cab and put one end of the hose down into the fuel tank. Blowing the air from his lungs, he sucked on the free end of the hose, then, snatched it from his mouth, and placed it in the bucket. As the diesel flowed, he spat to clear his mouth of the fuel. Passing the bucket down to Dawke, he told him to wash the filter. Dawke swished the strainer in the liquid and then started to spray it with the airline while he tried to justify his negligence.

"Jesus, Rath, it was just back from the service station. Who'd expect to—" he halted in mid-sentence as the radio crackled into life.

"Crowther, all vehicles," panted Dennis Crowther who had been following Rath and was now lead vehicle. The rest of his words followed in a rush. "There's a van parked across the track in front. Four...five fellas, with guns. They're waving me down—"

His transmission died. Spider, parked in the siding, cut in. "For Christ sake, Dennis, don't stop! Repeat, don't stop!"

—at me. Jesus! They're firing—" Crowther's transmission resumed for a few seconds then abruptly the words died.

"Quick, Dawke, the filter. That'll have to do. Let's get moving!"

Dropping the filter in the reservoir, Rath screwed the top back on. He jumped down and ordered Dawke to follow but to keep at least a hundred yards distance. With that, he scrambled into his cab and restarted the engine. He had no plan of action but was determined to get the other trucks back in sight so that he could at least see what was going on.

Spider, sandwiched between the fifth and sixth trucks as he had re-joined the convoy, cursed as he came to a stop with the rest. As he jumped down, the the attackers dragged Crowther from his truck and threw him against the rock face, where he collapsed. The driver tried to sit up. Spider was relieved to see that he did not appear shot or injured. The pair turned to the other vehicles and, brandishing their rifles, waved the remaining drivers down from their vehicles.

The men were shepherded to where Crowther sat and formed up in a ragged line. Raising his hands with the others, Spider managed to sidle into the line next to Rusty, who was the longest-serving driver and knew some Serbo-Croat.

"Who are they?" he whispered as the men slung their Kalashnikovs and began to manhandle the drivers in their search for weapons.

"Serb militia," muttered Rusty without taking his eyes off the ambushers. Spider looked around and counted a total of five. Two were unlashing the tarpaulin on Crowther's truck and two, who had completed the body search, had clambered onto the vehicle. The fifth man had stepped forward with a Kalashnikov to cover the drivers.

The men on the truck ripped the polythene covering off several pallets, gouged open the boxes and were throwing the contents onto the bed of the truck. The man on the ground looked up as one of the searchers shouted. With an angry gesture, he indicated the second vehicle with the muzzle of his rifle. The men sprang to the ground and began to remove the restraining ropes on that vehicle's canopy.

"So, what could we be carrying that they're after?" Spider wondered aloud. Crowther, standing on his left, turned to look at him but said nothing, then flinched as a guard stepped forward threateningly.

184

Minutes later, the searchers jumped down from the fourth vehicle and gathered round the leader who gesticulated and pointed under the trucks. The four returned to the first vehicle and, crawling on all fours, resumed their search.

Rath coasted his vehicle down through the wide section, searching ahead and then, as he caught sight of the white-painted trucks, pulled up. Several hundred feet below him, he could see the halted convoy in its entirety.

The trucks had stopped, because a van blocked the track just before a sharp, left-hand bend. From his vantage point, Rath saw one gunman holding the drivers at gunpoint, while three or four others were crawling under the trucks.

The road was not especially narrow and a germ of an idea began to form.

The leader of the Serbs stepped forward and indicated that the men should empty their pockets. He removed his combat cap to receive their valuables.

As Spider started to take off his watch, an immediate but muted movement to his right caused him to look back up the mountain. Rath's ten-tonner, only yards away, hurtled silently but relentlessly towards them, like the sweeping white wall of an avalanche. With both arms spread wide, Spider swept Crowther and Rusty up against the rock wall, roaring a warning to the other drivers as he did so.

The leader of the hijackers threw his rifle into the shoulder and took aim at the onrushing truck. Spider grabbed him from behind and pulled the weapon across his throat. Three of the searchers, on hearing the noise, had crawled out from under the vehicles, into the path of the oncoming truck. Pitched against the unbending sides of the stationary trucks, they then bounced back to fall under the wheels of the oncoming mammoth as it swept into the narrow gap between the standing vehicles and the side of the rocks.

Spider increased the savage pressure on the leader's throat as Rath's truck rocketed by. His cheek flamed and tears rushed to his eyes as the end of a tarpaulin rope on the hurtling vehicle lashed out and burned his face. It passed so closely, missing him by inches, that he could not be sure that he had not been the intended target.

The apparent runaway crashed into the parked van and propelled it to the edge of the drop where the smaller vehicle teetered then toppled from view. The Serb in Spider's grip had ceased to struggle and only the rifle under his chin kept him upright. Throwing the corpse from him, Spider brought the rifle into the firing position as he stepped forward to seek out the fifth Serb.

He moved alongside the row in a crouch, but several feet from it, peering under the trucks and cursing himself for not having kept a check on the specific location of each attacker.

As he neared the end of the line, the sudden appearance of the man as he rolled out from under the chassis of the second to last wagon gave him no time to consider. Reflexes took over, and he fired.

The Serb, who had already reached his knees, caught the burst in his groin and abdomen. Thrown onto his back, his legs thrashed fitfully, and his heels drummed against the dry clay of the track.

With his weapon still trained on the figure, Spider approached. He grasped the small of the butt of the downed man's weapon and pulled it clear. The body had stopped shuddering, and its sightless eyes stared upwards. He turned back to the others and saw Rath had joined them.

"What's next?" asked the big Irishman, watching Spider closely.

"First let's tidy up here. Throw them over with their vehicle. If they send anybody else out to check for them, we don't want to make it too easy. And get those rifles and all the ammo."

Rath continued to stare at Spider, then grinned widely, "Why not? Shouldn't litter, anyway."

He turned, and reaching down, grabbed a fistful of collar. Picking up the dead man's weapon with his free hand, and with little effort, he dragged the body to the edge of the divide and then released his grip.

"The rest of you mount up," Spider ordered. "Rath, a quick word." The two stood close together.

"If I thought for one moment that you intended to down me with that truck. . ." He left the sentence unfinished. Rath watched him stony-faced.

"We've passed no side roads. Grabovica is up ahead, so that's where these bastards came from. There are probably more of them there but we can't go back. We've got to go through there or give it up."

At the mention of going back Rath shook his head.

"It still makes sense to press on."

He nodded at the Kalashnikov in Spider's hands.

"And at least you're armed now."

The gradient had decreased, and the hillside fell away more gradually. The forest started to thin out, with the dark green of the pines giving way to the lighter hues and less compact shapes of deciduous trees.

Grabovica lay before them across the ragged patchwork of fields, some no larger than the area of three or four English gardens.

Spider slowed. Over the roar of the truck's power-ful diesel engine, he could hear the ominous crackle of small-arms fire. Warning the convoy over the radio, he gave the order to halt several hundred yards from the first house.

The village straddled the road, the only passable way over this section to Jablonica. The sporadic firing was clearer now and seemed to be concentrated in one location. From the tempo and sound of the bursts, the ex-soldier recognized the desultory shooting that takes place during mopping-up operations.

Spider jumped from his cab to join Rath.

As he jogged forward, the Irishman saw a thick black cloud blooming into the sky and then falling back to blanket the rooftops on the other side of the hamlet.

"Smoke to your right," he said with a nod towards the village.

Spider turned to look but did not respond.

"And we've got to go through? No other way round?"

"Afraid so," grunted Spider as he scanned the red roofs of the village.

"We could try the fields and open country."

Still looking in the direction of the smoke, Spider nodded, "If you want to risk the mines."

"Which direction do we take on leaving the village?"

"Any other time we'd take a left in the middle and be on the stretch to Jablonica, but now your guess is as good as mine. If we do go on, it's a case of balls to the wall; stop for nothing."

Rath nodded.

"Hang on here," said Spider, "but make sure all their engines are running. I'm going up there to see if we can get through. Be ready to push through and get the hell out of here if the proverbial hits the fan. Wish me luck."

Rath grinned but said nothing as he turned back to his truck.

Spider pushed through the meagre bushes that edged the fields and then broke into a crouching run. He hoped that the people firing had not posted sentries, or were at least too preoccupied to catch sight of him bee-tling across some peasant's land.

He reached the safety of a stone dyke behind the dwellings and started to edge towards a break in the wall that ran parallel to the buildings. Bent double, he crept through the gap as the roof of the nearest house collapsed, showering him with burning ash. Dark smoke billowed through the wrecked door and jagged windows.

He reached the rear of the next house and, keeping close to wall, edged round to the front.

The garden of the house bordered the main street. Keeping to the shelter provided by a dividing wall between the properties, Spider scuttled into the angle they formed, dropped to one knee and looked around. The ground appeared well cultivated and heavy with a ripening crop of vegetables. Fig trees, laden with fruit, lined the paved path leading to the front of the building.

He stiffened, as he heard shouts, then, risking a slow movement, he peered over the stones. Ten or twelve elderly villagers were in a group in the centre of the road.

They cowered in abject terror, as they tried, and failed, to avoid the blows of their tormentors. Four gunmen herded them towards the wall of the cemetery on the opposite side of the street. They were silent, their pallid faces streaked with blood, but Spider could feel their fear.

He looked beyond them down the street.

Ragged, crackling flames flared from shattered windows; fire was spreading unchecked through the torched houses. Mingled with the smell of wood smoke was a stronger, unmistakable stench. Sweet and cloying, hanging heavy in the air, it was so strong that Spider could taste it. He spat to clear his mouth. As the wind, drawn by the fires, swept along the street, the smoke at ground level, cleared to reveal several bodies sprawled on the roadway. He ducked back down, his thoughts racing.

Back to the trucks and wait it out? The Serbs had to leave sometime. He bit his lip in disgust as the realization struck him that it was possible they could leave from his side of the village and discover the convoy. He could hammer through at speed, relying on the heavy vehicles to force a passage. That had worked before, unless they had blocked the road with a stronger barricade.

He raised his head to see if the street was clear of obstructions.

Crowther sat motionless in the cab, his pupils fixed and glazed, his face deathly pale. Perspiration glistened on his cheeks, and a tic pulsed under his left eye.

Holy Mother of God, what were they doing here in Grabovica in the middle of a massacre? A burst of automatic fire rattled into his consciousness.

The Serbs seemed to be moving closer. Terror smothered his senses. His limbs felt heavy, lethargic, and incapable of movement, like a fly snared in gossamer, waiting for the spider to gorge itself on him.

He struggled to think constructively. Paroski's face, callous and indifferent, flashed before his eyes.

"Bastard," he screamed aloud.

His dread of Paroski alternated with the threat of butchery at the hands of these animals. He did not want to die in godforsaken Grabovica—a crude, peasant village in the depths of medieval Bosnia, the unwashed armpit of the Balkans.

Christ, he did not deserve this. He was going to die because of damned, stupid, useless Bosnians! Vivid, crimson pictures of hacking and stabbing blades swirled in his brain. His limbs felt leaden and lumpish: this was insanity, to be defenceless, weak, unarmed and waiting for slaughter by lunatics. He shuddered. All because the Bosnians needed weapons, weapons that *his lot* were crass enough to be carrying.

He locked his arms around his knees, and started to rock back and forth. Sweat poured down his cheeks, mingling with tears of desperation that trickled from his closed eyelids.

He started to moan softly.

He did not know how long he had been rocking, but gradually he became aware of his surroundings again, and of the mission Paroski had assigned him. God, how he hated the man!

Awash in his terror of physical harm, Crowther would have thrown caution to the wind and ignored the colonel's orders, but now calm was returning to his tortured thoughts. If he failed to follow the orders, he would risk charges in Croatia. Moreover, he could face jail for life or execution. Paroski would see to that—the man had even told him so. He bit his lip. He had not completed his other given tasks. The radio used by Spider to maintain contact with base and to reach UNPROFOR still functioned. Paroski had been specific about the early hamstringing of that set.

Its loss would gag the convoy.

Crowther lifted his wrist and stared at his watch. It would soon be time for him to contact Paroski, and he dare not make the contact without being able to report the sabotage of the convoy's radio.

It was now or never.

A look in the side mirror confirmed that the vehicle behind was empty, its driver probably having a nervous leak or a consoling cigarette with another driver. Crowther climbed out and edged around to the front of his vehicle. Peering around him and using the bulk of his vehicle for cover, he edged forward to the jeep.

He wrenched open the door and scrambled inside the vehicle. Pulling himself over the sleeping bag and cooking utensils, he reached the rod antennae mounted at the rear.

From his wallet, he pulled a thin wooden nail, which Paroski had instructed him to sharpen and take with him specifically for this moment. The colonel said that the nail would leave the radio ostensibly operable, but short-circuit the range-finding capacity of the antenna.

With a furtive look through the rear window to ensure he had avoided detection, he pushed the nail into the base of the aerial.

Forty or so yards beyond the villagers at the wall, a larger group knelt under the rifle muzzles of three other raiders. Spider searched the rest of the street. He saw no sign of a roadblock or additional gunmen.

A scream of pain brought his attention back to the prisoners.

The thick squelch of wood pounding bone and flesh reached him, with nauseating clarity, as one of the gunmen swiped an old man with his rifle butt. The other guards used their weapons, held chest-high in both hands, to push the terrified victims brutally into line against the wall. Grabbing the fallen man by the collar of his jacket, they dragged him to the wall and threw him at the feet of the others.

The enormity of what was about to happen bludgeoned Spider's senses. The gunmen stepped back a few paces, then threw their weapons into the aim. The prolonged burst of automatic fire cut the villagers down.

Spider ducked and chewed on his lower lip. These bastards were ruthless murderers, pure and simple. He swallowed hard, and then raised his head again. The executioners were prodding the bodies with booted feet. One fired a burst into the corpses.

A shout from a guard of the other group caused them to sling their weapons over their shoulders and move down the street to re-join the larger gathering.

Two stopped to share a light for their cigarettes before swaggering after the others.

A slight rustle behind him prickled the hair on Spider's neck, and before he could move, he felt the cold metal of a gun muzzle against his skin. He tensed, and then slowly, very slowly, looked round. Only inches away from his surprised eyes, he took in the face of Rath, devoid of expression.

Neither moved for what seemed to Spider like an eternity.

His thoughts raced. Surely, the Irishman could not be so shortsighted as to believe this an opportunity to settle the score?

Both men tensed, but as Rath shifted his gaze and studiously looked past him, Spider expelled his breath in a harsh whisper. Rath grinned malevolently, then removed the muzzle of his Kalashnikov from the Englishman's neck. Spider did not, could not, smile, knowing that Rath had shown him that their antagonism had not abated but remained in abeyance only until the current difficulties were resolved.

"Here," mouthed Rath, as he removed a full magazine from his shirt pocket. He raised his head to look over the wall, and then ducked almost immediately. Using his fingers and facial signs, he indicated that the Serbs were coming back to the wall with more villagers. Pointing towards his own chest and then Spider's, he signed that both should go into the house behind them.

Low to the ground, both men scurried towards the doorway and dived inside the house. Spider nodded at the stairs and, without a word, they ran up and entered a bedroom where they crossed to a window overlooking the street.

Spider pulled the bed away from the window and pushed it to one side.

"You take the group down the street. I'll sort these bastards," he said in a low voice. Rath nodded, then adopted a kneeling position behind a second window. Both quietly opened the casements.

In the street, four gunmen had returned to the wall with more villagers. Spider knelt on one knee, then settled back on his heel. He cocked his weapon and flicked the setting to single shot. With the point of his left elbow in the loop of the sling, he moved it up and around his upper arm to pull it tight. He lined the foresight up on the baseball cap of the leading guard and took up the slack in the trigger.

"Now!"

Both AK 47s opened up at the same moment. The head of the leading gunman exploded and showered the nearest villagers in blood and white bone splinters. Letting out a collective, wailing moan the prisoners half-collapsed, half-threw themselves at the base of the wall.

The remaining Serbs spun around, their shocked faces lifted with widened eyes as they searched for the source of the shot. One had raised his arm in a reflexive protective action.

In the ensuing seconds, Spider swung the muzzle of the rifle and snapped off two more shots. Before the raiders could identify his location, both rounds had struck home. Two men dropped, one remaining motionless, but the other, hit in the neck, rolled and thrashed wildly on the dusty road. The third dropped his weapon and ran in the direction of the larger group. Spider trained his rifle on the fleeing back and squeezed the trigger. The man staggered, then lost his footing as though pushed violently on ice. He crashed face down.

Rath's first shot hit a bearded gunman who, thrown backwards into the cluster of kneeling villagers, knocked several to the ground. Many had covered their heads in their hands. Others had turned inwards, trying to avoid the bullets by pushing and burrowing under the person nearest to them. An incongruous vision of puppies at their mother's teats flashed across Rath's consciousness. It disappeared as rapidly as it had come.

He switched his aim and sighted on another guard. He squeezed. One of the wiggling bodies bucked, then stiffened. The guard remained standing as though rooted to the spot. Rath sucked in his breath and grimaced. The next shot did not miss and the gunman went down heavily. The remaining militiaman took to his heels, and, despite two more shots by Rath, made the safety of the nearby houses.

Both men stopped firing. In the silence that followed, one of the villagers climbed to her feet and started to run towards the side of the road and the comparative safety of a doorway. Within seconds, others had followed her and were running along the street. Spider stood and applied the safety catch to his weapon.

"Back to the trucks, Rath. Now!"

Rath nodded. Both men made for the stairs.

NINE

Closed skies and dense dark clouds pressed down on the forest. The temperature had dropped and the cold was pervasive. Greyness surrounded them, and the moisture-filled air muffled the noise of the engines. The rain dripped from the ubiquitous pines, rattling down onto cab roofs. Huge puddles disintegrated and slashed upwards from deep scars in the track to drum against the metal bottoms of the trucks.

The water ran in sheets down windscreens, impeding visibility. It swamped the slow-moving arm of the wipers as they struggled to control the torrent flooding over the glass. No vehicle had a functional heater, and the dampness in the cabs, distilled by the body warmth of the driver, formed grey condensation that coated the windscreen. Diesel fumes corrupted the surrounding scent of pines, producing a heavy miasma that cloyed in their nostrils.

The huge, white vehicles bounced and swayed up the twisting incline in an elephantine conga. The climb, due to the limited distance of view, appeared endless, but Calum, close behind Crowther, dreaded the impending nightmare of descent that he knew would confront them on reaching the gorge.

He hated heights, and his nerves were already in tatters. The roughing-up at the hands of the Serbs before Grabovica and the sight of the murdered villagers had destroyed any equilibrium he may have had. This raw violence was all too real and immediate. The crumpled bodies had looked so broken. He could not chase the faces—slack, loose-jawed and staring—from his mind. White, pale limbs were impossibly juxtaposed and intertwined, nether regions obscenely exposed, dignity and humanity stripped away.

One old peasant woman had been a dead ringer for his own grandmother for Chrissakes!

The images of the dead vanished from his mind.

Crowther's vehicle had disappeared!

Calum's right foot stabbed instinctively at the pedal. The mammoth slewed as the brakes bit, and it slid to a halt. The curtain of rain pulled aside, and he looked down. The vast void of a threatening, bottomless abyss lay before him. The skin on the back of his neck prickled, and his head itched uncomfortably under the helmet; sweat trickled coldly between his shoulder blades beneath the flak jacket.

A sense of foreboding filled him. He shivered. He yawned nervously, stretching the muscles of his jaw against the tension of the chinstrap of the helmet, and gripped the steering wheel with whitened knuckles.

A sharp tapping on the window beside him startled him. He looked down to see Kurt gesticulating angrily. His eyes followed the direction in which the other driver was pointing. It dawned on him that the track turned sharply away to the left. A high wall of scarred rock bordered one side of the way forward. On the other, the ravine waited, implacably.

To Calum, it looked as if a gigantic cleaver had split the mountain crudely and unevenly. A planet away across the divide, but in reality less than fifty yards, the other wall of the ravine rose, blocking out the light. Deep, black and endlessly open, the maw of the abyss waited for the unwary.

He rolled his window down. "OK, Kurt, no panic. I've got it now," he lied.

The other shook his head in exasperation, then turned back to his own vehicle. Calum pressed down on the accelerator and gripped the steering wheel as the engine took hold and the truck rolled forward.

In the narrowest part of the gorge, the track left no more than eighteen inches clearance on either side of the vehicles. Calum concentrated on keeping the rock face on his left, as close to the side of his vehicle as possible without grazing the stone, but the road negated most of his efforts.

The track surface was broken, with deep ruts, and the gouges held the wheels and dictated direction. It was like travelling on rails with little or no deviation possible, and the pull of the furrows nullified any attempt to manoeuvre.

He tried to ignore the abyss on his right and forced himself not to look.

At every bend, and there were too many for comfort, the drag of the drop, with an irresistible magnetism, wrenched at his unwilling eyes. The rushing wind, heavy with rain and soaking him through the opened side window, helped to keep his vertigo from spiralling but the high walls of granite acted as sounding boards and the noise of the river thrashing and roaring in the ravine bottom, reverberating and mingling with the screams of the engines, tore at his already shredded nerves.

The convoy continued to travel at speed despite the difficult passage. The steering bucked and leapt in his hands. His upper arms and back ached with the strain of holding the vehicle on its path. At certain places, rock falls and scree formed uneven heaps of debris that the front wheels would mount, causing the truck to teeter and lean precariously close to the edge.

When it happened, it was with a nightmarish immediacy.

The furrows in the track became deeper. Crowther, driving the vehicle in front, was fighting his wheels as strenuously as Calum. The track narrowed, as it entered another of the prolific left turns, and as Crowther tried to avoid the drop to his right, the rock face buffeted his vehicle. The truck wobbled violently from side to side and the screech of scraped metal cut through the pounding noise of the gorge.

Close on Crowther's tail, Calum attempted to stay clear of the rock face and pulled his steering wheel to the right. The truck in front negotiated the bend, the heavy rubber of its spinning rear wheels at last biting fiercely into the ground. Calum feverishly pumped his brakes as a huge mass of road surface ahead vomited into the abyss but there was no returning pressure under his foot.

The pedal reached the floor but had no effect whatsoever on the wheels that continued to spin in the thin mountain air. His brakes had gone!

On both sides of him, the landscape disappeared and the emptiness held the truck a split second before hurling it out and down into the void.

Spider braked viciously as the short-range radio erupted in an excited babble of voices. Something drastic had happened. What, he did not know, but it would be pointless trying to gain control of the channel to find out. The track was too narrow to turn around at this point, and by now, the convoy blocked the way.

Cursing under his breath, he jumped down and ran back up the slope towards the other vehicles. He overtook Crowther as he ran toward the cluster of drivers looking down into the ravine. Kurt and Rusty were close to the brink; the others, more apprehensive of the height, were further back but nevertheless straining their necks to see over.

The absence of Calum's slender figure was obvious as he approached but despite that, he asked automatically, "Who is it?"

"Calum," several replied at once. Huddled together, they were blocking his way. He pushed his way through to the edge to look down.

His eyes rapidly assessed the scene. The sides of the ravine at this point were very steep but no longer sheer or perpendicular. The truck's cargo, pallets loaded with sacks of flour, spread drunkenly over a wide area of the descent to the river. Ripped sacks and swathes of flour littered the intervening spaces.

About a hundred and fifty feet below the road, the truck lay on its side, with the high flood of the river rushing and gurgling around and through it. The tarpaulin, secured only to the upper side of the cargo bed, flapped silently near the surface of the water as it streamed out the length of the truck. The cab was twisted and damaged. The driver's feet, the left one bootless, hung out of the passenger's window.

"Listen up, everyone! Move quickly when I tell you." Spider broke through the subdued murmur of voices. "Kurt, Crowther, get your first aid kits. Now!"

The two turned and ran in separate directions to their vehicles. "The rest of you, get all the chains and any ropes that you've got and bring them here. Make a lifeline. Move it!"

"Rath," he shouted at the Irishman's back as the man ran to his vehicle, "make sure they tie it together well."

He snatched the medical aid holdall from Crowther, who was the first to reach him. He noted that the buckles were intact with plastic strip. As it was still sealed, it would be complete. Putting his right arm and head through the strap, he settled the pack in the small of his back and turned to the ravine. There was no time to lose if they were to do anything for Calum: he could not wait for the rope.

He could get to the truck by making his way from pallet to pallet, if they would support his weight. However, would they? Or would they plunge to the bottom of the ravine, taking him with them? There was only one way to find out. He lined up with the nearest pallet, turned, crouched on all fours then lowered himself over the edge.

Taking a deep breath, he let go.

His feet slammed into the flour bags, and then he fell forward. Shock waves jarred and throbbed up his legs. The pallet lurched, started to slide, gained momentum and was away. It dropped, increasing in speed, then, with a sickening abruptness, stopped, coming to rest against another pallet.

Spider peered over, with still a hundred plus feet to go. Another pallet clung to the rocky slope about twenty-five feet below and to his right. Bracing his legs, he jumped. Surprise more than panic filled him on knowing that he had misjudged the leap and was going to fall short of his target. His body swept passed the pallet, but his outstretched arms struck the flour bags.

The contact broke his fall but his clawing fingers could find no purchase on the smooth sacks. However, the break in momentum slowed his plummeting descent. He fell again and hurtled past the last pallet. The angry, dark green water of the river rushed up towards him, and the last image he had was of a huge grey stingray waiting to swallow him.

The icy cold water engulfed him but, despite the force of his fall, he had not slammed into the riverbed. As he had fallen, his major concern was the lack of depth knowing that the river was only a few feet deep here because the topside of the truck was showing above the surface. As his head cleared the water, it dawned on him that he had landed on the tarpaulin.

He grabbed at the thick material as the wild current battered him and tugged his body back and forth.

He managed to pull himself slowly, strenuously, towards the truck. His fingers made contact with the front wheel, and he hauled himself clear of the water until he was crouching on the vehicle's door. The driver was upside down, and only his lower legs appeared above the water.

Spider reached forward to hold the youth's ankles as he tried to open the cab door. The door-catch was up but still it would not open.

It was jammed solid.

While holding the boy's legs, encircled in his left arm, he pulled his knife from his belt and, using the butt of the hilt, knocked out the remaining shards of glass from the window.

He replaced the knife in his belt, took a firmer grip on Calum's legs, and spreading his feet braced, his back for the heave. Fortunately, the body supported by the water came free relatively easily. Spider placed him face up on the door and felt for signs of life.

Nothing.

He held his fingers in position against the boy's neck for a few seconds more.

Nothing, but then—imperceptibly—he felt a movement, a soft, indistinct tremor, once, then twice against his fingertips.

A pulse!

He undid the chinstrap of the helmet and pulled Calum's mouth open, inserting his fingers to clear his tongue. Cupping the lower jaw with his right hand, he pinched the unconscious nostrils with his left and leaned forward to breathe life into his throat.

Spider heard the gurgle of water and felt Calum's neck muscles strain. He moved just in time as the Irishman regurgitated what appeared to be several pints of water. The water was discoloured with blood, and pale pink bubbles clustered at the corners of his mouth. Calum fell back but his eyes had opened.

"It's okay, easy now, easy. Everything's fine," Spider consoled him as he saw the confusion and panic. "You've had a fall but you're OK now. I am just going to check you out. Help me. Let me know if I touch anything too tender. OK?"

Calum swallowed then moved his head in confirmation. Spider reached down and started by feeling and gently squeezing the injured boy's ankles.

Several minutes later, Spider completed the check. The helmet and crushed flak jacket had provided some protection. However, the deep indentation, together with the blood he had thrown up, indicated that Calum's wounds were serious. His right femur was broken, and there appeared to be damage in his pelvic region, the extent of which Spider could not be sure. His right hand was crushed and his nose broken.

Spider had opened the medical pack and cleaned up the gashes and cuts, but he would need a splint for Calum's leg. He left the injured man and started to search for a suitable support. After a few minutes, he found part of a pallet caught in the rear wheels of the truck and locked in place by the rushing water. He pulled the pallet apart and returned with two slats. A short time later, and after several grunts and grimaces of pain from Calum, the splint was in place.

A shout from the cliff top reached him. The others had fashioned a rope, with chains and towropes; it was snaking down the rock face. Spider was relieved that it was relatively easy to catch the end of it, which he secured to the side of the truck. He would need a sling to get them up to the road. He edged along the truck side and reached for the few ties that still held the tarpaulin in place. Gripping the side of the tarpaulin in both hands, he tensed and then tried to pull it on to the truck. It would not move; the pull of the water rushing downstream was too strong. He pulled again but to no avail. He eyes fell on the lowered rope.

He untied the end and, threading it through one of the metal eyeholes of the sheeting, made it fast. It took far longer, however, to make the men up top understand, over the roar of the river, that they should pull the tarp out of the water.

At last, they understood and the rope tightened as they took the strain. At first, nothing happened, and then the canopy reluctantly rose from the water like massive, green, dripping tripe. Spider, balancing precariously on a sideboard of the truck, stretched for the end and swung it towards him. As soon as the end was over the truck, he signalled for slack in the rope.

Before the canvas was lowered, Spider had pulled out his knife and was cutting through the material. After wrapping the young Irishman in the canvas then binding it tightly in place with strips from the remaining tarpaulin, he fashioned a large loop that he tied to the end of the rescue rope.

Using more pieces of canvas, he then tied Calum in his improvised papoose to the rope above the makeshift stirrup. Spider turned on his side, and lying down alongside Calum, he placed his foot in the noose, and then gave the signal to the party on the cliff top.

Swinging and bouncing against the rock, with Spider trying to insert his body as a protective cushion for Calum, they moved jerkily up the cliff. Calum's eyes were wide, but whether from panic or pain, Spider could not tell. The injured man's face was inches from his own, and

Spider's muttered words of encouragement seemed to do little to soothe the apprehension the youth obviously felt. Ready and eager hands pulled them to safety.

Spider stood as the others carried Calum from the edge, and he then made his way to the jeep and switched on the long-range CODAN. The set crackled as it searched for the pre-programmed frequency. The crackling did not abate as the search continued—fruitlessly. After ten minutes of trying, Spider cursed, then threw the microphone onto the seat. Slamming the door to the vehicle in a barely controlled rage, he ran along the convoy to the group gathered around the supine Calum.

"We're going to have to detour to Zemor for the UNPROFOR medical unit. The CODAN is not hacking it. Get Calum into the back of the jeep."

The men crowding round the wounded man shuffled back widening the circle as Rath rose from his knees. He pushed his way out of the ring.

"There's no rush," Rath said, grabbing the convoy leader firmly but gently by the shoulders, as Spider threw himself forward to break through the cordon.

"Calum's gone. There's nothing more you can do, Spider, you've done more than anyone could rightfully ask."

Paroski sat bolt upright in the chair, and stared stony-faced at the wall map. Anger and frustration raged through him, but the only outward indication was his narrowed eyes and the small tic that flickered under his right eye. He resisted an overpowering urge to pound the desktop, and his hands remained in his lap.

How in God's name could that convoy still be on course for Tuzla?

There was a swathe of dead and wounded Serbs in its wake! What was that bumbling imbecile Kalosowich playing at? Was there some other agenda in progress that the Croats were not to know about? He fought against the suspicion.

In two hours' time, he was due to report to Radovic, and heaven help him if he could not report progress of some kind. Think, Paroski, think. However, what could he report?

"Sir, the Serbs shelled the convoy and destroyed a truck. No, sir. Yes, sir, that's correct; the weapons were not on the truck destroyed. What action did I take? I sent a detachment of White Eagles to intercept them. And? Well, unfortunately, these men have not reported yet. However, we made contact with the convoy in Grabovica. No, sir, I didn't say the convoy was halted; I just said that contact was made—with heavy losses to the Serbs..."

Paroski stopped his inane imaginings. *Think, man, think.*

He stood and walked over to the map. With his finger, he traced the progress of the convoy. Mostar, Grabovica heading for Jablonica. His finger stopped.

A germ of an idea started to grow.

Visibility was minimal; the natural gloom of the forest added to the premature darkness caused by the heavy clouds pressing down on the treetops. Dampness was perceptible, and the cool moisture clung in the mountain air. The first rounded globules splattered on the trucks, noisily followed by more, which within seconds became a teeming deluge.

The ceiling of pine branches did little to ameliorate the increasing force and effect of the rain. Unimpeded, the downpour whipped at the narrow track rapidly beating the wet surface into liquid mud. This filled the deep ruts and sucked at each oncoming wheel, then, failing to hold it fast, reached with unabated voracity for the next.

The rain thrashed down noisily on the metal cab roofs, adding a throbbing, persistent drumming to the whining crescendo caused by the screaming engines. It threw itself malevolently against the opaque windscreens with an unending violence, beating and slashing, swirling and ebbing as it tried to overwhelm the struggling wipers. The huge trucks battled uphill, slithering and sliding as the heavy treads frequently lost purchase in the slough beneath them.

Spider yawned involuntarily with fatigue. He forced his senses to concentrate on the climbing track. He was shattered. The other drivers must also feel exhausted. Tiredness was dangerous. On well-maintained roads, it was a threat: here it could kill—and often did.

His watering eyes searched through the gloom for the crest of the mountain. There would be an area on the top where a number of vehicles could park. They would stop; a hot drink and some sleep would work wonders. He opened the net and warned the drivers.

The drivers seemed refreshed just by the thought of rest. Although there was no laughing or joking, they were in reasonable spirits as they prepared bedrolls under the trees for the oncoming night. They fired up their Calor gas stoves; the very idea of hot drinks and food had revitalized them. The deluge had ended, but the warmth that followed was ebbing and a cooler dusk pencilled deep, lengthening shadows throughout the valley.

Leaning back against the tree, Spider could pick out the flickering glow-worms of light in the far distance. They punctuated the darkening valley as its inhabitants switched on lights to hold the night at bay.

Strange, he thought, that in most places where he had served, the armed conflict had taken place in beautiful countryside. Each had claim to its own brand of beauty, and this country had a stronger claim than most.

However, here, as in all those other places, the ugliness that lived in the hearts of men sought out the beauties of nature to revile and wantonly disfigure them. With a brutality distinguished only by its callousness, it desecrated the gems of all cultures other than its own.

Such mutilations would never heal.

Kalosowich was livid. The damned convoy was still *en route* for Tuzla; it was as if his intervention had been a mere gnat's bite. He had not even slowed its progress. With few reserves to deal with it, he would have to divert forces from another area. This time the force must be strong enough to put paid to what had grown from a meddlesome annoyance to an insult to his pride.

Breathing noisily through his nostrils, he surveyed the map. The company strength force of paramilitary on its way to Zepa would be ideal. It would have to travel cross-country, but even then, it would be doubtful if it could reach a suitable cut-off point in time, unless a delay could hinder the convoy. Narrowing his eyes, he looked around the Ops Room as he thought the matter through.

A delaying tactic? His eyes came to rest on the rifle with a telescopic sight leaning against one of the trestle tables. He swung back to his map.

Yes! The snipers at the cemetery!

TEN

The woman rolled slightly to lift the weight from her left side, slid her right hand into her jacket and tugged the bra strap to free her breast from the cleft between her upper arm and chest. Withdrawing her hand, she then squirmed into a more comfortable prone position and took up the slack of the weapon's sling against her forearm by repositioning her left elbow.

Aiming down at a target could cause a careless sharp-shooter to underestimate the distance. However, she knew the exact range to each point in her arc of fire, stretching from the corner of Stilovic Street, formed by two sides of the high-rise apartment block, and at the other extreme bounded by the arched doorway of the play centre.

On her first day on this sector of Sarajevo, the initial shot to test the range had bisected the head of a stray dog scavenging close to the roundabout. Four hours later, her assessment of the range was confirmed when she made the first kill of her assignment. The old woman was the beginning of a chain that included two other women, a middle-aged man and a French Legionnaire wearing a flak jacket. She brought him down with a headshot.

Not all of her shots killed instantaneously; she had seen movement after some strikes, but she was confident that the wounded would not get up. A hit with the Dragunov was invariably fatal. The tearing effect of the slug was horrendous, and the resultant hemorrhaging was massive, to say nothing of the shock caused by a strike anywhere on the human body.

There was no crosswind on the street; she could be sure of this because the thin ribbon on the wreath against the wall of the flats was motionless. Kevic had placed the garland, not out of sympathy for victims, but for sighting purposes.

Every sniper knew the hazards of discovery and to minimize risk, rarely fired a second shot. It was elementary that single well-placed shots and lack of movement, together with good camouflage, ensured survival.

The boy, with his bag of sparse shopping, had to be either suicidal or retarded to remain standing on that corner. Even if he were to walk away now, it would be too late. What was he waiting for? He looked around as if lost. Did the idiot want to die? A few moments more and it would not matter. The thought struck her that, if he had lived, her younger brother would be about the same age as this boy. She thought about Pero to stifle the feeling stirring in her breast and to convince herself that she felt no compassion: men, women or children were all legitimate targets.

As a young girl, she had lived on a small farm bordering the woods some three miles outside Trnovo, and had often gone hunting with her brothers, the elder one now serving with Zeljko Raznatovic's Arkanoci, the paramilitary unit providing the cutting edge of the ethnic cleansing program.

She had rivalled them both with her accuracy. On stationary artificial targets, her marksmanship was as good as her brothers, but her patience, tenacity and the inborn ability to remain motionless for long periods far exceeded their efforts in those earlier times, when the targets were deer or renegade foxes.

Later, at University, she had taken up skiing as a pastime and soon found that she was a natural at cross-country skiing. Before long, she was a member of the team representing the University, then her country, in the winter biathlon, skiing and target shooting her way to many awards. Her ability to suppress emotion, ignore empathy and tightly rein her imagination was a strength that contributed to success more than ever before.

Pero, who had joined the Army of the Republic of Srpska, died sometime after the November attack by the Croat Muslim forces on Kucin. There was no news of him until the following September when his remains were found near the Rajski Do hotel.

A noose of metal cable pinioned his ankles with a thick piece of wood attached to the other end. Most of his bones were broken and his skull smashed. His shredded clothing showed that his captors had tied him to a vehicle of some sort and dragged him to the hotel.

The young Muslim boy looked both ways, through force of habit, for non-existent traffic. He was about to step off.

The sniper took a deep breath, closed her left eye and took up the slack in the trigger. She realigned the crosshairs and releasing half a breath, paused, and then continued the even pressure on the trigger. Remaining relaxed, but channelling all her concentration through onto the target, she fired. As if the shot suddenly and inexplicably withered the supporting legs, the short figure wilted and dropped to the ground. The sniper slowly lowered the weapon and reached for the ejected casing.

She pulled her logbook towards her and made the necessary entry.

An air of total desecration pervaded the cemetery at Debelo Brdo. Toppled headstones, shards of memorials and tombstones lay scattered in the long grass. The ground under the trees was strewn with withered flowers and broken vases. Many of the uprooted gravestones formed windbreaks and walls for lean-to shelters. Here and there, sleeping figures were interspersed among the debris.

Kevic knelt beside the sleeping figure and touched her nose with a leaf. The nose twitched for a few seconds, then stopped. Her lips softened, the tension left her jaw and as the lines grew shallow again, her whole face gradually relaxed into that of a young girl. He slipped the stem into one of her dark, rich curls and grasped her shoulder. She awoke after a gentle shake and looked up at the young man assigned to her for training.

"It's time, Jelena," he said. "We leave in thirty minutes."

She widened her eyes and, as recollection returned, nodded. She partially undid the sleeping bag and sat up. For a few seconds she watched Kevic's retreating figure then, supporting herself on her right elbow, pulled the combat boots towards her.

With a movement of her legs, the sleeping bag unzipped completely and she removed her socks from the boots. The chill of the morning cooled her feet, and she hurriedly pulled on the worsted socks. She unlaced her boots and pulled both on without tying them. After tucking the laces into the top of the boots, she turned to the Bergen that she had used as a pillow during the night. She flipped the top open and pulled out a camouflaged toilet bag, which she wrapped in a dark green towel and headed down the slope of the hill towards the stream.

On reaching the water's edge, she removed her sweater and shirt and crouched above the fast-flowing water.

Why don't I ever bring a bowl?

She scooped some water up into the palms of her hands to wash her face, knowing full well that when tasked for this kind of operation a soldier only packed the bare essentials. Time enough for luxury out of the field. There were important things more worthy of packing in the Bergen than prissy little washbasins.

Her face washed and dried, she dipped her toothbrush into the flow and scrubbed her teeth. She missed the sharp tang of toothpaste but knew that it was not essential to dental care. She chuckled, as she thought that at least she did not have to shave, but the chuckle died as she remembered that none of the other twelve male snipers did either.

She strode back to the cemetery. As she reached her pack and equipment just below the crest of the hill, Kevic met her with a proffered mug of coffee.

"*Hvala*," she thanked him as she tucked her wash bag beneath her arm and took the mug that he held out with the handle towards her. He smiled and turned back to his weapon and gear.

The coffee had already lost its initial heat. She set the mug down on a piece of broken marble, and put on her combat jacket. Kevic, who was sitting on the waterproof ground sheet with his back against his pack, polished the cases of the rounds that she was to use. He finished and began to occupy himself with the portable gas cooker. Jelena poured water into the mess tin. Both heard the approaching footsteps and looked up as the sergeant came closer.

"Your tasking for today's been cancelled. The Colonel wants you for a special job. Now.

"Pack your gear, and I'll brief you while you're doing it."

Kevic was proving to be capable and had done well in preparing the position considering the limited time they had had. She had decided that, for this attack, a fully camouflaged hide was superfluous. The drivers would be unarmed, as UNHCR did not allow its employees weapons.

The position chosen was not ideal, but was adequate for what they had to do. It was grudgingly big enough for both of them, but comfort was not an overriding concern—at least not on this mission. A slab of upright rock standing almost chest-high topped with thin divots provided their cover. Kevic had dug up a clump of gorse and made a screen on top of the turf. He was now fashioning an unobtrusive gap to allow for the rifle's muzzle.

The road was less than two hundred yards away below them. She had a clear view of a longish stretch beneath her to the left, from which direction the convoy would appear. The road dipped into a valley of dead ground so the noise of the vehicles' engines would have to suffice as warning of its approach.

In front of her, the land covered in scrub, fell away almost to the road itself. Behind them, the slope dotted with stunted pines was gradual for about ninety or so yards before becoming too steep and bare to support any growth.

Jelena uncased the Dragunov, throwing the canvas holdall to one side, and then removed the plastic protective cup from the sight. Holding the weapon by the small of the butt with her right hand, she pulled Kevic to one side with her left and leaned forward against the front of the hide. Passing the muzzle through a gap in the spiky twigs, she then asked Kevic to check the front for any evidence of the weapon. Satisfied there was none, he re-entered giving her a quick shake of his head.

Sighting the rifle on a large outcrop of rock on the far side of the road, she loosed off two rapid rounds. Her efficient manipulation of the bolt and the rapidity of the second shot so quickly after the first never ceased to enthrall Kevic. One day he too would be a class rifle shot. The spurt of chippings and faint wisp of smoke at the rock confirmed her point of aim. She cocked the rifle and took it out of the aim. They lowered themselves to the ground and settled back to wait.

The sound of the engines reached them long before the first vehicle appeared. They both stood, and Jelena picked up the rifle. She adjusted her stance, took several deep breaths then brought the rifle up into the aim in readiness. Despite being alert, the alacrity, with which the jeep leapt over the crest of the road, surprised her.

It travelled on for a hundred yards as she took up the first pressure then squeezed off one shot, then a second. The glass of the window disintegrated. The chassis bucked wildly and swung violently to the left, scraping along the rock face before shuddering to a halt. The body and tail of the following convoy reacted like a punctured concertina.

The truck behind the stricken leader crashed into its rear, pushing it and its luckless driver another thirty yards. Before she could fire at the driver of the second wagon, he opened his door on the opposite side and was out of sight. With a surprising, swift presence of mind the other drivers switched into reverse and, in an awkward parody of a drunken caterpillar, shunted their trucks back up the road.

Jelena snapped another two rapid shots at them but without success. Concentrate, she told herself, but before she could fire again, they had reached the safety of the crest and disappeared below the skyline.

As she worked the bolt of the rifle to reload, she was off-guard as the driver of the jeep, whom she was convinced she had hit, leapt out and ran around the front of his vehicle to get to the other side.

Jelena fired before he had gone two paces. The man dropped, but instead of lying inert, he rolled sideways under the front wheels. She let the muzzle of the rifle sag but kept the stock tight against her shoulder. The crack of the shot reverberated and echoed in diminishing volume across the mountainside. She swore under her breath. Kevic started to say something, but an abrupt grunt silenced him in mid-sentence.

She scanned the vehicle. Nothing. Bringing the weapon back into the aim, she used the telescopic sight to traverse the length of the 4 x 4. No movement whatsoever. She felt sure she had hit him. Was it the force of the shot that had thrown him under the truck?

Rath's huge fist bunched on Spider's collar and he dragged him from under the Jeep.

"Now I am really pissed off," Rath snarled as they crouched beside the rear wheels. "We've got a sniper to deal with now."

"No self-respecting sniper would double tap like that," grunted Spider sitting back against a wheel as he tried to massage some feeling back into his neck muscles. "He could be overconfident, or he's new at this game."

Rath squatted back on his heels. "Self-respecting or not, his aim's bloody good," he retorted. He indicated the two vehicles with a nod. "He's got us bottled. What's next?"

"Is there any open ground between the wagons?" Spider craned forward to look.

Rath glanced along toward the next vehicle then shook his head.

"The AK 47s are in your cab?" Spider asked.

"One o' them; the other's in the tool compartment." Rath grinned as he realized the purpose of the questions. "Ah, time for the setpiece counter attack?"

"With textbook diversionary tactic," smiled Spider, "then we're going after the bastard. You get the weapons while I see how his reflexes are."

When Rath returned with the two rifles, Spider removed his helmet. Both men made their way to the rear of the second truck and crouched in its shadow. After checking his rifle, Spider stepped away from Rath and gave himself space to swing the helmet by its chinstrap.

"It's going out at the front of the Jeep. As soon as it does, we break for the other side of the road and the scrub."

Rath nodded, braced his legs and watched the swing of Spider's arm.

At the blur of movement, Jelena swung the muzzle and fired once. The helmet bounced, and then continued several yards down the road before rolling to a stop. She cursed and belatedly redirected her aim at the rear of the vehicles.

Too late! The diving rush of two figures from the rear of the second truck into the undergrowth at the near side of the road carried them into the cover of the rocks and scrub. They were once again out of sight. *Damn!*

Switching her aim to the point where they had disappeared into the bushes did not help, because the tell-tale branches that should have revealed movement remained undisturbed and motionless.

She marshalled her thoughts. The situation was changing and deteriorating rapidly. It was becoming dangerous for her and Kevic. She knew that the two hiding below them would not remain there. They could not be ordinary aid convoy drivers; their calculated reactions and the fact they had weapons proved this. In the seconds that the dash from the road had taken, she had seen that both men were armed. If those drivers over the crest also had firearms, then the advantage had changed sides.

She pulled at Kevic's sleeve. "Out. Up the mountain," she whispered harshly. "Keep low. Make for the trees."

Convinced that the men below were moving towards them through the bushes, she knew that their safety depended on both of them reaching the higher ground, where the bushes thinned and where she would have an unimpeded field of fire. Adrenalin coursed through her. She was conscious of the pounding in her temples.

"Now!" she screamed.

They threw themselves up the slope. Half stumbling, she fought to control her breathing as she followed Kevic in their crouching flight upwards through the gorse.

They reached the first pines and threw themselves down behind the protective trunks. Cautiously, she looked back down the slope. There was no sign of pursuit. Her ragged breathing slackened, and she swallowed hard. She struggled to subdue the fear welling within her.

They waited tensely. Her legs trembled, and try as she might she could not stop the shaking in her buttocks. The minutes dragged. She felt Kevic's eyes on her. With a sharp nod, masking the flooding terror, she indicated uphill and gathered herself together to make the sprint. *Christ, please make my legs work.*

Kevic rose and turned uphill. Almost simultaneously, he spun in the opposite direction to crash backwards against the trunk of the fir that bounced him forwards to lie spread-eagled at its base. The heavy, metallic twang of the shot assaulted her eardrums. His sightless eyes, which only seconds before had mirrored her own fear, stared unblinkingly in her direction. She pressed her face down into the pine needles and felt the strength drain from her legs. Her thoughts congealed. She could not think.

The shot had come from higher up.

The hunted, now the hunters, were above her on the mountain.

Spider laid his plate to one side, leaned back against the wheel, eyes hooded and wrists resting on his knees, watching the woman. Apparently oblivious to his scrutiny, she hungrily spooned the food from the bowl in her lap.

Under medium height, she was slim in build but far from frail. His eyes took in the well-filled camouflaged shirtfront and her narrow waist. She possessed a lithe physical presence that under different circumstances would have excited him and aroused more than clinical curiosity.

Still chewing, she raised her head and looked around her. Her eyes came to rest on him. Expressionless, she looked straight at him. Refusing to avert his gaze their eyes remained locked.

She dropped her head and returned to her meal.

Her short hair was thick and dark. Despite the brutal crop, the strong curls caught the light, reflecting auburn highlights in the evening sun. Left to grow, there was no doubt that it would be one of her strongest features. She had an oval-shaped face and full lips. The dark purple of the bruised swelling contrasted vividly with her translucent rose complexion that emphasized the depth of blackness and sheer intensity of her eyes. She looked up again, tilted her chin and held his stare. This time she did not intend to be first to break the contact.

Spider continued to stare stonily at her, but she would not look away. There was no doubt that she had overcome her initial fear of him. Still holding his eyes, she lifted another spoonful to her mouth and chewed stolidly.

Spider grinned.

Caught by surprise she swallowed, too quickly, half-choked, coughed then spluttered weakly. *Not as self-assured as she would like to believe.* His smile faded as his gashed arm throbbed. He remembered how viciously she had fought when they had caught her on the mountainside.

Rath's shot had taken the one nearer the tree squarely in the chest. There was no doubt he was dead before striking the ground. The other had remained face down at the base of the tree and appeared frozen with fear as he and Rath moved down the slope.

They had kept their weapons trained on the survivor and were surprised when they realized that the sniper was a woman. At first, Rath assumed that the dead man had been the sharpshooter, until Spider pointed out who carried the Dragunov.

Nevertheless, they had foolishly relaxed their guard.

As they approached, she climbed to her feet, threw the rifle to one side, then raised her arms. They moved closer but were still several feet away when, with a knife drawn from her boot, she leapt at them like an enraged cougar. Rath dived forward and blocked her attack.

The fury of the assault and the depth of the gash dispelled any doubts Spider might have had about her proficiency as a combatant. Rath obviously reached the same conclusion, and showed that he had overcome any reservations he may have had, by swiping her forcefully with his rifle butt. She went down heavily but it had still taken considerable effort from both of them to subdue her and tie her hands.

She finished eating and dropped the plate from the cab. Rising to his feet, Spider walked over and, without a word, reached up to grasp her left wrist and, far more roughly than he intended, re-fastened the chain that secured her to the steering wheel. He caught the flash of hate in her eyes and the savage curl of her lip.

She would require watching.

Spider enjoyed the hot, sweet tea. Say, what you like, he thought, about the virtues of coffee, you could not beat tea as a refreshing beverage. He turned to the truck and as he reached the front of the vehicle, he saw the woman was looking down at him. He took a swallow of the tea then held the mug up towards her.

She reached down and accepted the proffered cup. Blowing on the surface of the tea, she took several small, noisy sips, making a wry face as she swallowed then laid the cup on the ledge over the dashboard. She shook her arm, making the chain rattle, then holding up her hand and wrist, looked first at the chain then at Spider. He smiled, but shook his head.

"Sorry, but it's got to stay on." He could not be certain that she understood the words, but he was in no doubt that, she understood the refusal that lay behind them.

She swore at length in Serbo-Croat, but he had the impression that it was without real passion. She pulled her cigarettes from her shirt pocket, and he searched for his Zippo. Ignoring him, she awkwardly lit her own.

He shrugged and turned his back. His eyes took in the wide expanse of valley and wooded hillside that stretched below them. The landscape reminded him of summer in Austria, with grassy, sloping fields, climbing brightly upwards to the forested foothills, cradled at the base of dark but reassuring mountains.

However, this view lacked the uniformity and post-card prettiness of the country to the north. The patch-work of field and copse was similar, but not as cultivated and developed. The edges were torn, and the overall impression was coarser, less refined and rustically more primitive. It was as though nature had ripped the squares from rougher material to make Bosnia's quilt.

"Why did you come here to die?"

The soft, husky voice jerked him back to the present. The sheer unexpectedness of the sound threw him, and the shock was evident in his face. The timbre of the voice too had taken him by surprise. He would not have expected such a deep tone from a woman of her stature. She had a balanced rhythm and intonation, despite her accented English.

"I'm sorry, I missed—"

"Why do you all come here to die? Do you not have wives, children? Do you not have families who need you more than strangers?"

"We're here to help those less fortunate than our-selves. Why do you try to kill us?"

"We do not try to kill you. But if you interfere and get caught up in our fight with the Muslims and their Croat allies, then you should expect to be hurt."

"And taking food, medicine and other necessities through to starving families in Bosnian towns is interfering?"

"No, that is not interfering. However, your convoys do not just carry food; there are weapons too. Why do you laugh? Why do you think that Kevic and I were trying to stop this convoy? To stop milk and rusks going to Muslim babies?"

Spider's laughter died, and the smile left his lips. She obviously believed what she said.

"What else? You have a stranglehold on the supply routes. Your people harass or attack the convoys. You're accused of massacres. Every decent person condemns your actions."

Her look was venomous, but she did not respond.

There had been rumours in Croatia that the Bosnians were obtaining weapons through aid convoy conduits, but UNHCR officials summarily and categorically dismissed these as Serbian disinformation.

Nevertheless, the earlier attempts on the convoy, made before she had tried to stop them, could indicate that someone else, somewhere, also believed the scuttlebutt. The attacks had been concerted. Perhaps he should at least have considered the possibility that they were carrying something more lethal than medicine and food.

On the other hand, UNHCR had not received specific clearance from the Serbs for the convoy to start out. It had been a gamble. This might be retaliation. He had accepted from the first that this convoy would not be easy. As outsiders, they too had suffered at the hands of the Serbs, and he had sympathy for the Bosnians. Moreover, the convoy had come too far.

It had passed the point of no return.

Spider shrugged and decided. He certainly was not going to waste time and effort searching the cargo. He threw his cigarette down and crushed it with his boot. He had been about to warn her that he was going to secure her for the night when she asked if she could wash and go to the toilet. Looking around he saw that Dennis Crowther had finished his preparations and was sitting against the rear wheel of his vehicle smoking.

Spider called him, and he rose to his feet with a sullen expression.

"Dennis, take her over to the woods so she can relieve herself. I'll get her a towel and some water." Spider paused then, only half-joking, said to Crowther, "And don't lose her."

The driver indicated the woods with a nod, then trailed behind the prisoner to the edge of the clearing. At the pines, he pushed past her to lead the way into the trees. After ten yards or so, he stopped.

"This is far enough. No one can see you from here."

She stared at him in defiance, and he grinned back lewdly, as he realized she objected to his watching. He shook his head,

"No way, darlin'. Anyway, you are not my type."

They contested each other's stares, then, with an expression of obvious disgust she undid her belt and pushed her uniform trousers down. Crowther relented and half-turned his back. A few moments, later the rustling of clothing told him she had finished. Buckling her belt, she turned to go when Crowther caught her by the arm.

"*Da li govorite engleski?*" he asked. She did not respond but glared at him, then looked pointedly at his restraining hand.

"Do you speak or understand English, damn you?" he whispered harshly. "Come on, you stupid cow, do you or don't you? We're on the same side, see?" He caught the flicker of puzzlement that crossed her face but he felt sure that she had understood.

"Listen to me! We've not got much time, but I'm working for Croatian Military Intelligence and—"

The blob of spittle splattered on his cheek and ran down his jaw line. He managed to hold the blaze of rage in check and lowered his fist.

"Listen, you crazy bitch, how do you think your people found out about the weapons on this convoy? Because the man I work for told them! You do not want them to get through, and we do not either. We can work together to stop them." He paused for breath and knew he was getting through to her, because, although the loathing had not left her face there was something else there.

"I'll prove it to you," he snapped and pulled the cellular phone from inside his anorak. "I'm going to call Colonel Paroski, and he'll explain it to you." He pressed the select button for the pre-set number on which he reached Paroski.

As the phone rang, several times, he wiped the sweat from his face with the palm of a wet hand.

Answer, you Croat bastard.

"Colonel Paroski, Crowther here. We are several hours from Tuzla, a couple short of Vares. Odds are that we will take route Skoda early tomorrow. However, there is something else. We have captured a Serbian woman soldier and—No, no, you listen," he rushed on, surprising himself at his temerity in interrupting and silencing his nightmare. "She could help me."

At the other end, Paroski thought quickly. Perhaps the pervert did have something. This woman could be the sniper employed by Kalosowich. At least she had proved she could kill, and as a soldier, be expected to carry out instructions, unlike this pig-dropping of an Englishman.

"She's here," Crowther volunteered, ending the brief but uncomfortable pause.

"Put her on," the colonel ordered.

Crowther, who had been holding the phone in two hands, pushed it towards her. She took the instrument then almost timidly in English said, "Yes. Hallo?"

"I am Colonel Paroski," replied the intelligence officer in the same language. Then he switched to Serbo-Croat. "Your commander, Colonel Kalosowich, has been very concerned about you," he lied, "but he is also very angry that you failed. However, there is a way to redeem yourself. Listen to me very carefully then pass me back to the foreigner."

She turned from Crowther as though it was a private and intimate call.

What's keeping them?

Spider finished the mug of tea and, rising to his feet, was about to go towards the woods when the two emerged. He glanced over at the bowl of water. It would be tepid now. He passed a towel to the woman and raised an enquiring eyebrow at Crowther.

"She decided to take a dump." The driver grinned nervously, which Spider misinterpreted as part of the man's natural shiftiness. "And we had to improvise on paper."

Spider woke without movement and listened. He held his breath but—nothing.

He waited.

He heard the call of a hunting owl, followed shortly afterwards by the cough of a nocturnal four-legged predator, but he knew instinctively these sounds had not woken him. He continued to listen, then, as he was thinking that it might have been imagination, he heard the noise again.

It was the stifled sound of sobbing. He sat up slowly and peered through the gloom to where they had chained the prisoner the night before. The sobbing was subdued, restrained but nonetheless heartfelt. Spider left his bedroll and crawled over to the supine figure.

He unlocked the padlock on the chain and removed the fetters from her arm. Reaching out, he touched the woman's shoulder. The crying did not stop but, although not becoming louder, increased in intensity. He lay down beside her, grasping the material of her sleeping bag, and pulled her toward him, pressing her to his chest and thighs. The tears continued as he cradled her in both arms and tentatively touched, then stroked, her cropped head.

As the crying ebbed, she made a half-hearted effort to pull away, but when Spider did not release his hold, instead lowering his face to the nape of her neck to nuzzle the soft fragrant hair that grew there, she sighed and relaxed. They lay together quietly for several minutes.

He tightened his grip when she moved, then relaxed as he realized that she did not want to break free. She lifted her head, turning her face so that her lips brushed lightly against his. They returned to press, at first softly, and then firmly, then even more wildly, unveiling the sexual hunger her eyes had only hinted at during the day.

His tongue probed between her lips, tasting and revelling in their milky freshness mingled with the saltiness of the tears, when they widened even more, and her tongue was probing and, unashamedly, vigorously exploring his.

Their breathing was ragged and uneven, and she helped to free herself from the restraining sack as he tugged and pulled the material away from her body.

His searching hands found her breasts as her fingers tugged his shirt free from his trousers. The unexpected coolness of her fingertips on his naked groin triggered a spasm of unadulterated pleasure. He gasped as his abdominal muscles quivered violently.

Shifting his hands to her waist, he worked at her belt before she, with a moan of impatience, pushed his awkward hands aside and undid the restraining waistband herself. She pushed her trousers down past her knees, and with a movement of her legs, kicked the garment free. In almost the same movement, she then pushed at his shoulder and he rolled onto his back, pulling her astride on top of him.

His fingers dug into and kneaded the firm soft flesh of her parted buttocks, as simultaneously, her fingers found the column of his hardness.

Gripping his flesh firmly with one hand, she pulled the material of her pants away from her body. With a low moan, she lifted her hips and guided him into the waiting wet warmth between her thighs. A nipple between his teeth and his face pressed against the yielding overhang of her naked breasts, he gripped and pulled down on her shoulders as she bucked and thrashed above him.

How long it lasted, he did not know, but he felt sure that they had climaxed together—she with a wracking body shudder as she fell forwards, and he with the overwhelming ecstasy of exhaustion. The weight of her body pressed his shoulders against the carpet of pine needles, and he grunted in total lulling relapse. With his hands still on her buttocks, he felt her sit up, but the glorious heat that seemed to weld them like strange Siamese twins at the groin drew all the strength from his very body. Even his eyelids refused to open.

The torrent of searing agony, when it swept over him, was horrendous, and he yelled involuntarily.

His eyes flared open wide. The blade had sliced through his shoulder muscle down to the collarbone, narrowly missing his neck. His brain screeched hysterically at his arms to block the second blow that his whole being intuitively knew was coming, but his right arm flopped pathetically at his side.

The second plunge of the steel grated on bone as his left hand struggled furiously but ineffectively, failing to lock onto one of her wrists. She held the weapon in a two-handed grasp and, now restricted to being one-handed, he was no match for her. With a grunt, she heaved her arms upwards, breaking the tenuous clasp of his fingers, and then reared above and away from him in a determined attempt to strike the *coup de grace*. He was as helpless as the day he was born.

The blast bludgeoned his eardrums.

Simultaneously with the explosion, she was no longer above him. The shot triggered in him the desperate exhilaration of his survival instinct, and he rolled wildly to his left coming to a halt against a pair of muscular legs. His nostrils detected the smell of cordite, and he heard the reassuring and calming flat tones of the Irishman.

"Easy, man, easy."

Rath bent and pulled him to his feet. Despite Spider's efforts, dizziness swamped him, and he could only look bemused as he turned his head to Rath.

"For someone who's called Spider, you know shit about arachnids."

Spider tried to smile but could only produce a pained grimace. There seemed to be an indistinct yet increasing buzzing as he took in the other drivers around him.

Then, as Rath said something else, and the meaning of the additional words seeped through the mire of darkness that was swallowing him, he grinned vacantly. His legs crumpled and he muttered inanely as he slumped to the ground.

" 'Specially Black Widows."

ELEVEN

The light filtered through the trees and cast dappled images onto the windscreen. Their movement flickered over Rath's face and was enough to waken him. He opened his eyes, stretched, appreciating the sensation that flooded his arms and back as the movement eased the sleep-cramped muscles. He yawned.

He wiped the thick condensation from the inside of the windscreen with a piece of rag. There was no movement outside. Opening his cab door, he jumped down. Arms above his head, he enjoyed another luxuriant stretch then went to the tool compartment, where he unloaded the small gas stove and kettle. He fired up the stove and enjoyed the sibilant sound of the released gas as its flames licked at the bottom of the kettle.

Standing upright, he looked around him. He took a deep breath, and relished the strong sharp aroma of pine in the atmosphere. Tantalizingly, it conjured up thoughts of home and it was moments before he recognized it as the familiar scent of his mother's freshly scrubbed kitchen.

He smiled. His spirits were always higher at this time than at any other point of the day.

The air, at first damp and cool, began to warm. Needles of the surrounding pines glistened with sparks of liquid in the rays of the sun as it climbed in a sky devoid of clouds. The only sign of yesterday's torrential downpour was the occasional wisps of vapour rising from the floor of the forest, where the heat of the sun warmed the overlay of pine needles.

"Mornin", Spider."

Rath looked up from his stove to greet Spider, whose flushed face threw the pallid scar into prominence. The convoy leader nodded wordlessly and then stood shakily beside him.

"Thanks for last night. I owe you," Spider held out his good, left hand.

Rath touched it briefly, then diverted his attention to the soggy bandages on the injured man's shoulders.

"I'll have a look at that and change those dressings. Sit down." He helped Spider to sit and then removed the dressings, somewhat brusquely, but without causing too much discomfort. Spider could not turn his head, but from the corner of his eye, he could just see what appeared to be large black spots, which he guessed were stitches. He could remember nothing of the sewing-up operation and realized that Rath must have completed it, while he was unconscious.

"Not too bad even if I say so myself," said Rath.

The subdued whistle caused them both to turn towards the small kettle; the Irishman removed it from the flame and dropped two teabags into its stained interior. He turned to the vehicle cab and brought out two mugs and a plastic container of sugar. Spider opened the container with one hand and the aid of his chest, and held it while the other spooned sugar liberally into the teas. The dash of milk provided the final touch.

He sipped the hot tea staring reflectively at Rath.

"Morning."

The dark eyes twinkled, and the big man grinned at him as he chuckled, "Civilized, now that you've had a cup of tea?"

"Never make the mistake of thinking I'm ever civilized," Spider warned with a tight smile.

Both men knew that something—intangible, indefinable—had changed in the nature of their relationship.

"Before you start asking embarrassing questions, let me tell you what happened," said Rath with a wide grin that was so infectious that Spider found himself smiling too, though he had no idea what the other was about to say.

"Last night, I heard noises," his grin faded as Spider flushed. "But I didn't come to the conclusion you did. So, after I got one of the AKs, I looked around. I saw you with the woman and thought, what the hell? Then I saw the knife, but not quickly enough."

Spider tried to shrug but failed as the pain sweltered across his neck and shoulder.

"She's over there," Spider looked over at the woods and felt a sense of relief.

"But there's more," said Rath.

"Bad?" asked Spider.

The other man shrugged.

"Crowther has disappeared with his truck and load."

"Didn't anyone see him go? Or hear him?"

Rath shook his head.

"After the fracas, some of the drivers relocated their trucks, you know, pulled them up closer. Crowther must have taken the opportunity to get his on the rear slope. When he was ready it was just a case of releasing the hand-brake and coasting down until he was out of earshot."

Spider frowned.

"Why?"

The big man flipped an evil-looking blade, thick with congealed blood, to stick in the ground at Spider's feet.

"From last night. Dawke says that's Crowther's knife."

"So what time are we leaving?" Rath asked.

"We'll wake the others soon but let's enjoy the world for a few minutes while we've got the chance."

Spider sipped from his mug, relishing the pleasure the drink gave him.

"We'll continue to lead the convoy with a truck and keep the jeep in the body of the column. We'll have more chance crashing through roadblocks with the weight of a truck up front. The driver of the truck must still keep his wits about him, though, and go for broke if a barrier looms up.

"Would you be up for lead truck today?"

Rath swallowed the last of his tea and threw the dregs to the ground.

"No problem, as long as the radio stays open."

"Great. Let's get the others up and on the road."

"Okay, that's your numbers for order of driving. Switch on." Engines coughed, barked and spluttered into noisy life as the vehicles started.

"Any problems? Everyone up and running? I will call your numbers now, so give me a response. Okay, One?"

"One, okay."

"Okay, two?"

"Two, okay."

The radio check continued until the last vehicle responded.

"Right, get ready to pull out in sequence. And, keep the convoy closed up. Okay, One, when you're ready."

Rath slid his vehicle into gear, released the handbrake, then as he increased the pressure on the accelerator, he pulled the steering wheel in a long turn. He leaned toward the mouthpiece of the radio,

"One, pulling out, now."

The convoy had been under way for three-quarters of an hour. The sun had climbed high above the ridges, and it was unbearably hot. Several miles behind them, the forest faded, and as the road descended, they were once again travelling through barren rocky wasteland.

All around, the rocks threw the reflected glare of the sun onto the road. Rath licked the sweat from his lip and wiped his wet forehead with his sleeve. Rolling his window down, he was grateful for the initial coolness of the breeze caused by the forward motion of the truck as it coasted downhill and round the bends.

Suddenly, his eyes caught sight of three or four irregular bumps in the road ahead.

He slammed his foot hard down on the brake pedal and dragged the handbrake upwards. As the rubber bit, the heavy vehicle slewed to a shuddering awkward halt, and he snatched at the radio.

"Problem up ahead. Slow down, slow down, and get ready to stop."

The convoy behind braked, reduced speed then one by one pulled up.

"Spider, it looks like mines on the road up ahead. I'm going forward to check."

"Careful. If they're mines they might under observation by paramilitary."

"Understood. You had better standby to hightail it. Over and out."

Rath reached for his rifle and climbed down from the cab. He cocked the weapon, then scanned the way and banks ahead. There appeared to be no one lying in wait in the immediate vicinity of the road, but he could not be a hundred per cent sure, as he could not see both sides from his present viewpoint.

He turned his attention back to the objects in the path of the convoy. They appeared to be of varying sizes but were like circular shallow domes, in silhouette. It looked as if they were made of dark brown and green plastic, and from this distance looked to be several inches in diameter.

He inhaled. Then, rifle at the ready and turning his head constantly to watch both sides of the highway, he moved slowly forward. As he drew closer to the suspected mines, the shapes took on an almost familiar definition. They looked just like...*No, they couldn't be.* He had seen one as a boy.

Silent laughter started to shake his shoulders; then as the incongruity of the situation became stronger, and the sense of relief heightened, he threw back his head and roared. His impish sense of fun surfaced and he looked back at the convoy where the others were sheltering under the trucks. He slung his rifle over his shoulder and went forward to pick up one of the 'mines'.

"Jesus, what's he doin'? Oh, he's not, is he...?" Scouse croaked.

"He bleedin' well is", Dawke gasped, "he's bringing the fuckin' thing back here."

The group tensed collectively, ready to take to their heels.

"Bloody mad Irish..."

Scouse had risen to his feet as Rath drew closer. The remainder of the drivers edged in retreat but without taking their eyes off the approaching figure. Spider frowned and moved forward to meet him.

"That's far enough. We don't need...Rath, that's far..." but he broke off as he caught sight of the other man's broad smile. Rath raised both hands in front of him, and the group exploded into laughter as they too recognized the distinctive shape of—a tortoise!

Mahmud leaned back against the stunted wild olive and sucked his teeth. A sun that, for the first time in weeks, was reaching a temperature to which he was more accustomed, was now burning off the haze that had lasted most of the morning. The rays seemed to bounce in a white glare off the rocks, and he revelled in the harsh heat.

If he closed his eyes, which of course he would not, dare not, since Tadim had ordered him to observe all movement in the valley, he could be back in Nuristan. True, he did have to stretch his imagination. Much of his country was not as fertile as these valleys, and the Bosnians, although always complaining, were rich men in comparison to his people. In these valleys much was different—even the enemy.

The Russians. Ah, now there had been a worthy foe. As the enemy in Nuristan, they had been highly proficient, more ruthless and far more pervasive than these wearisome Serbs. In the early days, one would dread the darkening of the skies and the huge prehistoric shapes of the forecasters of doom.

The high mountain passes that had been the invasion and trade routes of bygone times, which had cost attackers and travellers alike a high price, were no longer easily defended due to the aerial leapfrogging by the Soviets. Their helicopters, capable of transporting incredibly heavy loads of front-line cargo, weapons and ammunition, would swoop down in flocks. Each would disgorge eight fully-equipped battle-ready troops to surround villages, and create mayhem and destruction.

The Mi-24 or Hind was the ubiquitous, and, according to Simmons, the CIA agent in Pakistan who had trained him and three other villagers on the Stinger, the world's number one combat helicopter. It had deadly wing-tip launchers and nose gun turrets that spat wholesale death. It could hear, see and render ineffective, weapons aimed against it. It was invulnerable, unbeatable; until the arrival of the Stinger.

The mighty Stinger, destroyer of Russian sons; the "widow maker". He, Mahmud, had played a great part in taming the eagles of the peaks. Twelve missiles he fired in all, not including training rounds, and the mighty wings of twelve Hind-Ds had ceased to beat. Their ruptured carcasses plummeted into the walls and depths of the Hindu Kush canyons. His proficiency became legendary, and his skills as a warrior caused Tadim to choose him, as one of the first, to carry the flame of Jihad to Bosnia.

From his vantage point, high on a southward facing slope of the Bitovjna Mountains, he could see a huge stretch of the Neretva valley. The deep, wide river, reflecting an artificial hue of lapis lazuli, took up most of the valley floor, but grudgingly made space for the road.

The surrounding mountains that edged tightly against both were unbroken until the Grogtu gorge, which cradled the Limojica and breached the walls of the valley. At this natural fork, the main road then branched and sent a tendril close to the tributary. It mimicked its form to steal into the gorge before climbing far above the river. The lower reaches of the road were clearly visible.

Holding the circular mess tin in his left hand, he shaped a ball of cold rice. Flapping his wrist to shake the clinging excess grains free from his fingers, he carried the lump to his mouth and chewed stolidly.

With two others, he had been laying mines in a protective cordon around Konjic, but Tadim reassigned him post-haste to act as forward scout. His orders were to pay particular attention to that part of the road leading to Grabovica. He was to report movement of any kind. He glanced down and nodded at the mobile phone resting on the flat stone beside his water bottle, as though confirming its presence.

He pulled his bag containing the plastic-bodied TMA-2 landmines closer. His rifle lay across his lap, making it immediately accessible. Kneading another ball of rice, he continued to enjoy the warmth of the sun as he ate. Without taking his eyes from the panorama below, used as he was to scanning rolling mountainsides from distant points, he continually adjusted his focus.

His thoughts had started to drift towards his homeland when a movement far below him, which would have been imperceptible to many other eyes, brought him back to Bosnia.

He concentrated on the spot where the movement occurred. A miniature doll-like soldier, clad in black, scuttled across the yard of a peasant's smallholding. Within seconds, several more figures in dark uniforms left the barn to join the first, near the road. At that point, a long narrow strip of trees shielded the road from view.

After several minutes, they had still not emerged from the line of trees. *An ambush perhaps? Possibly, but not for my group.* The HOS, an extremist Croatian militia, had members who were brutal, cruel and greatly feared but, in his opinion, only by women and children. Perhaps, maybe, even crippled men but the Croats could not intimidate true believers. They could not share the field with holy warriors.

He thought it unlikely that the paramilitaries below him could have any inkling of his or his comrades' presence, since they had made the move from Konjic during the previous night. No, the infidels were lying in wait for some poor road travellers. He picked up the phone.

Tadim took the mobile phone from the pocket of his camouflaged jacket, flipped it open, then answered. He listened to Mahmud's description of the deployment of the HOS, and ordered him to remain in position and continue to observe the ambush. Snapping the instrument closed, he told the driver to pull over. The Range Rover, stolen from Salzburg only three weeks earlier and now brush-painted a matt olive green, rolled to a halt.

Tadim lit a cigarette and expelled the smoke with a hissing sound. He was surprised. The Croats were not what he expected. His latest intelligence, based on information from local people, who meant well, but were not always reliable, indicated that a group of Serbian para-militaries, Arkanoci or even White Eagles, were in the immediate area.

No one had mentioned Croatians. The nearest Croatian enclave would be Grabovica, but most of their men, the able-bodied ones at least, were serving in the HVO. Despite the village being devoid of fighting men, a HOS unit would not be here to defend it in their absence; that would be too dangerous. They shunned armed confrontation.

Their skills and preferences lent themselves more suitably to looting and rape under the guise of ethnic cleansing. The likelihood that they were present to do battle was zero. Something must be about to happen, and he currently did not know about it. However, since he controlled the real fighting men in this part of Bosnia, he would make it his business to find out.

One thing was certain; it would not take place without his consent.

The sun slid from view behind the distant peaks, darkening the sky and bringing a chill to the air. Mahmud had just pulled up his collar and hunched back against the rock when he saw the first white truck emerge from the gorge. *United Nations' vehicles.* He raised the glasses. They were not armoured vehicles. No UNPROFOR insignia. No soldiers, no weapons. *Could these be aid vehicles?*

He nodded to himself in appreciation of Tadim's skills and respected his all-seeing wisdom. The leader must have known that the food vehicles were coming and had placed him here to give early warning. They had hijacked food trucks before and were obviously going to do so again. Mahmud reached for the mobile phone and pressed the number, keeping his eyes on the valley floor. At that same moment, the doors to the barn on the smallholding below swung open and a tank, bearing the insignia of the JNA, rolled forth.

Mahmud squinted in surprise and puzzlement.

From its markings, the tank appeared to be Serbian, but the black boiler-suit overalls worn by the men around it identified them as HOS members. What would armed Croats be doing in the company of Serbs? What unholy alliance was taking place below? Then Tadim answered, and Mahmud reported the appearance of the convoy and described the puzzling events in action below.

Once again, his orders were to remain in position.

Spider spiralled his right hand in an upward motion, and the convoy sprang back to life. Drivers pulled themselves up into cabs, doors slammed, and heavy diesel engines roared as the convoy readied itself for the descent into the valley. The first truck rolled forward, closely followed by the second. Soon, the whole column was under way and picking up speed. Returning familiarity, confidence and skill in their own ability dissipated the inhibiting influence of the events of the immediate past on the drivers.

Within no time at all, the all-terrain trucks were bouncing robustly down the mountain road, pushing through the rain that was growing heavier by the minute.

The sun's rays, becoming ever weaker, reluctantly probed the edges of deep pockets of mist, which thickened and muted the strident colours of the valley floor. The blue of the lake faded, then diluted to the reflected grey of the sky. The rims of the mountains blunted as the peaks lost their definition. Dark green shawls of pines on the middle and higher slopes turned to black and merged with the dimming plant hues of the lower reaches.

The valley darkened.

A horseshoe of glowering mountains appeared, forbidding and formidable, in the distance. Spider knew they were virtually impregnable and, with the exception of the road to Tuzla, there were no breaks in their fortress-like walls. The way forward, the only way they could take at this point, lay through those mountains. In places, the road would be nigh impassable, but he had committed the convoy and even if he wanted to, there could be no turning back.

The Commander of the HOS detachment munched on a mouthful of bread and pork fat as he watched the camouflaging of the T-72. Unscrewing the cap from the metal flask, he wiped his greasy lips and took a long swallow, relishing the bite of the harsh liquor.

It would not be necessary to devote time and effort to making the tank invisible, or even disguising its shape too much.

He belched.

It would be enough that in its present position the tank would remain out of sight until too late. The netting, with branches and twigs from the surrounding trees and bushes, would be sufficient.

Encroaching darkness provided an additional guarantee. The oncoming convoy would be well within range of the tank's heavy main armament and secondary machine gun before anyone in the convoy could see it. Hull down behind the wooded bank that bordered the road, its weapons had a clear field of fire from the curve of the bend down the approach stretch of road. The JNA markings, removed when the Croats captured it west of Konjic several months ago, were repainted. If there were survivors from the impending onslaught, they would be convinced that Serbs had attacked them.

He pulled the sheepskin jacket over his shoulders while still on his knees and buckled on the holstered Makarov. Pushing his dirty plate and the remaining lump of bread into his knapsack, he threw the bag to Marcos. He would collect the excess kit and place the black uniforms in the barn until the action was over. The camouflaging of the tank was complete.

His men assumed their assigned positions in the area in front of and around it. He watched as the two with the machine gun pushed their way through the undergrowth to a position several yards in front of the tank but to the left. They would be able to fire down the slope and into the side of the convoy and cut off any attempted flight.

Satisfied that his preparations were complete, the commander lowered himself into a prone position and settled down to wait for the convoy to enter the ambush.

The Bosnian-Serb general slammed the door of the car, then scowled at his watch.

"Two hours," he snapped at the driver through the open side window. Flexing his powerful shoulders, he eased his neck muscles by turning his head in alternate directions. He turned away from the car and scanned the rows of windows above his head. There were no curious onlookers.

With a bodyguard on both sides and one in front, he strode forward briskly to climb the six steps to the entrance of the government building in Pale. Waiting for him at the top was the president's aide.

"Good morning, General," the assistant said, almost on tiptoe as he tried to see around the leading escort to talk to the general directly. He caught the glowering scowl before the rush of bodies forced him to pirouette, then sidestep. He broke into a trot after the bulky figure in a futile attempt to keep pace, as they swept past.

"He's waiting for you in the conference room," he squeaked breathlessly as the uniformed figure mounted the staircase, taking the steps two at a time. The civil servant gave up any attempt to follow, and, with a piqued shrug, slowed to a walk. He ignored the mocking grin that one of the minders threw over his shoulder.

The general did not pause at the door to the conference room but, indicating with a short gesture that his guards should wait, he shoved open the heavy oaken door. The room was empty except for a seated figure, which appeared dwarfed by the massive table. The soldier strode to the end of the long room, approached the head of the table, and gave a curt salute.

"Thank you for coming, *Druga General*," the president of *Republica Serbski* said, half rising. He ran a hand through a heavy mane of grey hair, crowning a pallid face, then indicated that the soldier should sit.

"If you will give me a moment." He waved a slack-fingered hand at a sheaf of papers he had been reading.

"Naturally," responded his visitor pulling a heavy chair away from the table and placing his holstered pistol and cap in front of him. As the other read, the general studied him openly.

What shall it be today, Mr Poet.

Despite the impression of closeness given by the two men in public, the general had no high regard for this would-be verse monger. He had been a less-than-mediocre practitioner of psychiatry. His wife, also his partner in the practice, was more competent. The president was an erstwhile peasant who had considered himself Montenegrin rather than Serb until a few years ago. Now he was a convicted fraudster who had chosen politics in his thirst for power.

The man's megalomania did not allow him to empathize with anyone whose presence on the world's stage could challenge his own. The general knew there was little or no danger to his own position of authority by this Fuehrer, since his standing and reputation amongst the troops in the field guaranteed all the protection he needed. His military prowess, validated by the success of the Republic of Bosnian Serbia Army, ensured the support of the People's Assembly. Though ruthless and ambitious, the general did not frown per se on others with the same trait, but as a soldier, he could not but distrust politicians.

Discretion, when needed, was another of this soldier's traits, and he was astute enough not to let the other see his distaste. The square face remained impassive. For the time being, their mutual aim of an ethnically pure Greater Serbia harnessed both in a formidable yoke.

As he read, the president was under no allusions as to the loyalty of the man seated on his right. In all probability, he was still Milosevic's man. The Bosnian Serb directed the efforts of his soldiers with a cold sense of purpose, and he could very easily turn this against him. World opinion, for what it was worth, considered them bedfellows and, for the present, this suited his plans.

Today, as usual, this *prima donna* would require careful handling, especially in view of the pressure from *Gospoda Milosevic* in Belgrade, whose own position could turn out to be untenable if sanctions continued against Serbia.

"Belgrade is very uneasy over our..." the president carefully used the plural pronoun in all conversations with the general. "our reluctance to negotiate on the subject of boundaries."

"Mr President, I feel that I am about to be asked to agree to something that will be unacceptable to me."

"No, no, please. I have no demands to make of you, *Druga Ratko*. I just want you to understand my position."

"Let me reiterate. On each occasion that I have allowed military strategies to bow to political considerations, we have gambled with the success of our aims. No one should be more conscious of this than comrade Slobodan."

"General, when have I *ever* hindered your efforts?"

"With all due respect, there have been several instances where I have reluctantly conceded for the sake of political expediency. I have accepted the lines laid down, initially by Belgrade and subsequently from here in Pale. You will remember that in '91 my plan to take Zadar and Sibenik failed to meet with approval, despite the fact that this would have split Croatia in two. In '93, I could have easily taken Srebrenica, Zepa and other enclaves along the Drina but received directions to withhold action. It is becoming more and more difficult to accept that restraint is beneficial to our aims."

"General, it is not, and never has been, my intention to restrict your efforts, and please accept that this is not why I asked you here today." He brushed away a stray lock of unruly hair. "No one is more aware than I am that a snake is never held by its tail, but by its throat. But we have to be sure that retaliatory action by the UN does not undo all our efforts."

"If, God forbid, you should be coerced into agreeing to relinquishing territory my men have died for, then would it not be better to have more than we have now, with the Turks driven out in such a way that the memory of their expulsion would smother any desire to return?"

"But of course, General." The president turned his gaze to the mountains framed by the window and fixed his eyes on a faraway peak. "My concern at present is Sarajevo and the likelihood of its capitulation in the very near future." His voice rose, implying a question.

"Mr. President, you obviously want a realistic and frank appraisal." The general barely hid his satisfaction. "Despite the concentration of troops I have around the city, I cannot contemplate its fall. UNPROFOR has a strong presence in Sarajevo and, despite their reluctance to oppose us substantially in the past, a concerted effort to crush the city might very well be the trigger."

The president's face darkened as he belatedly realized where Mladic was heading. The general was not slow to notice and hurried on.

"In the short term, politically, it may be expedient, but militarily the game is not worth the candle. If our aim is to control the greatest land mass possible, prior to a cessation of hostilities, then I would recommend a scaled withdrawal from the area to allow me to concentrate on the other pockets; Srebrenica, Gorazde, Zepa and," he paused for effect, "Tuzla."

Karadzic's mind was furiously working overtime. What his general was saying did have possibilities. However, there were complications.

"Tuzla would indeed be a prize, but UNPROFOR have armoured troops there, and of course, they hold the airbase. The risk would be enormous."

"Not necessarily, Mr President. The Norwegian and Danish joint units are professional, I admit. I am not gambling on their inability to strike back, but rather on the indecision and lack of backbone of their politi— civilian masters in the UN. I would not attempt to wear the defenders down but, given leave, blitzkrieg Tuzla so that within 24 hours - 36 at the outside, it would be ours."

"I like your proposal, General. Indeed I do. But I cannot agree to the withdrawal of the guns from Mount Igman."

"It was not my intention to propose such a thing," replied the general, enjoying the nonplussed expression that flooded Karadzic's face. "Only the armour. Only my tanks."

The president stared at the soldier. Trust this Serb from Kalinovic to know how to have one's cake and eat it. Slowly, he smiled in begrudging admiration.

"When would you propose to redeploy?"

The dawn sun strengthened and chased the remnants of night from the valley. Dewdrops glistening on the pines surrounding the clearing reflected the rays and glowed in the grey diffusing light, like a myriad of miniature campfires dying as the day pushed its way through the thick foliage.

Crowther stared blankly through the condensation on the windscreen. How long he had been awake, he did not know. He did not even know if he had been asleep. Stiff and cold, he shivered as the stale reek of body odour filled the cab and assailed his nostrils.

Blinking, he stretched to relieve the cramp and tried to orientate himself. The panic, triggered by the events of the previous night, that had unnerved him, and caused him to bolt, flooded back. He wound the window down to thrust his head into the moist dawn, gulping the fresh morning air which slowly, gradually, subdued the shivering which had taken over his body.

His fear abated, but not the helplessness that accompanied it. He had no plan of action, no survival scheme, not even a rational thought. Lowering his head to his crossed forearms on the steering wheel, he wept. What could he do? Where he could he go? Where could he be safe?

Until yesterday, the distance he was from Paroski, and the fact that he had survived the various tribulations of the convoy, had seeded in him a resistance that was slowly burgeoning into defiance. Until yesterday, when the colonel deadheaded any semblance of courage or right thinking that he might have regained.

It was obvious that the woman had had no liking for him prior to the contact with Paroski, but afterwards—she could not control the loathing in her face. It was clear that the Croat had told her everything. She had thrust the phone into his hands, and the colonel had told him who was now in charge. She demanded his knife, which he handed over.

Hardly had his fingers left the hilt, when a forearm of steel barred his neck, and he was on his knees between her legs. The bitch had pricked him with the blade under his ribcage, forcibly enough to draw blood. Moreover, she had enjoyed it!

She had asked him if he could get his hands on any of the Kalashnikovs. Not if Spider was around, he had told her. And, if Spider was not around, she persisted? He told her that if they could nobble the convoy leader, he felt sure he could get one.

In reality, he thought it unlikely, even if the other drivers were unarmed.

After she had dealt with Spider, he was to get a Kalashnikov and give it to her. While she was dealing with Rath and the other drivers, he was to prepare the vehicles for torching. It was cold-blooded but seemed straightforward enough. He had closed his mind to the fate of his comrades; in his thoughts, they had already become "the others".

There might have been a chance of success if they had taken out the Irishman first, but they had not, and that is how it was. The woman was dead and now he was out here in the wilds of Bosnia, alone and with no hope.

He had been on the other side of the vehicle with the cab door open when he heard the shot.

He knew, instinctively, that everything had gone wrong.

Closing the cab door quietly, he had run in a crouch along the the vehicles, before coming into the clearing behind the other drivers. They were milling towards Spider's truck. No one gave him any special attention in the gloom.

The convoy leader was not dead but the woman, recognizable as such only by her naked form, certainly was; most of her head had gone.

The shooting had made each one conscious of his vulnerability. The drivers nervously rechecked their vehicles for parking position, fuel availability, quick starts, and security of the load - everything that drivers do, so as not to dwell on the present situation.

He had joined in.

Then the thought struck him. Dawke and Scouse had been with him in the old part of Split when he had bought the knife. Scouse might not be a threat, but the talkative Dawke had paid great attention to the knife. It was the only one at the stall, and Dawke, who had seen it first, was irritated because he had offered cash before Dawke could. How long would it be before it someone realized that it was his knife? If they suspected him and recollected he had been alone with the woman, then a resultant search would reveal Paroski's phone.

As some of the drivers repositioned their vehicles, he was able to get his truck onto the forward slope, release the handbrake, then slowly, gradually, allow it to pick up speed and momentum. Several miles away from the original location, he turned off the northern route and followed a track leading into another of Bosnia's ubiquitous pine forests.

In a clearing, he pulled over and switched off his engine. He called Paroski, and with trepidation, told the colonel that the woman had failed. The silence at the other end was more intimidating than any abuse would have been. The Croat said nothing and then the connection was broken. The tension and stress of the night, together with the strain of driving solidly flooded his consciousness.

His eyes closed and he slumped in his seat, the instrument dropping from his nerveless hand.

Thin beams of vehicle lights far down the valley flicked left and right to pierce the darkness as the trucks negotiated the winding road, disappearing periodically as the convoy snaked down through the dips and then reappearing as the convoy mounted the rises.

Even at this distance, Mahmud could see they were travelling at speed. Yet there was still no sign of Tadim or any of the other warriors. What would he do if the unbelievers attacked the convoy?

Peering down over the edge into the denser darkness below, he spat to one side in disgust. Despite the effort the HOS had taken to conceal their presence, three or four glowing red fireflies showed in the darkness; his keen sense of smell detected the aroma of tobacco.

He opened the phone and tried the number. No response. Closing the phone, he gnawed his bearded lower lip in thought. One thing was clear; Tadim would not want this convoy hijacked by the pig-droppings below.

What to do?

As the answer came to him, he dragged his knapsack toward him, pulled out the first of the mines, and then unwound the long strip of cloth that formed his headdress.

The leader of the HOS heard the growl of the trucks as they approached. The convoy was less than a mile away and closing rapidly. *Almost time.* He got to his feet and moved a couple of paces to the left to stand behind a nearby tree. He withdrew the pistol from its holster and cocked it. Peering around the trunk, he saw the first vehicle, closely followed by the others, climb towards them. He glanced around to ensure that his men were ready. He took a deep breath, bracing himself, then raised his pistol.

A searing white brilliance ripped through the darkness.

The ground around him heaved, then erupted explosively.

Then again.

And again.

He dropped to his knees, covering his head with his hands as the tree behind him toppled.

Eyes straining to penetrate the night, Spider could feel the mountains waiting for them. The scant light from the night sky, hindered by the heavy patches of cloud, was diminishing, and the blackness ahead became even denser. The vehicle lights created the effect of a dimly-lit stage backdrop, with the dark figures of cloaked trees waiting in both wings.

Steady, Spider, steady.

They were making good time on a road surface that was relatively unbroken. It was just possible that Tuzla would not be—

Light flared, from the darkness to his right, silhouetting the pines and several wildly gesticulating figures. He swerved involuntarily and the vehicle swayed, tilted then righted itself. The force of the explosions buffeted the cab, and the dull thuds vibrated through the thin metal. Despite the close proximity of the eruptions, he knew intuitively that the convoy was not the target.

Grabbing the handset of the radio, he roared, "Convoy Leader to all vehicles. Don't stop! Repeat, don't stop! Go, go, damn it, go!"

Mahmud primed the last mine. Laying it as carefully as he had the others on the cloth, he gathered up the ends. Straightening, he lifted the looped sling and once again sidestepped cautiously to the edge of the drop.

He started to swing the loaded cloth like a pendulum in both hands, gradually increasing the momentum and speed. As the mine reached the end of the outward swing, he loosed one end and pulled his makeshift sling back towards him.

The bomb spun and arched through the air then seemed to hang before plummeting downwards.

Paroski slammed the telephone down on its cradle and swore through his clenched teeth. His sallow complexion suffused, and his jaw muscles bunched tightly. Veins in his neck throbbed as he tried to rein in his anger.

Bitch!

The supercilious tones of the secretary echoed in his ear.

"Please be prepared to brief the general at half past eight tomorrow morning with details of progress so far—if any."

If any, damn her, if any!

He struggled to bring his rage under control. This was all he needed. Several moments later, his breathing slowed, became more even, and the colour in his face faded. Realist that he was, he had to admit to himself that there had been a singular lack of success.

But, why?

Yesterday, when Crowther had called, and he had spoken to the woman, it looked as if the matter was resolved. He would have wagered money on it. Then at half past two, the clown had rung to say that the whole thing had disintegrated. Kalosowich's woman was dead, and his paedophile had run off in abject terror.

What had gone wrong?

He had identified all the courses of action open to the convoy. By a process of elimination, he had deduced the only viable options left to it. The conclusions that he had reached had been logical and rational. He had made all the necessary preparations to prevent its further progress. All the right things done, and all the right stops pulled out, but still the maverick convoy eluded him.

Perhaps he had been too consistent, too much in context, too systematic.

Pushing himself out of the chair, Paroski crossed the room to stand before the map. The overlay was marked with chinagraph pencil; black showing the convoy's probable route or, more precisely, what had been his best guess as to its intended course, and red showing the actual road taken. The wide variance between the two lines highlighted just how wrong he had been. Despite the narrow choice of alternate passages, the two lines coincided for the first twenty-five miles only.

Eyes narrowed, he continued to stare at the topography of central Bosnia Herzegovina for several more minutes. The most recent information he had was that the convoy had rested up overnight in the woods south of Rankovici. Its goal—Tuzla—now lay only a few miles to the north. The convoy was within four hours of the town. His options became limited since, the nearer the trucks got to Tuzla, the less he could do with the curtailed resources he had left. The Army of Bosnia-Herzegovina controlled the countryside and the approaches to Tuzla from the north-west.

His attempts to destroy the convoy to date had depended on divining the course of travel, then positioning ambushes and artillery barrages in its path. The convoy's presence in Rankovici showed how miserable a success that had been.

Something more direct, more drastic was required now.

He moved closer to the map and located Rankovici with his finger. Tracing the road north leading out of the village to the intersection on the tarmac road to Tuzla, he read the name of the next village. Mind made up, he reached for the red pencil and slashed a vigorous cross on the overlay. He could see from the information passed to him by his informant that the convoy would have to pass through or around this small town.

Vares.

So be it. Stop the convoy at Vares, permanently. But how? Before he worked that one out, however, he would take steps to roll up the smuggling operation here in Croatia. If Stösser, Ovasco and the English convoy manager were conveniently in custody, at least that would prevent any further developments at this end and might even provide some drastically needed answers.

He picked up the phone to initiate the round up.

TWELVE

Spider was crouching at the side of the road, over a map spread on the ground, as Rath approached with two mugs of coffee.

"What have we got in front of us?"

Spider took the mug offered, then located Tuzla with a forefinger and traced the route back to their present position.

"Thanks. Not far now. Another three, four hours maximum should do it to Tuzla." He sipped the hot, sweet liquid. "We've come a long way but we're not there yet."

Rath chewed the inside of his cheek as he nodded, then bent over to look at the map.

"What's the likelihood of being bumped again?"

"It's hard to say. But if we work on the assumption that we're fair game until we get to Tuzla. . ."

"We've just passed through Sutjeska and the next place is Vares. There is a UNPROFOR unit there, so it might be worthwhile pulling over to see if there is any possibility of an escort. On the other hand, if we want to get this nightmare over it would make good sense to push on. What do you think?"

"From the beginning we thought we were likely to attract more attention with an escort than without one," responded Rath. "Wrong! So, since we've got to go to Vares, let's make up our minds about the escort when we get there."

Spider shrugged, then nodded.

"We'll get under way in..." he checked his watch, "ten minutes."

Rath swung round, shouting to the members of the team that they should get ready, then moved towards his own truck.

The radio net crackled open.

"Mount up, and wheel 'em out."

Seconds later, they were on the road to Vares, but one question dominated everyone's thoughts.

Would they make it?

In the basement of the regional Headquarters of the OS-BH in Tuzla, Captain Zelim lay back in a chair with his booted feet on the cluttered desk. He held a magazine before him, but his thoughts were not on its pages. Zelim was bored. He lowered the tattered magazine, then abruptly threw it sideways across the room.

Another ennui-filled day stretched ahead of him.

The mortaring was prompt on the hour at six o'clock that morning. The Serbs on Mount Majevica, to the east of the town, always laid down fire on them at the same time each day—never more than three grenades. Quite desultory, really, almost as if they had something more interesting to do, but, since the programme called for mortar firing on Tuzla, then fire they would. It was three hours since that day's quota, and there would be nothing more until early next morning.

No real diversions.

He sighed.

The telephone buzzed. Listlessly, he picked up the receiver and listened with no real interest.

"Zelim, 5th Company HQ."

"Colonel Tabara here, Zelim. Is Major Abdic there?"

"No, sir. He was in Zenica yesterday but has not returned. Can I help?"

"I did particularly want Major Abdic, but yes, yes you can. I have a mujahedeen group, about thirty in all, due in any time now from Konjic. We have reassigned it for special duties under the command of Central, and I have instructions to brief them on those duties. After I have seen them, they will come to your compound. Major Abdic agreed they could draw rations. After that, they have billets back down in Breza with the Seventh. Do you have anyone who could go with them and act as liaison?"

Zelim thought it would be ideal to get out of the cellar for a few hours. He could act as escort himself. The major was due back anytime now, and the situation was quiet.

"Yes, sir. No problem."

"Good. Fine. Make sure I get a call as soon as they reach the Seventh. Thank you, Zelim."

The captain felt immeasurably cheered up. He belted on his pouches and holstered his weapon. Whistling and in higher spirits, he left the cellar and headed for the guardhouse at the main gate to await the arrival of the Afghans.

Paroski checked his watch. The time available to destroy the convoy and its cargo was dwindling.

Rapidly.

After a few moments of deep thought, he reached for the packet of *Opatiya* on the table and lit one. He blew the smoke into the tent of light made by the desk lamp and absently watched as it curled thinly upwards.

Every action so far had failed. He wished that he could be there himself, to make sure that his plans reached fruition. If only he could fly.

As the thought struck him, so did the possibility that he did have wings.

The Air Detachment at Pleso had several helicopters. Three of these had been brought over to the Croatian side in the early days by the air wing's current officer commanding, Major Peter Markovic, following Croatia's declaration of independence. The Gazelle helicopters, manufactured by SOKO in Yugoslavia under licence and in service with the JNA, had been at the plant for refit. Markovic and two other Croat flyers in the JNA had agreed to steal three of the helicopters and bring them to Zagreb to be the nucleus of the fledgling Croatian Army Air Corps. The remaining seven stayed under the control of the Serbian-run JNA.

So, if a Gazelle without insignia or markings was to show up in Bosnia and create mayhem in a Moslem area, who could be sure that the Serbs were not responsible? The more he thought about it, the more the plan appealed to him. He pulled the phone towards him.

"Get me the airport at Pleso," he told the operator, "then put me through to military aircraft section. I want to talk to Major Markovic."

Within minutes, the operator rang back, and he had a surprisingly clear line to the head of the Army's air reconnaissance troop.

"Paroski, Head of M.I. I have a tasking for you, Markovic. It will not be a recce. I need one of your birds, without markings. Yes, without markings, fully fuelled and with a full complement of air-to-ground missiles. The destination is Vares. That's—hold on." Peering at the map, he read off the coordinates to the waiting Air Corps officer.

"How long do you need to get ready? Good. Excellent. I will be with you in forty minutes. Yes, you heard correctly. I will be aboard."

The three long-wheelbase Land Rovers, all sitting low over their axles due to the weight they were carrying, climbed the hill, then pulled up before the barrier. The drivers of the second and third vehicles jumped out almost immediately but remained by their Rovers.

Tadim climbed out of the leading vehicle, signalling to his driver, Mahmud, to remain behind the wheel. As he strode to the gate, a young officer left the adjacent building, and walked towards him. The Afghan shook the grinning Bosnian's hand, but he felt no need to return the smile. They conferred in English; Tadim was pleased and surprised that his usage of the language surpassed that of his host.

After observing the normal courtesies and greeting protocol, they agreed that, while the mujahedeen collected and loaded the food held ready for them, the officers would drink coffee. The Afghan leader passed the loading instructions to his men, then followed the Bosnian officer into the guardhouse.

After loading, which would take at most fifteen minutes, and then a meal, the party would set out for Breza.

Captain Zelim opened his map case, located Breza on the map and pointed it out to the towering mujahedeen leader.

"Breza. Not far from here. Very easy to find."

Tadim was expressionless as he looked at the proffered map. He nodded as he sipped the thick black coffee. They had already passed through Breza that morning on their way to Tuzla.

"I will come with you. To your new camp."

Tadim raised his eyebrows, then shrugged. If the Bosnian thought it necessary, why not? He finished his drink and, setting down the cup, casually saluted the young captain then left the guardhouse to return to his vehicle that was now loaded with combat rations.

Mahmud leaned over the passenger's seat to open the door for him. Tadim stepped aside to allow Zelim to get in first so that the captain could climb over into the back of the vehicle. The load area was full of boxes, cooking utensils, folded blankets, tarpaulins, jerry cans and ammo boxes.

Two other vehicles arrived, but before they came to a stop, Tadim made a circle in the air with his index finger and pointed to the gate of the compound. He lowered himself into his seat in the Land Rover and stared straight ahead, as Mahmud glanced quickly in his side mirror, then pulled out.

The smell of cigarette tobacco from the rear of the vehicle caused Tadim to look round and frown at the young Bosnian. He shook his head, then pointed at the equipment filling the bed of the vehicle. Zelim sighed but nodded. He cupped the cigarette in his hand, and putting his hand out through a gap in the canvas, flicked the butt away.

Cheatham, preoccupied, toyed with the soupspoon. Despite attempts over the last few days, he had been unable to contact Webb or any other members of the convoy. He had no idea where the vehicles were or, more importantly, their cargo. He was the first to admit he was not a "people person" and did not lose any sleep worrying about his employees, but the lack of information did place him in a quandary.

Cheatham half turned to look for what seemed the umpteenth time across the other tables at the entrance to the restaurant. Stösser and Ovasco were twenty minutes late. When they did arrive, Stösser would want to know about his property, and that presented Cheatham with a dilemma.

He would have to lie so as not to jeopardize future business opportunities. He spent some time revising and honing the story he would tell the German arms dealer.

They still had not appeared, and he was hungry, but it did not make sense to order without them. Irritated, he flipped open his mobile phone and selected Ovasco's number on speed dial. He had tried twice already, and this time was no different.

There was no reply.

He waited a further ten minutes with ill-disguised impatience before pushing his chair back and leaving the restaurant. Once in his car, he decided to drive to Ovasco's home and find out exactly what was amiss.

He knocked at the front door.

As Cheatham waited, he looked over at the workshop but could see no sign of any movement or activity. He turned as the door opened, and Ovasco's wife stood before him. Her face was red, and he could see she had been crying.

Before he could say anything, she burst out:

"They took him away. The police took him away!"

Cheatham blinked rapidly and felt the panic swoop upwards inside him. Without a word, he spun round and staggered awkwardly to the car. Fumbling with his keys, he managed to insert the ignition key and start the engine. His instincts told him that this was it.

Time to move on.

Cheatham put the bulky envelopes containing the money he had just withdrawn into his briefcase. While it was open, he checked the plane ticket and his passport in the other envelope. It would take forty minutes to reach the airport. A taxi could take him there, and he would leave his car where he had parked it, a few hundred yards from the bank. It was a company car, so it was no financial sacrifice.

He took off his sunglasses, polished them, returned them to his face, took several large deep breaths and headed across the marble floor of the bank to the door.

Paroski lit another cigarette from the butt of the first one. He leaned forward to extinguish the stub in the ashtray behind the driver. As they waited for the lights to change, he saw the Englishman, Cheatham, walk down the steps of the bank into the square. As he walked towards the taxi rank, Paroski leaned forward and ordered the driver to pull up alongside Cheatham.

Paroski barely waited for the car to stop before jumping out and grabbing the surprised convoy manager by the arm. He pushed the Englishman roughly towards the open rear door of the car and bundled him inside. Shoving Cheatham further into the car, Paroski climbed in and slammed the door.

"Drive on," he snapped at the driver. "Pleso, and go straight to the hangars."

He half-turned to Cheatham.

"So, what do you know about the whereabouts of your vehicles?"

Cheatham swallowed and tried to get his thoughts in order. but did not reply. Paroski stared at him for what seemed an eternity.

Without warning, Paroski slammed his elbow into Cheatham's solar plexus and as the man's head shot forward, the Croat swung the back of his fist upwards into the unprotected face. Cheatham felt his ribcage explode and then excruciating pain barrelled its way through his nose, mouth and head.

As the Englishman spluttered, then gasped for breath, Paroski picked up the fallen briefcase and opened it. He tore open the manila envelopes and emptied the notes into the open case. He pulled out the passport and airline ticket, and then turned his attention back to Cheatham.

"You will not need these any time in the near future."

Markovic stood with the co-pilot, Peter Naric, at the entrance to the hangar, watching the red and white Air Croatia planes that landed, taxied and took off from the civilian part of the airport, with clockwork regularity. There was nothing more for them to do.

He had devised a flight plan and calculated the necessary airspeed to maintain sufficient fuel for the mission. The helicopter, which had been "sanitized" so that no trace of evidence existed to suggest it was Croatian, stood on the concrete apron in front of the shelter. He and Naric had also cleared all traces of their identity and nationality from their flying gear; not even identity disks remained.

Despite Paroski's assurances, he still felt uneasy about the next few hours. UNPROFOR had a standing ban on all aerial activity over central Bosnia, and although he was convinced there was little they would do to enforce it, he was not confident that they would reach Vares without incident. Fuel, too, would be at a premium since they would be operating at extreme range for the aircraft. Naric, who would be the gunner on this mission, in addition to his usual duties as navigator and observer, had prepared the SA 341H that stood ready on the concrete apron.

As the colonel had ordered, the cantilever tubular weapon beams, mounted on both sides of the helicopter, now held the UV 16-57 pods containing the rockets. The 7.62mm calibre machine gun, belted up and loaded, jutted out from under the nose of the Gazelle. With all safety and control checks completed, the aircraft, like a sleek thoroughbred at the stable door, was ready to leave as soon as the colonel appeared.

Markovic heard his name called across the floor of the workshop and above the roar of the engines. Turning back to the hangar, they saw that the colonel had arrived. Naric moved across to the helicopter as he walked inside to meet Paroski.

They briefly clasped rather than shook hands. Paroski was impatient to leave, and it showed when the flyer asked for more specifics on the mission ahead. Paroski then curtly briefed Markovic on the purpose of the flight and his intentions.

He brushed aside the major's concerns about the flying ban, assuring him that it was improbable that they would experience problems en route. They would be able to deal with the convoy once there with little difficulty, since it was unescorted and unarmed. The mission was straightforward, and there would be no complications.

Paroski did not feel it necessary to inform Markovic that all his own best efforts to date had failed.

Markovic nodded, and then noticed the civilian who accompanied the colonel. He looked at Paroski then nodded, with raised eyebrows in question, at the presence of the man.

"He comes with us," Paroski answered.

"That is not possible—"

"He is coming with us and—"

"—as the aircraft will be on extended capacity already. I have not calculated for the extra weight." Markovic completed his sentence. He stiffened noticeably as he said, "I must insist, Colonel."

Paroski bit his lip in vexation, then spun round to address Cheatham.

"You are free to go for the time being. But this," he snarled holding the briefcase at shoulder level, "goes with me!"

Cheatham stared at him in mute dismay.

The major indicated the aircraft at the front of the hangar and, lightly touching the colonel on the arm, walked towards it. Naric, already helmeted and waiting beside the helicopter, opened the passenger side and assisted Paroski into his place behind the co-pilot seat, then passed the colonel a helmet. When Paroski had put on the helmet, he then plugged in both sets of radio and intercom cables and climbed in.

Cheatham walked, with leaden legs, to the entrance of the hangar and watched the helicopter. He could not believe his bad luck. The fact that he was temporarily free meant nothing. He could not run without a passport. More importantly, and more immediate, was that his money, the result of months and months of intricate plotting and hard work, was in the hands of that psychopath heading out to deepest darkest Bosnia.

His lower lip started to tremble. He could not control the movement. He blinked several times, but his eyes filled with tears of frustration and self-pity. He struggled vainly for self-control.

Of its own volition, his mouth forlornly formed the words.

"My money, my money."

Markovic belted up and then, after adjusting the position of his throat mike, called for a three-way test over the system. Satisfied, he switched on the ignition, and the Astazou 870shp engine sprang to life. With all checks carried out and completed several minutes before, he turned to the colonel with raised eyebrows and gave the thumbs up sign, jerking his thumb skywards. The colonel nodded his assent.

Feet comfortably resting on the rudder pedals, the pilot reached for the collective lever with his left hand, and gently worked it until the upward thrust of the rotors dissolved the pull of gravity. This reduced the weight of the aircraft until its wheels were resting lightly on the concrete. He held his hand steady as he scanned the instrument panel. Reassured that all functions were stable, he applied collective to increase power. Simultaneously, he applied pressure to the left pedal to counteract the increased torque and keep the nose of the Gazelle in line.

The helicopter lifted several feet off the ground, nose-down and swinging gently under the rotating blades. Instinctively, he edged the cyclic stick minimally towards him, adjusting into a level hover. Another brief glance at the engine instruments on the panel assured him that all was well. Increased pull on the collective lever, together with simultaneous forward pressure on the cyclic stick, and on the left pedal, allowed the airspeed to increase.

A moment later the aircraft shuddered as it passed through transactional lift. A soft constant pull on the cyclic stick continued the climb. His feelings of disquiet about the mission had disappeared now that they were actually airborne. The Gazelle climbed swiftly and steeply over the hangars, up and away from the rapidly shrinking trees and buildings.

Moments later, it broke through the light cloud layer, above the airport.

Markovic eased the stick forward and increased airspeed as they headed west toward the coast.

Still heading west, and soon after leaving Karlovac behind, they gained height as the helicopter followed the climbing gradient of the wooded valley up towards the narrow Vratic pass.

As the huge panorama of the wide seascape leapt up before them, they swooped down across the snaking bends of the road towards the coast. The cabin, almost completely glazed with transparent mouldings, was flooded with the early morning sun like a huge translucent bubble. The sudden beauty and the latent power of the sea, unveiled as a broad expanse of blazing ultramarine, never failed to affect Markovic, whether he travelled over the pass in the air or through it on the ground.

The helicopter chattered over the red roofs of Senj to the water, then, as he banked to change course heading south along the coast, swung steeply to port.

He adjusted the airspeed, then noted the fuel level and time. The metallic surface of the Adriatic, under an azure arch of cloudless sky, glistened as far as he could see ahead of the aircraft. Later, he checked the fuel and time again, to verify the burn-rate and was pleased to see that his previous computations were correct. There should be no problem with fuel on this flight.

To their right, clusters of islands, reflecting myriad hues of greens and reds seemingly propelled by an invisible current, swept past below like multi-coloured flotsam. For Markovic, sights such as this made flying a joy. He glanced sideways at Naric, then turned to grin happily at Paroski.

The colonel returned his smile with a sour stare.

A short time later, the dry, barren, pink-tinted contours of the Kornati islands, denuded of trees by the insatiable appetite of the medieval Venetians for wooden piles on which to support the expansion of their city-state, rushed towards them. Then just as rapidly, they receded. To their left, the grey jawbone of the Dinaric Alps yawed jaggedly alongside the narrow strip of fertile coast.

Markovic checked his watch. In a few minutes, the horseshoe formed by the towns of Split and nearby Trogir, with their outer ring of white tower rises, would appear below the mountains. Naric tapped his arm and, with gestures, pointing inland then turning an open palm over and under several times, asked whether they should fly over the port to the interior. Paroski pre-empted Markovic's response over the intercom, and leaning forward between them shook his head violently.

"—kovic," he shouted, then repeated it, as he realized the voice-activated intercom had dropped the first syllable. "Metkovic," this time less loudly but more emphatically. Markovic gave a thumbs-up to signal that he understood and would comply.

Forty minutes later the colour of the sea changed as the Neretva delta spread like an open fan below. The Gazelle banked, whirring noisily, across the stark skeletal derricks and angular cranes of Ploce. These showed up dark in contrast to the lighter shades of the ships moored alongside.

Soon they were flying over the dark green lines of Opuzen's orange and lemon trees towards the Herzegovina border. Markovic dropped the aircraft down low over the groves and commenced nap of the earth flying.

They were now operational.

The heat from the sun increased as it rose, but Crowther was not aware of it. He remained motionless in the vehicle with the sweat running unheeded down his face. His thoughts were in a feverish cyclic turmoil. *I've got to do something, but what? I don't know; think man, think! I've got to do something, but what, I don't. .* The cacophony of gibberish thrashed and jerked in his head. Should he try to head for Tuzla? How could he, without using the same route as the rest of the convoy? *Back to Mali Prog, and Croatia? And Paroski?* He shuddered. *Think, man, think!*

Try as he might, he could think of nothing logical that would help. He tilted his head back against the rest and closed his eyes. He drifted off into a disturbed and restless sleep, twitching and turning and dreaming of Paroski.

It was either afternoon or early evening when he woke—he could tell by the shadows—and still he had not worked out a plan of escape. He would have to dream up some lie to tell Paroski. He pulled out the phone but was not yet ready to dial the number.

The jolting and swaying of the vehicle increased and eventually broke through into Zelim's consciousness. He woke from the light sleep realizing that he had been dozing. Leaning forward between the Afghans, he peered through the windscreen.

"This is not the best way to Vares," he said, tapping Tadim on the shoulder. "You must have turned off?"

"We turned off."

"But why? It will take hours to get there on this track. You should have stayed on the main road." He pointed up ahead. "Just up in front, soon, there's another track going back down into the valley. It'll be easier."

"Easier is not always safer."

"But—" The young captain tried weakly to make his point.

"Captain," said Tadim evenly but not unkindly and placing a forefinger on his lips, "Captain, you are along for the ride. I decide the route we take. We are not amateurs. We have been operational in your country for more than a year now. We will remain operational, because we are always alert and never take things for granted. We remain vigilant. This route is difficult and not used often, and that is why we take it." The vehicle continued to sway and bounce as Mahmud fought it up the steep incline. "We will be in Vares soon enough, have no fear. Besides, we are eagles. It is in the mountains that we live, fight and travel." He smiled at the young Bosnian.

Zelim sighed but nodded.

Tadim reflected on the mission he had been given. His orders were to intercept an aid convoy and escort it to Tuzla. The convoy should be heading towards them on the road below. It had done well to get this far. He thought of the HOS unit and was convinced that the convoy they had engaged was the one that he now had to escort.

He grinned mirthlessly. The Serbs would no doubt be the first to endorse the efficiency of his men in protecting travellers in Bosnia. The interest his military command was now showing in this convoy indicated that its problems were not all over.

The Land Rovers reached the top of the climb. He nudged Mahmud, signalling that he should pull over, under the trees. They would stop here while he surveyed the land ahead. As the vehicle rolled to a halt, he sprang out and, jogging easily to the crest, leaned against a pine on the edge of the track while focusing his binoculars on the valley below.

The mood among the drivers had lightened and, although the chitchat that had broken out was a breach of radio discipline, Spider allowed it to continue. They were in better spirits, and the thought that the end of the journey was near was obviously uppermost in all of their minds. A hot bath and a decent meal filled his thoughts too, but faded as the valley started to close.

Running parallel to the road was a river whose flood leapt and gurgled over the rocks, racing the road to the base of the mountain ahead. For centuries, these wild waters had sought the line of least resistance, and over time had dissolved part of the limestone base of the mountain. The constant worrying and frenetic gnawing of the water enlarged the fissures into which it vanished, and slowly but implacably, had fashioned a huge cavern which now penetrated the barrier and acted as a tunnel through to Vares.

This type of natural action was, Spider recalled, named Karst after a barren limestone plateau in Slovenia where it occurs. As the rain descends through the atmosphere, it picks up small amounts of carbon dioxide, and when this mixture makes contact with limestone it initiates a dissolving action. In Karst landscapes, many burns, streams and even rivers disappear down into these cracks, which are enlarged into holes and vents in the limestone. They flow for miles underground, forming sinkholes, subterranean lakes and caverns where rainwater percolating from above forms stalactites and stalagmites. The flowing waters reappear on the surface, often at great distances from the point where they submerged, when the geology changes and no longer provides the line of least resistance.

Casting an apprehensive glance at the river once more, he saw that the water level seemed to be very high. The mass of the mountain loomed, throwing the end of valley into deep shade. Beyond the shadow, like an empty eye socket, was the gaping black yaw of the cave that they had to negotiate to reach Vares.

Spider made up his mind to reconnoitre the tunnel and gave the signal for the convoy to halt.

"Jablonica Jezera," said Naric, pointing down.

Paroski could see the aquamarine links of lakes stretching from the dam at Jablonica to the outskirts of

Konjic that lay at its eastern end. They were now close to Vares. His hands sweated in anticipation. Without warning, the helicopter veered to the right , causing him to look sharply at Markovic.

"No problem, colonel, just standard practice. We do not normally cross open water because of the danger of radar interception. I am also going to take us nearer to the mountainside from here on in. It will increase the probability of turbulence because of the danger of downdrafts, but if there are any UNPROFOR fighters roaming above us, it will make it just that little bit more difficult for them to spot us down here."

The helicopter gained some height in its slide to the right to avoid the centre of the valley. The sight line of any pilots flying above them funnelled naturally into the bottom of the valley.

Paroski showed no great interest and returned to the map on his lap. No longer in the centre of the valley, the helicopter followed an invisible line close to and halfway up the mountain.

Naric reached above and pulled the down tube of the gyro-stabilized sight across in front of him. It connected to the Ferranti AF532 mounted on the port side of the roof of the cabin. He adjusted the settings to 2.5 magnifications for search, and then checked the weapons systems once again.

Twenty-eight minutes later, Naric reached round, tapped the colonel's arm and pointed to the valley below.

A solitary white vehicle was slewed across a narrow track, partially hidden by the surrounding trees. Paroski could not help but feel excited. If there was one nearby, then the rest could not be too far away.

"I want that vehicle destroyed, Major Markovic."

The pilot frowned slightly but swung the helicopter into a wide swinging loop.

"Weapons check." The Major concentrated on the banking turn.

"All weapons armed and ready," responded Naric.

"Entering approach run now. Fire at will."

Crowther listened anxiously to the distant ringing of the phone. He heard an additional noise through the open cab window: the sound of an approaching helicopter. There was a click and the connection made. It was with difficulty that he heard Paroski as the background noises grew louder.

Markovic looked over at the incongruous trill of the mobile phone, which Paroski took from his pocket, but Naric had locked on to the vehicle below and would not allow his concentration to be distracted by the ringing.

As the colonel answered the phone, Naric depressed the firing button and the missile streaked away in a burst of orange.

Paroski kept his eyes on the truck below as he spoke. "Paroski."

"Crowther, I—"

The truck leapt several feet into the air like a gigantic, scalded, white cat but with none of the natural grace. It turned in the air and fell heavily on its side.

"Yes, hello, go on. Hello?"

Paroski scowled at the phone before turning back to the stricken vehicle. The connection had gone: the phone was dead in his hand.

"Excellent shot, gentlemen." He collapsed the short aerial on the phone but did not put it back into his pocket. The firing of the missile had probably affected the phone transmission, and the paedophile would probably get back to him in a few moments.

"Now for the others!"

They soon located the objects they were seeking. Under a row of trees, lining the road to the entrance of a huge cavern, they saw the remaining convoy trucks.

"Markovic, I want them all destroyed. Obliterated. Each and every one."

The major nodded. The Gazelle reacted to the gentle push on the stick swinging into a long looping circle.

It came round for a run and approached the rear of the convoy.

Spider flashed the torch around the gloomy, cathedral vaults of the cave's interior. Thick strands of darkness diffused the beam. Like smoke in the wind, it dissipated into the black recesses above his head. Moisture, glistening and shiny like sweat on ebony, ran down the steep walls. As he expected, the water was high, desperately so. The spring rains had increased its volume, and the road had disappeared.

He sniffed. The smell of faded, sour mould assailed his nostrils. The gurgling of the river on its way forward over the rocky floor filled the cavern, jumping up past him, then rebounding down in echoes from above. The cold in the cave was intense, and he shivered. Still, the trucks would be able to make it providing everyone kept their heads.

He waded on through the underground passage and as he came closer to the far end the atmosphere lightened somewhat. Standing for several minutes under the huge irregular arch of the exit, he checked the immediate external area. Everything seemed normal. He turned and re-entered the cave.

Blinking as his eyes gradually became accustomed to the bright sunlight, he saw that the drivers had gathered in a group and were all looking skywards.

"There's a helicopter," shouted Dawke as he approached. "Could be UNPROFOR."

"What markings has it got?" asked Spider.

The man looked at him blankly, then turned, seeking confirmation from the others.

"It's got no markings," snapped Rath.

"Everybody! In the trucks! Make for the cave. Now!" roared Spider.

"But if it's got no markings—" said Dawke querulously.

"Now, damn it," roared Rath, turning and running to his truck.

At that moment, the chattering noise of the oncoming helicopter swept before it and filled the valley. Spider revved up his engine and jerked the wheel round to pull out.

Glancing in his side mirror, he saw with relief that all the trucks behind him were in motion, then he stiffened in horror as the glass filled with the dark green shape of the Gazelle as it swept into view a few hundred yards from the tail vehicle.

He saw the flash of orange and then heard the exaggerated hiss of the release of the first missile. A heartbeat later, the surface of the track exploded, showering his vehicle with rock, earth and gravel as the force rocked his cab. He stood on the accelerator, leading the pack as the vehicles scrambled for the safety of the mountain.

The vehicles of Tadim's group had stopped for the second time to allow him to scan the valley floor with his binoculars once again. He stiffened at movement in the trees of the slope opposite but relaxed as the field glasses revealed only the presence of a group of children. He focused on the floor of the valley and saw more figures under the trees.

Closer inspection revealed a group of men smoking. He counted them; numerically they could be the drivers of the convoy, the ones he was looking for.

He swung the glasses across to the area in the shade. In line and parallel to the river were the trucks; this had to be the convoy that he was to escort to Tuzla. He lowered the glasses and was about to return to his Rover, when a commotion among the drivers caught his eye.

The figures had abruptly scattered and were leaping into their vehicles.

At that moment, the sound of a helicopter engine reached his ears. Mahmud had joined him on the lip of the slope. Before he could locate the helicopter, Mahmud was pointing down towards the mountain and pulling on his arm. He caught sight of the aircraft just before it fired.

"The rocket, Mahmud. Get the Stinger!"

Mahmud dived back to the loaded Rover and reached it just as Zelim was clambering over the front seat to get out. Mahmud pulled him, without ceremony, forward and out on to the ground. He then sprang into the rear of the vehicle and pulled out the MANPAD. In a matter of seconds, he had armed and primed the weapon and was running over to his previous position beside Tadim.

"Wait, Mahmud. Get ready, but do not lock on until I tell you. I don't want our missile chasing his."

Mahmud nodded; he knew exactly what his commander meant. In Afghanistan, a Hind-D had escaped when he had fired his Stinger at the helicopter, but the missile had swerved and chased a cluster of AT-3 Sagger anti-armour missiles fired by the Russian.

Without warning the helicopter lifted, soared skywards then disappeared from sight over the ridge of the mountain.

"Markovic! Up! Up and over! Close the other side!" screamed Paroski. "Block the tunnel! Block the tunnel!" He pulled at the major's shoulder. The helicopter swung violently as the pilot tore the colonel's hand savagely from its grip.

"Colonel, please! Control yourself!"

Annoyed, Markovic put the helicopter into a wide turn, and as he started the run approaching the mountain, he put the aircraft into a steep, upward climb towards the mountain peak.

"The tunnel. Seal off the tunnel. Now, damn it!"

Once over the top the helicopter plummeted, the steepness and speed of the drop showing Markovic's anger. Paroski's face blanched as the descent halted sharply.

The pilot lifted the Gazelle a few yards higher and manoeuvred its nose round square to the slope as Naric lined up on the exit of the cave and then fired three consecutive missiles into the earthworks above the arch.

As the smoke cleared there appeared to be no damage, then slowly, the side of the mountain moved and slid downwards, picking up momentum as it went. In a rush to the bottom of the valley, it buried the opening of the tunnel.

"Yes, yes!" the colonel shouted. "Now back to the other side before they can turn round."

In the cave, the driver of the leading vehicle slammed on his brakes as the roof ahead of him collapsed. Clouds of dust blanketed the beam of his headlights, and stones and scree showered the cab and windscreen. Unable to avoid the collision, the truck behind pushed his vehicle forward several feet as the following driver belatedly saw his emergency stop.

Heavy diesel fumes filled the air together with the mounting roar of water and shouts of confusion as the drivers leapt down from their trucks and waded forward to see what had happened. The rock fall had blocked the fast-flowing river. The water had reached the axle of the front truck.

Panic was imminent, and Spider moved quickly to suppress it. Shouting to make himself heard over the hubbub of voices and the noise of the river, he called on the drivers to converge on his position.

"OK. Keep it under control. You can see we can't get out by going ahead. What we're going to have to do is reverse out of here. Start backing up now, but don't leave the cave completely. Stay under cover until we are sure the helicopter has gone and it is safe to do so. Move back and be ready. Rath and I will check the other end."

He nodded to Rath and, over the din that resumed as the drivers returned to their vehicles, he mouthed the words, "Get your weapon."

Armed, both men hurried past the line of trucks towards the light at the entrance to the tunnel.

Despite the distance involved and the cushioning effect of the mountain between them and the other valley, the mujahedeen heard the detonation of the three missiles. Mahmud had dejectedly accepted that he had missed his chance to down another helicopter when, to his surprise, the Gazelle hopped over the crest and returned to its previous position in front of the tunnel.

The elated Afghan controlled his excitement and sighted on the helicopter once more. He locked on and waited for the signal from his commander.

"Now!" roared Tadim, closing his open palm on Mahmud's free shoulder.

The gunner pressed the trigger.

In the helicopter's cabin, both crew members were engrossed as Markovic held the hover stable to facilitate Naric's launch of the missiles at the remaining entrance to the underground passage. The Gazelle's exhaust stack had an upward deflector to give protection against ground-fired infrared heat-seeking missiles. It also had an incoming missile detection system that Markovic had switched on before leaving Zagreb. As part of the aircraft's defence system against missiles seeking a heat source, the infrared counter measures (IRCM) had diversionary flares capable of manual or automatic release.

Despite the close proximity of the Stinger launch, two hundred feet above and less than two thousand yards distant, the Gazelle's IRCM system was infallible. It worked perfectly. Within the space of a breath, it detected the launch, activated the panel warning-lights and initiated the audio warning-tone that filled the cabin.

The supersonic Stinger missile, in a flash of orange and grey, locked unerringly on target and hissed towards the aircraft.

Markovic's eyes flicked downwards.

Comprehension screamed across his consciousness. His eyes widened, as he watched, almost in another dimension, his own groping, grasping, sluggishly desperate fingers moving to the launch switch of the defensive flares. The switch might as well have been a hundred miles away.

It had been set at manual.

Orange flame engulfed the Gazelle, silhouetting the stark figures of its dying crew and passenger for a nano-second before the sound of the explosion tore the sky apart and scattered burning debris over the trees below.

One of the children playing on the higher reaches of the hillside spotted the white trucks below. His shout caused the others to scamper in a giggling group down towards the valley floor. The explosion above their heads halted them in their tracks. They stared skywards from behind their raised hands as the debris hurtled down.

However, there were other fragments, descending more slowly than the rest, spiralling and swirling their way to the ground. Throwing caution to the wind, the first child to reach the paper whooped in joy and exhilaration.

"Money! It's money!"

Soon they were all snatching at the pieces of windfall and stuffing their pockets with the unexpected treasure.

One small girl found a small, dark blue book among the treasure and paused to open it. She saw a round face staring myopically and glumly from one of its pages.

What a sad man, she thought, and threw the passport aside as she re-joined the others in harvesting their find.

THIRTEEN

The two men reached the area of daylight. The air was heavy with the smell of burning aviation fuel. Only yards from the cavern entrance, clusters of flaming debris dotted a wide area of the road and both verges. Two large segments of wreckage were still recognizable as parts of an aircraft; a section of the cabin with seats, occupied by two charred and featureless effigies, and a length of tail together with the twisted fenestron.

The pieces continued to blaze, with sparks and black smoke hustling and crackling, as they consumed the alloys and fabric of the fuselage. A heavy, thick pall of metallic grey smoke hung overhead.

As they emerged from the shelter of the cave, Rath grabbed Spider's arm with a restraining hand. He pointed to the unfired rockets still mounted on the burning tubular steel framework of the downed helicopter. No sooner had he done so than the missiles exploded, detonated by the engulfing flames. The force of the explosion threw both men across the road and down the riverbank. Both lay winded for several minutes. Lying on his back, Spider saw the sky through the branches above his head; several were burning, as were many of those of the nearby trees.

He had lost his AK 47, and the wound in his shoulder throbbed. He wiped the sweat from his eyes and rolled over to search for Rath.

The sight of several pairs of combat boots at eye-level brought him up short. Raising his head, he saw that he was under the muzzles of several rifles behind which were dark visages of mujahedeen. Other soldiers had pulled Rath to his feet and were dragging him to the top of the bank back to the road. Hands reached for him, and he too was half-carried, half-dragged back to the road to join Rath in the presence of a black-bearded giant in Bosnian army uniform.

"You have our weapons?" the mujahid asked without preamble.

Spider did not respond but cast a glance at Rath, who was expressionless.

"The weapons," repeated the soldier. "Time is short."

"I don't know what you are talking about," replied Spider.

"We have very little time to discuss this issue. You are the convoy from Opusan?"

Spider nodded, trying to fathom the intent of the questioning.

"Then we are to take over a consignment of weapons that you are carrying for delivery to Tuzla."

"If we've got weapons for you, then we certainly don't know about it," said Rath convinced that the Bosnian soldier was hallucinating.

However, comprehension had dawned swiftly and harshly on Spider. He knew now the reason for the persistent and determined attacks.

"Our need for one of your vehicles is almost as great as our need for the weapons," Tadim said, looking under bushy, black eyebrows at Spider. "We will take one."

The convoy leader, who appeared calm and resigned, although his mind was working furiously, not least at the probability of Cheatham having set them all up, coolly agreed. He was under no illusions; his refusal would not have changed anything.

By this time, the vehicles were emerging from the tunnel. Spider beckoned Rath to join him as he headed towards the approaching trucks. He told the men about the alleged arms shipment, frowning at the attempt of Dawke to raise a question, and said that it was essential that they segregate the weapons from the relief supplies. After the trauma of the past few days he was determined that, *they* would deliver the supplies. Nothing less would do.

"Start bringing the trucks out into the open and line them up at this side of the road," he ordered, pointing in the direction of the trees.

The group turned back to the cavern to collect their vehicles as Spider took Rath by the arm and pulled him to one side under the watchful eye of the huge Afghan.

"As soon as the trucks are out of the tunnel, we'll empty the first one, and it'll be on this vehicle that we'll load the arms. That vehicle will be going with these people to Tuzla. Our guys will follow with the rest of the supplies."

No sooner had the first vehicle come to a halt than the mujahedeen were swarming around it, untying the ropes and removing the tarpaulin covers. Restraining bands on the pallets were broken and the cargo unloaded. Obviously aware of the identifying markings of the boxes containing the contraband, the fighters segregated the cartons and passed them along the chain of waiting hands.

A pile soon formed under the trees while the relief supplies went to build a similar heap at the other side of the road. As soon as the truck was empty, three Afghans detached themselves from the main working party and started unpacking, cleaning and re-assembling the various weapons.

They also opened the ammunition.

"Rath, I'm going to ask them if we can radio Zagreb and get clearance for the handover."

"Why bother with Zagreb? We—"

"I know what you mean and I agree with you but I want to speak to Cheatham. I've got the feeling that our manager knows exactly what's been going on."

Rath just shrugged.

"They appear to be in a hurry," he said to Spider in an aside that was overhead by Tadim.

"Yes, we are," the huge Afghan said. "Tanks have been withdrawing from Sarajevo. They are on their way to Tuzla. We need those weapons to stop them. The tanks will be vulnerable once and once only, and that's when they are still loaded on their trailers."

"Where are the tanks now?" asked Spider.

"The latest I have is that the first group has reached Vlasenica and has halted there to wait for their re-supply vehicles to join them."

"Well, if you want to hit them before Tuzla," Spider said looking at his watch and calculating the distance from Vares to Vlasenica, "you should have left an hour ago."

The Afghan ruefully agreed.

"Fortunately, their re-supply appears to be delayed. If we leave within the next forty minutes, I can get to Zivinica just after dark. I can engage them before they reach Tuzla."

"Commander," said Spider using the title since he was not sure of the man's actual rank, "I need your permission to use your radio to contact my base in Zagreb. They will need to know where we are and the condition of our men and cargo."

The Afghan stared at Spider as though he had not understood, but just as Spider was about to reiterate his request, the soldier nodded once, then again more emphatically.

"Come with me." He started toward his vehicle with Spider and Rath close behind him. "You have your frequencies?" he asked over his shoulder as he opened the passenger door of his Range Rover.

"Yes, no problem," replied Spider as he edged past the mujahid and eased himself onto the passenger seat. He reached for the controls on the radio. "May I?"

The Afghan nodded again and Spider changed the channels, then reached for the mike.

"Hallo, Zulu Charlie. This is Sierra Whiskey. How do you read me? Over."

Only the crackling of the ether was audible, and Spider repeated his opener three more times before, very faintly, he could hear an unidentifiable voice.

"Sierra Whiskey, this Zulu Charlie. I read you 2 by 5. Send." The use of 2 by 5 indicated that the reception of the transmission in Zagreb was exceptionally poor.

"Zulu Charlie. Is Romeo Charlie available? Over."

"Sierra Whiskey. Wait. Over."

Several minutes passed. Spider was beginning to think that the transmission had been lost when the radio came to life again.

"Sierra Whiskey. Romeo Charlie is in down town Zagreb. He should have been back by now. What is happening? Where are you now? Over."

Spider kept his tone level and decided only to report the current situation. Cheatham could sweat over the rest.

"Zulu Charlie. This is a Sitrep. The situation is as follows. We are minus—I spell numbers—t-h-r-e-e, three trucks. Michael and Calum are dead. Crowther has deserted with vehicle and load. Convoy intercepted by non-UN armed force. Over."

"Sierra Whiskey. Cheatham's instructions remain current. Deliver to Tuzla. No deviation. Over."

"Zulu Charlie, understood."

"Sierra Whiskey. He'll go ape about the losses. Over."

"Zulu Charlie. Tell Cheatham I will proceed to Tuzla. Over."

"Sierra Whiskey. Great. Excellent." The relief in the base operator's voice was evident. "I will inform Cheatham ASAP. Out."

Tadim looked askance at Spider who nodded and said, "I got through. Thanks. Now, can we move on to Tuzla with the supplies?"

"I would prefer that your vehicles remain under our escort to Tuzla. Unfortunately, we will not be going directly to the city. We will have to backtrack several miles for an alternative route."

The statement left no room for question or refusal.

With the jeep containing the escort troops in the lead, the column of heavy tractors pulling the low-loading trailers rolled down off Mount Igman and headed eastwards to join Route 19 and Zvornik in the north. Route 19 paralleled the road that made its way north to Tuzla. Less than two miles out of Zvornik, the column would swing westwards.

The thirty-five Soviet-made tanks would unload and become operational at Tojsici, less than fifteen miles across country, southeast of Tuzla. The tank force comprised mainly T-72s, of more recent production than the several T-55s, which made up the balance. The crews travelled in the middle of the column in one of the three open-backed civilian lorries. The other two trucks, filled with helmeted troops and a heavily armed M-980 carrier, brought up the rear.

Spider hated wearing sunglasses, but the slanted rays of the sun made it unavoidable. He was driving the lead ten-tonner in the wake of the Bosnian land rovers, hurtling along the asphalt road. All the drivers had long given up any attempt to avoid the pits in the road caused by previous shelling.

Rath, in the passenger seat, was trying, with a degree of success, despite the swaying and bumping of the vehicle, to read an opened map. The vehicles had travelled at a consistently high speed from Ocevjla and were now approaching the larger town of Kladanj.

"It's hard to say if we'll have a problem going through here," he said loudly, to counter the noise of the engine.

"I don't think it's going to worry them too much," replied Spider, nodding at the Afghans manning a heavy machine gun mounted in the back of each land rover.

"Yeah, the good old GPMG is a great confidence booster. Why do you think they want to escort us in?"

"He's using us as cover." Spider managed the bucking steering wheel. "With our supply trucks, his force will look like an authorized UN convoy. Until his action kicks off, it should be enough to confuse any observers."

Rath did not comment but returned his attention to the map.

Corporal Moeller, the duty radio operator at NORDBAT, the Norwegian and Swedish contingent of the United Nations' force based at the airfield at Tuzla, pencilled the details of intercept of the Bosnian Army transmission and passed it to the runner.

"For the commander."

Colonel Ekland gnawed his lip in thought as he read the message. A relief convoy had reached their area of operations, only to be hijacked. Under his current mandate, he could take no specific action, based solely on this scrap of information. However, he was in no doubt that something more would happen. When it did, his unit would be ready.

"Put the crews on standby for imminent action," he informed the duty officer.

Any reservations they had about Kladanj evaporated as the column swept through unimpeded and without reducing speed. They pushed on towards Zivinica. The effort to maintain the speed set by the Afghans taxed the supply truck engines, but the drivers brought their skill and expertise to bear, resolutely keeping the convoy intact.

"Looks as though we won't be stopping in Zivinica," Spider said, causing Rath to look up from the map.

As they approached the town, Tadim indicated by hand signals that they would continue without halt. They travelled for almost two kilometres through the built-up area and into the farmland on the other side before turning right for the last village before Tojsici and the confrontation with the tank force.

The sun had almost disappeared, and it was dark when the convoy left the main road and turned left for the outskirts of Tojsici. The scouts sent out by Tadim returned with news that left little room for optimism. The leader of the mujahedeen was unable to hide his disappointment when the reconnaissance team reported the downloading of the tanks and that they had moved out in formation in the direction of Tuzla.

From where they were, they had easy, direct access onto the main road leading to the city. Equally frustrating was the news that their logistic support vehicles had successfully re-supplied them. The scouts reported that all the armoured vehicles now carried external fuel tanks, which were disposable and could be jettisoned when empty. Unloaded and re-supplied the tanks were no longer vulnerable. The rush to catch this coven of vampires, while helpless and ineffective, each chained to its trailer, had been to no avail.

The moon was up.

On the ground with a full complement of forty main armament rounds, ammunition for the machine guns and fully fuelled, a single tank would create terrible problems for the defenders of Tuzla. A force of thirty-five would spell doom and disaster.

Tadim considered his limited options and finally gave the order to follow the tank force at a distance. He would need the intervening interval to devise a plan of attack.

The tank pack appeared to be slowing and after a brief halt, the lead mastodon slewed right, crawled through the entrance to a derelict coke-making plant sited on the outskirts of the city. It crunched its way across the open space to stop in front of the main building. The balance of vehicles followed and lumbered across the gravel to form up in herringbone formation.

Tadim sent three scouts forward to reconnoitre the Serb position as night fell. The only good news from the reconnaissance party was that, although readied to launch an attack, there was no evidence that a move was imminent. This was puzzling, because the Bosnians had learnt, on more than one occasion to their cost, that the T-72s were equipped with night-vision equipment. They were capable of carrying out operations during the hours of darkness.

The tanks were not currently manned. The tank crews and the supporting infantry were using the administrative buildings and had set up a field kitchen.

The mujahedeen leader gathered his fighters together in a sitting group at the side of his vehicle. His plan, he told them, was relatively simple. The assault would concentrate on the destruction of the tanks, accomplished by two units, each armed with the available Stingers and M72 LAWs. These groups would attack by approaching the tank lager from the rear, using the buildings of the coal plant as cover.

He positioned a third smaller group, with some anti-tank weapons, in cover at the other side of the road. If the Serb force tried to break free and head for Tuzla, they were to thwart any such attempts. The briefing lasted all of four minutes.

As the men were getting to their feet, Tadim spoke to Spider and Rath.

"I have told my men that the destruction of the tanks is my priority."

He turned to answer a question put to him by one of his fighters, who had approached. Spider moved closer.

"Might I make a suggestion, Commander?"

Tadim raised his palm for his fighter to wait, frowned at the two members of the convoy, and then nodded with ill grace.

"You will be stretched to destroy thirty-five tanks with the few missiles you've got. The destruction of that armour, with all due respect, is not your priority: the elimination of the tank crews is. Without the crews, the tanks are going nowhere. And besides, thirty or more serviceable tanks would be a welcome addition to the Bosnian inventory, or so I would have thought."

The Afghan's sour expression did not change, but he snapped out several words in Pashto and the dispersal of the group halted. He waved his hand, and the Mujahedeen returned to their cross-legged sitting positions on the ground.

"So, we should attack the buildings and not the tanks?"

"It makes sense to me," replied Spider. "If that is where the Serbs are, task your third group to cut off any attempts to crew the tanks. We need to initially deal with the sentries. If we can do that quietly then the rest can be taken by surprise."

Tadim gave a brief nod and turned to address his men, then explained to the two foreigners that he had taken their advice. There had been no mention of prisoners, and Spider gave the big Afghan the benefit of the doubt for not being over confident. He knew that, despite any element of surprise that they might have, the imminent conflict would be severe.

He silently wished the Afghans well.

Spider and Rath had returned to their vehicle and were sitting in the cab. Rath felt no urge to break the silence. Spider appeared lost in thought. After several minutes, he nodded, as though to himself, then looked at Ralf who had been quietly watching him.

"Change of plan, at least for me," said Spider.

Rath made no comment but raised an eyebrow in question.

"After the debacle at Queen's, I wasn't sure of anything. What I did know was that I was through with killing. I was sure of that. Chopping down someone else because it was part of my job no longer made any sense.

"My reason for leaving the Army was that I could avoid any involvement in that. I took this job believing that working for UNHCR, getting food and relief to homeless and displaced persons, working for a peacekeeping outfit, would allow precisely that. This run, and the crap we've had to take, has shown that the bad bastards don't go away just because we pretend they are not there.

"We've been trying to get through to Tuzla with these supplies, because we know there are thousands of men, women and children desperate for the extra few days' respite the provisions will bring. We're almost there, having got through some major hassle, and then out of the woodwork comes this tank force obviously set on destroying the very people we're here to help.

"I can't let that happen. I just can't sit by and watch it happen, especially not when others are trying to stop it."

Rath remained mute.

"So, I'm going to tell Tadim that I want to be involved, to take part in the next step."

"Tell your man to make room for two," said the Irishman before he swung his door open and leapt down from the truck.

"So, we're going with them?"

Rath nodded. For him, it was not only a question of accompanying the fighters.

He, too, intended to take part.

Tadim showed no expression when Spider and Rath told him.

"I want you two to remain with me during the action," the Afghan commander said before turning away.

Spider looked at Rath, who, after a brief pause, shrugged and grinned mockingly.

"Tell him it's out of the question—Boss."

The commander of the mujahedeen had calculated the remaining distance to Tuzla. It was logical to assume the Serbs were now intent on a dawn attack, confident that the timing would be detrimental to the defenders' morale. If that premise were correct, and with the knowledge that the tanks could easily travel at a consistent speed of thirty miles per hour on the tarmac road, he estimated that the column would move out around three o'clock in the morning.

To pre-empt them, the mujahedeen would launch their attack at one o'clock. There would be no signal to attack. The leaders of the three groups synchronized their watches to ensure a simultaneous offensive.

After shaking hands with Tadim, Spider and Rath joined their assigned group with their weapons. The group, their equipment already proofed against rattles and clanks with clothing and masking tape, moved out silently and headed away from the plant.

The plant covered a huge area, including its own railhead, which had fallen into disuse since early in the conflict. At the rear of the plant, the tracks followed the river for some distance before branching off towards the south. The intention was to make for the river that flowed past the rear of the installation then to follow its banks to the perimeter fence.

Low blanket mist was rising from the darkened waters and seemed to follow them at knee level as they made their way downstream. They reached the fence without incident and crawled up to the wire.

The barrier was in good order. There were no obvious breaks. The group waited in the gloom for signs of patrolling sentries, but the night remained silent and unbroken by coughs, shuffles or other disturbances that one could expect from guards.

After a longish delay, the two leading Mujahedeen inched forward and cut through the wire netting surprisingly efficiently, since they were using only knives. The mujahid leading the group pantomimed with his hand that they should move through the fence, and the body of men moved silently through the gap in the wire.

They were now in the plant area. The leader lifted his upper body from the prone position, indicated his watch and then gave the universal sign to wait. As one, the group sank down to the grass and settled in the dark solid shadow of the buildings to wait for zero hour.

Spider rested his chin on his arms and was scrutinizing the darkness for movement when he felt a gentle but persistent tap on his boot. He pulled himself back alongside Rath.

The Irishman pointed to the installation buildings and whispered, "Looks like the Thunderdrome from *Mad Max*."

Spider frowned but nodded. The stress and tension of the past few days, and now this apprehension, was making him irritable.

He tried to relax.

Several minutes before one o'clock, the two men sensed the collective air of anticipation and were immediately alert. Without haste, they carried out a final weapons' check. Spider looked at the luminous face of his watch - three minutes to zero hour. The group, as one, started to crawl forward towards the three-storied administrative building where the click of a lighter, followed by the small red glow of a cigarette, identified the precise location of their first target.

The gaunt, skeletal mass of corroded meccano that was the conveyance systems rusted its way into the sky, high above the huge, bottle-shaped kilns squatting over the firing units. Propelled by a rising east wind, which was damp, cold and heavy with moisture, dense impenetrable clouds scudded low across the night sky.

Shivering from the cold, the sentry stiffened as he heard the eerie, weird whistling made by the wind in the mares' nest of pipes and metal tubes above his head. As it continued, he leaned back against the building to relax and tried to guess whether it would snow or rain during the night. Probably more snow, he thought.

He closed his eyes and thought of the sun on the land back in Montenegro. So vivid were the pictures in his head that he forgot the cold and could almost feel the sun's warmth on his body and smell the fresh lake air. He took a deep breath to suck in a lungful of it when a palm of immense strength grasped his nostrils and mouth, a blade slashed and the sun exploded in a warm, wet, red pool over his eyes, face and neck.

With the first sentry down, the second proved to be even less alert, if that were possible. He made an obscene, gurgling grunt as the mujahid drew the knife across his throat.

Spider reached the corner of the building and edged around to the front.

Through the dirty glass of the office window, he saw the guard commander seated at the trestle table with his head bobbing spasmodically as he struggled to stay awake. Spider pulled the pin on the grenade, and holding it firmly in his grasp, showed it to Rath and the mujahedeen around him.

There was a movement at the front of the next building some distance away, and several Mujahedeen had dropped to their knees in the firing position before they became aware that it was their other group manoeuvring into position.

Reassured, they pressed back on both sides of the door, and Spider lobbed the grenade through a broken pane. Snatching a quick glance through the window before lunging for the door, he saw that the Serbian had heard the grenade strike the floor but was so sleepy that he remained seated and the disturbance did not cause him to react.

The ensuing explosion blasted the window, together with its frame and shards of glass, from the building. The door was thrown open and the men on both sides charged in; those on the right continued straight up the stairs and Spider, with those on the left, burst into the main ground-floor room.

A burst of machine-gun fire into the fallen Serb jerked the body about on the floor. Spider crossed the room as swiftly as he could to reach the adjoining room, firing at the darkened doorway. Two lifeless figures sprawled on the floor.

The sound of firing from above his head, followed by the clatter of heavy footsteps pounding down the stairs, caused Spider to run for the door, and the rush of the mujahedeen swept him up as they ran from the building. A second later, the office block appeared to leave the ground in a blaze of brilliant white light. It hung in the air momentarily, complete and whole, before disintegrating. Slabs and chunks of concrete flew in all directions.

A new sound, the cries and wails of the wounded, mingled with the explosions and more Serbs, more than they had expected, streamed from the neighbouring building, firing as they ran towards them. Spider dropped to one knee and fired directly into the body of men. Empty cases splattered on his shoulder, and he looked up to see Rath for the first time since he had thrown the grenade.

Rath quickly changed magazines and continued firing. Silhouetted figures, rapidly moving black cut-outs highlighted against the burning buildings and vehicles, ran helter-skelter without apparent purpose over the yard.

"Look out, Spider! Tank!" Rath roared as he dived, rolling across the yard. The Englishman spun on his knee and saw the massive, ugly shape of a T-72 lumbering towards him. A searchlight mounted on the hull blazed out and cut a swath through the darkness to pinpoint him in its beam. He froze as a 7.62mm machine gun yammered, and he felt the bite of stinging concrete as the first rounds narrowly missed him.

Throwing himself out of the spotlight into the shadow, he heard the screech of tortured stone as the giant tracks chewed their way round to bring the tank's cyclopean orb to bear on him once more as it followed his flight.

The machine gun continued to fire, and Spider knew fear, as the Afghan on his right seemed to fumble in slow motion with the LAW. The mujahid swung the missile launcher into his shoulder and fired at the tank. The explosive reptile streaked through the thickening billows of burning, black diesel hanging low over the compound towards the squat frog-shaped bulk of the tank.

It missed and streaked unimpeded into the far distance.

Inexplicably, the tank changed direction in a ninety-degree turn and rumbled towards the main gate.

More and more Serbs were joining the fray, and inexorably the Mujahedeen were pushed back. The snarling, metallic cracks of the small-arms fire increased, and it was clear to Spider that the outcome of the battle would not be a foregone conclusion.

Several Serbs had formed a breakaway group and veered towards Tadim's third party on the other side of the road, laying down heavy concentrated fire.

The Afghan's wayward missile tore into an empty ambulance, awaiting a new clutch assembly, on the maintenance park of NORDBAT.

The Scandinavian unit was a hive of activity stirred into action by weapons fire, some apparently from heavy armaments in the immediate area. Tank engines were revving up, and the mammoth Leopards were already slewing their way onto the main road to Tuzla, which ran past the camp.

The LAW round, fired with apparent malice at a vehicle on site, was the catalyst, if one were needed, that galvanized reactions and influenced the mind-set of the Nordbat Force colonel.

"We are not here to take 'incoming'," he snapped at his deputy. As they neared the battle site, the forward tank commander reported that his infrared detector system had picked up hostile tank-aiming systems that were active, and hot barrels indicated tank weaponry in use.

The response from his colonel was short and to the point.

"Fire at will."

Gradually, the night was dissolving and the attackers regrouped.

The main source of danger to them came from a dark-green M190, a wide low carrier, with two 7.62mm machine guns and a 20mm Hispano-Suiza cannon that had swept around the cluster of buildings. It was now hurtling up and down and across the wide forefront of the plant with the four ports on each side open and fully manned by gunmen spraying bullets at any perceptible movement.

Spider crouched with Rath, who had joined him behind the pyramid of fuel drums, all of which appeared to be full, and wracked his brains for a solution.

The vehicle, which was creating havoc among the mujahedeen and taking a heavy toll, screamed into a sharp semi-circular curve at the end of the yard and rocketed back across the forecourt.

"Rath, do you think you could hit it with the grenade launcher?"

"No problem,"

Spider sprinted across the tarmac in front of the vehicle, which seemed to accelerate at the same time. The driver, at the front left-hand side, swung the heavy carrier to his left to follow Spider, leaving its side exposed.

Rath fired, and the grenade passed through one of the open portholes and exploded inside. The vehicle thrashed, and the front glacis plate buckled violently outwards, then the carrier slewed awkwardly to a halt only a foot away from Spider.

The first round fired by the Nordbat leading tank hit the carrier a second after Rath's shot. For the first time, the combatants, Mujahedeen and Serb, saw the huge, white shapes of the UN tanks. The destruction of the carrier seemed to provide a signal to the remaining Serbs, and within seconds, they had turned and were streaming across the nearby grass to the rear of the plant and safety.

Tadim bellowed after some of his men who were giving chase. He did not want to lose any more warriors and now, the remaining unmanned tanks were of more importance than the fleeing Serbs.

The air filled with a weird, throbbing hush now that the heavy machine guns and grenade launchers were silent. The sky lightened. A new dawn was beginning.

Spider grabbed Rath's arm. He had already thrown his own weapon to one side. He snatched Rath's weapon from his grasp and threw it.

"Let's get back to the convoy before this lot start taking names."

Rath needed no encouragement.

FOURTEEN

The trucks rolled along on the final lap to Tuzla. They slowed as they entered the heavy palls of smoke that were only now dispersing and swirling across the road from the burning coke plant. The lead driver, once clear of the wrecked installation, saw the solidly filled profile of Tuzla visible against the dawn sky.

Even in better times, Tuzla, named after the Turkish word for its prime commodity, salt, had been a gritty mining and manufacturing city, with drab high-rise apartments.

That morning before the sun rose, thick fog blanketed the town and its surrounds. A clinging yellow haze of pollution, only slightly ameliorated since the war had halted the manufacture of chemicals, textiles and paper, seemed held in place by the surrounding hills. It hung over the city, making the air acrid. The unaccustomed eyes of the drivers watered, their noses and throats felt raw.

Spider knew that deadly verges filled with lurking landmines bound the approach roads to the city, like many of the roads in Bosnia. Deep potholes left by Serb shells that had rained down almost continuously for four years of war pockmarked the narrow strips of asphalt. Before long, the convoy reached the slip road that led to the UNHCR depot.

In the town itself, most buildings carried the scars of the shelling. Plastic covered some of the open ragged sores; others had only bed sheets. In addition to the damage caused by the Serbs, the years of indiscriminate mining of the salt beneath the city and the lack of shoring up in the disused shafts had caused widespread subsidence. Many of the dwellings had tilted or sunk and were too dangerous to inhabit, due to the regular and progressive collapsing of subterranean burrows. Several hours after the convoy had unloaded the supplies into the wide low warehouses, the drivers were shuttled in the convoy jeep in parties of six to the Hotel Tuzla. The hot water that was available was too sparse for a reasonable shower, so the drivers made do with a most, welcome strip-down wash. Before long, they stretched out on the beds to enjoy their first night's sleep for what seemed an eternity, but which in reality had been only four, albeit seemingly endless, days.

No one made the bar that night. The first they saw of each other was at breakfast, sparse and scanty as it was.

Both men were silent as they took their drinks to a table and sat down. The café was quiet, and only one of the Muslim waitresses was present.

The trip back down country had been uneventful compared with the run to Tuzla. It had taken only a day. Their debriefing at the UNHCR depot by the Head of Station had been brief but not pleasant. The loss of lives and vehicles marred the relative success of the operation. The Head of Station seemed sceptical about certain elements of Spider's report.

He had decided beforehand that there were specific issues that he would avoid. As the possibility did exist that the authorities might implicate him in the weapon smuggling, once known, he made no mention of the illicit cargo. He was determined to say nothing about the contraband, at least until he had spoken with Cheatham.

At this stage, he could not be sure that Cheatham was involved, although the man's absence did point to some degree of connection.

"What now?" asked Rath.

Spider shrugged.

"We could carry on here. We have the vehicles, the people and the accommodation, and UNHCR will probably be ferrying supplies up-country for a while yet. Though, personally, I'd rather move on."

Rath stared at him, his face devoid of all expression.

"I was thinking more about our personal situation and where we stand now."

Spider got up, unsmiling and just as impassive as Rath.

"I like to believe that I'm a logical man. In my opinion, after all that has happened over the past few days, we gain nothing by continuing the Belfast saga. I don't know if you have a reason to think otherwise, but for me it is over."

Rath looked down at his beer, then raised his glass to drink. His gaze when it returned to meet Spider's was contemplative. He nodded.

"There are a couple of things I need to do. For one, I need to go back to Frankfurt on a personal matter. And two, some unfinished business needs to be closed out with my previous employers."

He stood and extended his hand. Spider took it.

"I've got some unfinished business too, which I think you have an interest in as well." He watched Rath closely, then saw his erstwhile enemy grin wolfishly.

"Cheatham," the Removal Man said.

Both lifted their glasses, touched them together briefly and then drained them to seal the new accord.

THE END

10148665R0

Made in the USA
Lexington, KY
04 July 2011